"*Deadly Stra*... that combine... compromising either aspect of the story."
—*RT Book Reviews*, 4.5 stars

"Danger and desire mix in the perfect balance that kept me glued to my ereader all night.... I'm hooked and I believe you will be too."
—*Night Owl Reviews*, 4.5 stars, Top Pick, on *Lethal Game*

"Julie Rowe writes with a fast-paced, engaging style full of emotional honesty. Her three-dimensional characters are sure to tug at your heartstrings."
—*New York Times* and *USA TODAY* bestselling author Lori Wilde

"Julie Rowe blends the perfect cocktail of action and romance."
—*New York Times* bestselling author Brenda Novak on *Icebound*

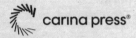

carina press®

Recycling programs
for this product may
not exist in your area.

ISBN-13: 978-0-373-00386-0

Lethal Game

www.CarinaPress.com

Printed in U.S.A.

JULIE ROWE

LETHAL GAME

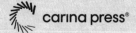
carina press®

To my daughters, Koryn and Megan,
because they're awesome.

LETHAL GAME

Security is mostly a superstition

~ Helen Keller

ONE

IT HAD TAKEN him three airplanes and over twenty-six hours to travel more than seven thousand miles, and now he was going to have to kill someone.

Ten feet from his room in the Navy hotel at the American Naval base in Bahrain.

All Special Forces Communications Sergeant Connor Button wanted was to find a bed and crash for a few hours.

What he did not need was witnessing some idiot striking out with a hot blonde and not taking it well.

She'd just removed his hand from her waist.

The man put it on her shoulder and tried to bring her closer. "Aw, come on, sweetheart."

She slid away, her voice clear across the short distance. "No."

Okay, dude, time to retreat. Only, the guy didn't. He grabbed her by the back of the neck, hard enough to make her gasp in pain, and leaned down, his mouth aimed for hers.

She slapped the moron, but he didn't get that hint either, just grabbed her hand and twisted it behind her back.

Con had to make himself stand still for a second. One second, so he could throttle back the instinct to beat the stupid fuck to death.

Fine. His jaw flexed. He wouldn't kill the asshole, but he could hurt him real bad.

Con dropped his duffel on the floor and stomped toward the woman and the moron whose arm he was about to break.

Into several pieces.

Small ones.

The stomping got the moron's attention. He glanced up, saw Con coming and his eyes went wide. He let go of the woman so fast she wobbled off balance and fell to the floor. Con stopped to help her while the moron ran like a track star down the hall and around a corner.

Good call, asshole.

Con bent down and offered his hand to the woman. "Are you okay?"

Her head jerked up and she stared at him with eyes that didn't miss a thing. She scooted away, leaving his hand hanging in the air, then stood. Her shoulders went back and her chin rose.

He almost smiled. She was so not interested in another man getting all up in her business. He'd make sure she was all right, then he'd back off.

"Ma'am, did he hurt you?"

"I'm fine," she said, retreating a step.

Blue-green eyes stood out in a face framed by white-blond hair hanging in a sheet down to the middle of her back. She was also stacked, though she wasn't showing it off. She was following military clothing requirements, wearing long pants and a collared shirt one size too big, buttoned up to her neck. An asshole had just tried to sexually assault her, but Con would bet a year's pay that had he not come along, the moron would have had his hands full with a pissed-off female trying to smash his balls into paste.

He glanced down.

Her mouth was pressed into a thin angry line, but her hands were shaking.

For the first time in months something other than anger or despair slammed into him.

He knew just how she felt. Hyped up on adrenaline and looking for a target.

It surprised him so much he opened his mouth to make some inane comment or other to show her he was no threat, but she raised a hand to stop him.

She spoke a quick, firm "Thank you." And then she was gone, inside the room closest to her. The click of the lock being engaged echoed down the hall.

He blinked at the empty hallway. He wasn't sure she was okay, but those shaking hands and that locked door sent a pretty clear signal that she didn't want another man anywhere near her.

Sometimes other people just made things worse.

He sighed, strode back to his bag, checked his room number again and discovered he was next door to the blonde.

At least he wouldn't have to go far if Moron came back.

SO MUCH FOR getting some sleep. He'd lain awake, alert for any noise that might indicate a problem in the room next door, but it had been church-quiet. He got up at 0700 base time, then went in search of his new commanding officer, Colonel Maximillian. The man had an interesting reputation, but he trusted what his buddy, Jacob "Sharp" Foster, a former Special Forces soldier, had to say about him. Everyone else said the colonel was one bullet shy of a magazine. Sharp had warned him that the colonel wasn't exactly regular army, but he gave a shit about his people, and that was number one for Con. If your CO had your six, at least you didn't have to take your attention off what was coming at you.

The colonel had a fancy lab that didn't exist on the base, according to official records. Officially, the lab that did exist on paper was rated for level two containment. Good enough to run the sort of tests any big city hospital conducted. In reality, the lab was capable of level four containment testing. The stuff you needed to wear a bio-suit for and breathe your own oxygen supply.

Con had to pass through two internal checkpoints to gain entry to the nondescript building that was his destination. Colonel Maximillian's office was the first one inside the prefab rectangle that housed the lab and offices. A soldier who didn't look a day over sixteen sat typing on a computer facing the entrance to the building.

The kid's gaze darted over Con's uniform, then he stood and saluted. "Private Eugene Walsh."

"Sergeant Connor Button, Special Forces."

"Yes, sir. Colonel Maximillian is expecting you." Walsh extended his hand in the direction of the first office. "Go right in."

Con gave him a nod, then walked into the office.

He saluted the salt-and-pepper-haired man, who stood and saluted back. "Sir, Sergeant Button reporting for duty."

"Welcome, Sergeant." The colonel came around his desk and offered his hand.

Con shook it once, twice, then released a hand that

hadn't tested him beyond what would be considered polite.

"Take a seat," the colonel said, gesturing at one of the chairs facing his desk. "I'd like to go over your assignment and answer any questions you might have."

"Thank you, sir." Con sat and adopted a neutral body posture, back straight and hands resting lightly on his thighs. It was harder than it should have been.

The last time he'd been in the Middle East he'd been deployed with his unit, attempting to ascertain the military strength of two groups of extremists in Northern Iraq and Syria. Both groups had threatened multiple American and allied targets, as well as calling for sympathetic citizens to carry out terrorist acts inside their own countries.

The last time he'd been in the Middle East, he'd been the only survivor of an IED that took out their vehicle. Fortune had smiled on him that day. He'd been thrown clear.

More and more often, he wished he hadn't been so lucky.

Colonel Maximillian continued to stare at him and seemed content to not say anything for several moments.

Con waited with the patience of a man who'd waited days for just the right moment to take a shot at his target.

Finally, the colonel asked, "How much do you know about your mission here?"

"Probably not enough."

Maximillian's face didn't change. "Sharp said you were smart. Are you, Sergeant Button?"

"That would depend on your definition of *smart*."

"Observant, creative, organized, able to see unusual relationships between people and information."

"Sir, you're looking for Sherlock Holmes. He's a fictional character."

A brief smile crossed the colonel's face. "How would you describe yourself?"

"Flexible, determined, fuck the box."

Colonel Maximillian's forehead lowered over his eyes. "Were you aware General Stone had some reluctance in assigning you to this mission?"

"Not directly, but it doesn't surprise me."

"Oh?"

How many conversations like this had he had recently? Five, six? "Sir, I received injuries in an attack that killed all the men in the armored vehicle with me. I'd be surprised if he wasn't hesitant." No officer wanted to have a suicidal or homicidal soldier on a mission. Survivor's guilt could lead to either one. Or both.

"Do you consider yourself fit for duty?"

"Yes, sir."

"Why?"

Goddamned why-questions. *Why* judged, weighed and measured what was in a man's head. What was in his head was not pretty, and not to be shared.

"Sir, I signed on to serve my country. My service isn't done."

Maximillian tilted his head to one side. "That is one of the best non-answers I've ever heard."

Fuck it. Con leaned forward and said in a less civilized tone, "I got thrown off the horse. I need to get back on and finish my ride."

"And if you don't?"

Con's throat closed up. "That thought can't be in my head."

The colonel's face lost its sharp inquisitiveness for a moment, replaced by a surprising level of comprehension. A second later it was gone and he was flipping through pages on his desk. "You've had some problems with your temper since you returned to duty."

"I'm working on that." Anger was easy. Acting on it was even easier.

The officer considered Con for a couple more seconds, then nodded briskly. "My Biological Response Team is tracking a very dangerous man who's created his own extremely deadly strain of anthrax. We managed to prevent an attack on a base in Afghanistan, but not before nearly one hundred people died of the infection. We think he's not done. We think he'll continue to strike at high-quality American or allied targets, and we don't know where he is or where he will attack next."

Con straightened. Hunting down a homicidal nutcase wasn't the sort of duty he'd taken on before, but it sounded dangerous. Good.

Holy fuck he was messed up.

Maximillian continued. "We were successful in preventing the last attack because we had one of our infectious disease specialists embedded with an A-team training members of the Afghan military. General Stone agrees with me—until this man is found, we need more cooperation between my team and army Special Forces. I asked for specific men to work with my people. Men who are not only well trained and smart, but also creative and who can take a step back and support his teammate or take charge of a situation if that's what's needed. Jacob Foster says you're that kind of man. Are you?"

It might be nice to have a specific enemy, with a face and a name, rather than a faceless one who could be anybody. The need to kill, to avenge his dead, was a relentless voice in the back of his head. This mission could get him the opportunity to give himself that, and maybe a measure of peace.

"Sir." He paused, trying hard not to come on too strong. If he lost this chance, he might not get another. "I'm a team player. That means I'll play whatever role is needed by the team."

Colonel Maximillian smiled. "Do you mind working with a woman?"

"No, sir. Sharp mentioned the possibility I'd be paired with a woman." Man, woman, two-headed alien, he didn't care as long as they shared a common enemy.

"You're okay with that? No hesitations?"

The colonel seemed unusually concerned.

What the hell? While he might smack down a fellow Special Forces soldier, he'd *never* lay a hand on a woman.

"Sir, I'm the youngest of five children with four older sisters. Working with or for a woman is nothing new to me."

"Good." Maximillian nodded. "I don't mean to sound paranoid, but the doctor you're going to be working with is somewhat high-strung."

"High-strung?"

The colonel shook his head. "That's the wrong description. She doesn't trust…people. I've been trying to find a suitable partner for her, but I've been unsuccessful."

"Unsuccessful?"

"Most people look at her and see a young woman who looks as if she'd have trouble with breaking a nail. Coddle her in any way and she'll find a way to make you miserable."

The bottom of Con's stomach grew cold. "So why me?"

"Growing up with sisters is part of it."

This interview was a personality test. *Fuck*.

"You've also been through some challenging combat situations and I think that will give you a level of experience she'll respect."

Con had to work to keep a growl out of his voice. "I'm not going to sit around the campfire telling her war stories." What he'd seen wouldn't instill confidence in anyone.

"I don't expect you to. She works best with people who are highly competent, who *don't* brag or try to impress."

First time he'd been complimented on his ability to keep his trap shut.

"Another issue is her age. She's young, she's a genius and she has absolutely no idea how to talk to anyone who isn't a scientist or doctor."

That didn't leave a whole lot of people. "Genius, as in graduated from medical school really young?"

"She's twenty-four and is the youngest physician in the USA to have a double speciality in virology and hematology."

"Virology, I get. Hematology?"

"The study of blood cells."

If she was an overachiever, he could work with that. "So, work is her life, and before that, it was school?"

"Exactly."

"S'okay. My second-oldest sister is married to a physicist. He speaks math, and we get along just fine."

Maximillian quirked an eyebrow. "You speak math?"

"Nope. I speak barbecue. Everyone has something to say about properly grilling a steak."

The colonel laughed. "You'll do. Time to meet her." He stepped out of his office and led the way down a hall. "Oh, and call me Max. It's shorter."

"Thank you, sir."

Max sighed as he opened a door with a key and preceded Con inside.

The room they entered was part office and part lab, with a couple of desks and two tall microscopes set up on the end of each. Papers and boxes of slides littered both surfaces. Only one of the desks was occupied.

A woman sat looking through the lens of one of the microscopes. Her hair was white-blond and pulled back into a severe bun. She wore an army uniform with a lab coat over top. When she saw Max, she pushed away from the scope, stood and moved to meet them.

The blonde from last night. With her hair pulled back, she could have passed for even younger than twenty-four.

Fucking gorgeous. He took that thought, hog-tied it and shoved it into a dark corner. His personal mission left no room for anything beyond a professional relationship.

She also looked ready to rip someone's head off.

"Sophia," Max said. "This is your new partner, Communications Sergeant Connor Button." He turned to Con. "Connor, this is Captain Sophia Perry." Her mouth, pressed into a thin line, convinced him to pretend last night hadn't happened. He nodded at her respectfully. "Good to meet you, ma'am."

"Ma'am?" she asked, crossing her arms over her chest and displaying a huge bruise on her right hand.

Must've hurt.

"This is who you found to babysit me, Max? A fossil?"

Damn, she came out swinging. Maybe he'd let her win this bout. Con managed to keep a straight face and said in a hesitant voice, "I'm only twenty-nine."

"Would you rather I pair you up with someone who follows *all* the rules and regulations?" Max asked her, irritation showing in his rigid posture. "This guy—" he pointed a thumb at Con "—hates inside-the-box thinking as much as you do."

"Oh yeah?" she said, looking Con full in the face. A challenge. Why was she so pissed off? Because she didn't think she needed a babysitter?

He shrugged, then coughed to hide a chuckle. If he laughed now, she'd think he was laughing at her. "I don't like boxes. They're never big enough, and they're too…square."

She blinked at him, then narrowed her gaze. "What did you do to draw this duty? It had to have been bad."

Max opened his mouth, but Con didn't want to escalate things, so he spoke first, and went with the unvarnished truth. "I got blown up. I spent almost seven months in hospitals and physical therapy. The last three or four months I've been instructing and getting back into shape." He smiled at her. "When I found out what my first mission was going to be, bodyguarding some army doctor, I thought *what the fuck?* I sure as shit didn't want *easy* duty. But having talked with Max here,

I've changed my mind." He shifted his gaze to Max's face. "This isn't easy duty, is it, sir?"

"No. It's not a matter of *if* there will be another biological weapon attack somewhere in this part of the world, it's *when*."

"My role isn't just to bodyguard Dr. Perry, is it?"

"No." Max began pacing back and forth between Con and Sophia. "We have intel that points to the Biological Response Team as a specific target. I don't want you to just protect Sophia, I need you two to be a team. All of us are being paired with Special Forces soldiers, even myself."

"Assassination?" Con asked. The idea of it made the back of his neck itch.

"Very possible. Sabotage is another danger."

"Have any attempts been made?"

"Yes. Dr. Samuels and her Green Beret were nearly killed in a trap I believe was set for them. We have an enemy who is intelligent, ruthless and fearless."

"Can I get everything you have on this guy?" Con asked.

"My assistant will have it ready for you in an hour or two." Max turned to him. "Have you been assigned quarters?"

"Yeah."

"I'm going to have you moved to the room next to Sophia's."

The woman in question opened her mouth to say something unpleasant—he was sure from the way she'd screwed up her nose—which is why Con spoke first again. "Are you sure that's necessary?" He looked down, like he was thinking hard. "Do you want to advertise to the whole base that I'm her bodyguard, or would you like to keep it below the radar?"

Max gave him a dirty look. "Whose side are you on?"

"Hers, sir."

"Fine," Max said, with bit of an impatient edge to his voice. "I'll check to see where you're housed now. If it's not too far, you can stay where you are." Max pressed his lips together, glared at them both, then stomped off.

Con looked at Sophia.

She looked back at him, snorted and went back to her microscope. "Nice attempt to come to my rescue. Again. But I don't need anyone to rescue me."

She needed to talk to someone about the moron. To prevent fear and anger from getting too deep a hold on her brain.

Despite how fast things had happened, the human mind had a way of warping events so the memory of them seemed to take a thousand times longer than the reality had.

Hell, he was a walking testament for how three seconds of hell could totally screw up the rest of a man's life.

Or take it.

Listen to him passing judgment on her mental state, when he'd done his level best to keep the shrinks out of his. Right now, he just had to convince her he was on her side. He *wanted* this assignment. "I know."

"Really?" Sarcasm turned the word into something sharp and heavy. "You just met me. How would you know that?"

"I saw you in action last night."

She froze, and for a moment the expression on her

face was a mixture of anger, fear and disgust. A second later, it was gone, smoothed away as if it had never been there.

Whoa. What was that?

Without looking at him, she said, "Babysitting me is going to be a complete bore for a soldier's soldier like you. I'll tell Max to find someone else."

TWO

OUT OF THE corner of her eye, Sophia saw the big man tense up. A lot of people would have missed it, but she'd become a student of body language long before any child should. How else could she know if the doctors were telling her everything was all right when everything was all wrong?

Sergeant Connor Button had already seen her in the most vulnerable moment conceivable, struggling to fight off that clumsy jerk. She didn't want his pity or his protection. What she needed was a partner who looked past her youthful exterior and recognized her ability and determination to do the dangerous work she'd signed up for.

So far, none of the potential partners Max had brought her had bothered.

The sergeant shifted his weight and crossed his arms over his chest. "Guys with my skills don't grow on trees, Doctor."

Here it came, another rant from a muscled-up warrior who thought shooting a rifle made him qualified to tell her what to do. She rolled her eyes and continued studying the slide on her scope. "Uh-huh."

He sighed like she was the dense one. "Look, my job isn't to get in your way, it's to make sure you have the freedom to do your job no matter where you end up."

Freedom? She looked away from the microscope. An

interesting choice of words for a man who worked for one of the most rigidly organized groups in the world. "Explain that to me."

"You're the expert," he said. "So, if you're deployed to an area where there's a possible outbreak, my job is to make sure you're free to concentrate on your work. I'll worry about security and coordinate with any locals if you have protocols they need to follow."

It all sounded rational, but his body language just moments ago told her there was an underlying desperation that shouldn't have been there. None of the other Special Forces soldiers had seemed as determined to get this assignment. "Why are you so gung-ho about working with me?"

His lips tightened and she knew she'd hit a nerve. There was more to this than he was saying. If he didn't come clean with her, he was out. Max would throw a fit if he had to find yet another partner for her, but she couldn't work with someone who wouldn't treat her like an equal.

"Look," he said, rubbing the back of his neck with one hand. "I made it back to the active duty roster by the skin of my teeth. Most guys in my shoes would be transferred to a desk job or some other role not out there." He used his chin to indicate outside. "I've got something to prove."

"To who?"

"Myself."

She studied him. That sounded like the truth.

All well and good, but that didn't necessarily make him the right partner for her.

"Are you prepared to spend eighty percent of your time planning for possible missions that might never

happen?" she asked him. "We might never get *out there,*
but if we do, I need you focused on this job, not your
old one."

His jaw clenched. "When I take on a mission, a partner or a team, I give that mission and those people everything I've got."

Sounded like macho bullshit to her, something she
had no time for. She went back to her microscope, mut-
tering, "You don't even know what I do."

"Give me a chance to find out." He took a step toward her. "I have a buddy who works with one of the
other doctors in your team. He says it's the most challenging work he's ever done. That's what I want. I want
to push myself and expand my skills." He spread his
hands out in supplication. "I want to make a fucking
difference, even if only the two of us know it."

Make a fucking difference.

The same goal she set for herself every morning
when she woke up. She didn't want to be impressed,
but of all the things he could have said, that was the one
sentiment she'd been hoping to hear.

Now that she had, she couldn't quite believe it. Everything he'd said and done tumbled through her head.

"Fine," she said. "I'll give you twenty-four hours to
prove to me you're in this for the long run, you have
something to contribute and you really can work with
me. If you don't, you're gone with no bitching to Max."

He gave her a slow, calculated smile that shot Arctic
air through the room. "Deal."

CON LEFT THE captain's office with the adrenaline of an
accepted mission speeding through his system. She'd
thrown down a gauntlet, one he was happy to pick up.

Someone should have warned her not to goad a Special Forces soldier like that. He wouldn't back down from a challenge. He *couldn't*, not if he wanted to maintain his reputation as a man who got the job done. Period.

What he needed now was information.

"Walsh," Con said to the private. "I need the names of the previous Special Forces soldiers Captain Perry washed out."

The kid didn't have to think about his request at all. He immediately wrote down a list of four names and handed them to Con.

He knew two of the four. Both were good men who had plenty of experience in adapting to whatever mission they were assigned. The other two he didn't know, but he could find out more without difficulty. What the fuck could they have done to get rejected and ejected?

Eugene was staring at him like he was one of those impossible-to-solve mind bender puzzles.

"What?"

"She didn't fire you yet." He sounded almost disappointed.

"This is the Army. We don't fire people, we tell you exactly how you screwed up at a volume that makes it obvious to everyone within a mile." He didn't want her to scurry behind his back to get rid of him. He'd have to make sure she didn't.

"She doesn't do that."

Con's smile came back. This kid was sharp, and Con would bet his left nut the private knew all about Sophia, what she wanted and how she operated.

"So, what did the other guys do wrong?"

"Everything."

"I'm gonna need more than that, kid."

Con found himself on the wrong end of a measuring glance he himself used on newbies who thought they were king shit of Turd Island, but balked at doing the dirty work when shit hit the fan.

"They took one look around here and rated us way down on the priority list. Then they looked at Captain Perry and dismissed her because they decided she was too young to have any real responsibility or authority."

"That was dumb."

The kid shrugged and turned away to read a document on his computer.

Con studied him. His shoulders were so tense they were up around his ears.

Had he done the same as the other soldiers Max had auditioned?

Con took a moment to look around, really look. This wasn't a typical Army medical building. Along with the lab coats hanging on the wall outside of the colonel's office door and the faint smell of bleach that lingered in the air, there was a stillness to the place that made him feel like he was twenty feet underground.

In a bunker.

Protected.

Who needed to be protected? The people inside the building, or outside the building?

The work being done here wasn't way down on any priority list.

On the wall behind Eugene's desk was a big map of the world with colored flag pins stuck in it.

Con walked over to give it a closer look.

There was a cluster of pins in West Africa, specifically Liberia, Sierra Leone and Guinea. Another cluster of pins decorated Northwestern Afghanistan, and still another in a couple of Middle Eastern countries. There were also a dozen or so solitary pins dotted across the map.

"Is this a disease hot-spot map?" he asked Eugene.

"Current outbreaks, yeah."

"That's a lot of pins." Too many, and he didn't know much about any of them. "Is there a summary of all this? One for regular Army idiots?"

"Right here," Eugene said, holding out a file folder.

Con took it, still staring at the map. "How many of these is Captain Perry working on?"

"All of them."

All of them? "Shit, I have a lot of reading to do." He knew the best place to do it, too.

It was an odd feeling to have such a large man sitting at the desk beside her. Usually she was alone, or Dr. Samuels occupied the other workspace. Not this behemoth in a uniform her peripheral vision couldn't miss with blinders on.

At least he didn't talk to himself or make much noise.

Though, that didn't lessen the impact of him sitting barely five feet away. He was a distraction she didn't need. She sighed and adjusted her position in her seat for the fiftieth time.

He frowned at her and asked, "Am I disturbing you?"

Funny you should bring that up. "Yes, you are. Could you read that somewhere else?"

He looked at her like she'd said something ridiculous. "I'm not doing or saying anything. How am I bothering you?"

By being an alpha male? She couldn't say that. "I like working alone."

"Is this an antisocial thing or is it a result of that jackass who manhandled you last night?"

"What?" Where had that come from? "No, I haven't given that another thought."

Now he looked at her like he'd caught her hand in the cookie jar. "Maybe not consciously, but shit like that doesn't get written over in your short-term memory. It sticks with you, and fucks with your reactions to all kinds of things."

How would he know that? Was he emotionally compromised? "Does that explosion you lived through still affect you now?"

His expression turned glacial. "The murder of several of my best friends, my *battle brothers*, will always affect me."

Way to stick your foot in your mouth. Stupid. She sucked in a breath with the intention to offer some kind of apology, but he spoke first.

"All I want is a real shot at this assignment. I didn't come here to waste your time or mine, but you've got to meet me halfway." He turned and leaned toward her. "How can I earn your trust if you've already decided this isn't going to work?"

She raised her chin and met him stare for stare. "I just don't know what you, or anyone else with your type of training, can do for us. The first couple of guys assigned to me got the benefit of the doubt, then got in the way. One of them treated me like a first-year med student and argued with me about everything." That was being polite. He'd been a complete ass. "I just don't know how this is going to work."

"It works for Sharp and Dr. Samuels."

"I've met him and their situation is different. They worked together and became friends over a period of months during a training mission. We don't have that kind of time."

"You're going to have to give someone the time. The colonel sounded like he wasn't going to back off on finding you a partner."

She didn't have an answer for that.

"Look." He tapped the file of papers he was reading through. "I've been going through this summary of all the outbreaks your team is observing, and this shit is scary."

"So, how do you think you can help?"

"By staying out of your way, and keeping everyone else out of your way, too." He lowered his voice. "There's one other thing. I'd like to give you some remedial self-defense training, so you can kick ass the next time an asshole gets handsy."

"Remedial? Try initial."

"Huh?"

"I wasn't given any self-defense training."

"During basic everyone gets—"

She cut him off. "Except me." She gave him a tight smile and stood. "I'm in the level four lab the rest of the day." As soon as he found out why they hadn't trained her, he'd turn into every other big brother who saw her as a little sister in need of protection.

No thanks.

CON STARED AT the door long after Sophia had walked out it.

What. The. Fuck.

How did a guy get a straight answer out of these people?

He left the file on the desk and went in search of Colonel Maximillian. The man's office was empty.

"Where's the colonel?" he asked Eugene.

"In the level four lab."

"Fan-fucking-tastic." Con fixed a laser-guided glare at the kid. "Is there a reason why Captain Perry received no self-defense training during basic?"

"Yeah. She has a blood disorder called ITP." He shrugged "She gets massive bruises sometimes."

The one on her hand was pretty big. "Is this a life-threatening disorder?"

"It can be," Eugene replied, "but she's been taking medication that keeps it from getting worse."

The only person who could explain what it really meant was in an airtight outfit only slightly less complicated than a space suit, in an environment no more accessible to him than the moon.

THREE

CON WAS A patient hunter. He read through the file and waited for Sophia to come back to her office. What he discovered could've easily turned his hair gray.

He'd heard of Ebola in Africa and MERS in Asia, but there were dozens of other hot spots of one infectious disease or another all over the world. The file focused on cases in the Middle East, Africa and Asia, but also listed places in South America and the United States where outbreaks of malaria, West Nile and antibiotic resistant E. coli were putting people in hospitals, and a few of them in the ground.

Also included were task lists of what responders had done to combat these outbreaks. Some of them required more work than others. Months of medical support for the areas affected might be needed, while others were resolved in a few weeks, or even days.

It all depended on how many people were infected and how easy it was to determine which bug or virus caused the outbreak.

The Army's policy of using Standard Operating Procedures wouldn't work. SOPs only helped if the situation was predictable. Infectious diseases typically weren't.

Sophia walked into the room as he was trying to figure out how any one doctor could be involved in all these cases.

She gave him a tight smile and asked, "Learn anything?"

"Yeah," he said giving her a once-over. "You've got to be half octopus to be involved in all of these outbreaks."

She blinked.

Not what you were expecting to hear, sweetheart?

He watched her mentally regroup and tilt her head to one side. "What are you reading?"

"It's a summary of all the current outbreaks your team is monitoring. What I can't figure out is how any one group can keep track of all this without having a whole lot more people working for them than I see around here."

"We obtain a lot of information from other groups with people on the ground at the site of the outbreaks. The Centers for Disease Control, the United Nations, Doctors Without Borders and others all share information."

"Does the information flow both ways?"

"Yes and no. Max determines what information we pass along."

"Do you have any input?"

"Some. It's usually case by case."

She was talking to him, giving him no attitude for the first time since meeting her. "Speaking of cases... I asked why you hadn't been given any self-defense training. Eugene said it was a medical condition. Can you tell me more about that?"

Her back went rigid, but she still answered him. "It's a blood disorder."

Hmm, not a lot of help there. "There are a couple

things I could show you right now that could help if someone ever grabs you like that moron did."

"Really?"

"Moves every woman should know."

"I'd have to get permission—"

He cut her off. "Nah, we don't need to go to a gym or anything. I can show you right here."

She paused, a tiny frown pinching her brows together. "Okay. Show me."

He stood and moved to the middle of the room, which gave him about five feet of space on all sides. "What you want to do is make whoever has a hold of you let go. That close, neither one of you has a lot of leverage or room for a powerful punch or kick, so there are three or four top spots you want to aim for."

"The testicles," she said right away.

"Yes, but sometimes that pain takes a second or two to register. The kneecap and the toes are equally accessible and hurt like a son of a bitch immediately." He waved his hands at her to come at him. "Go through the motions."

"Right now?"

"Yeah, now, so if you really have to do it, you won't hesitate."

She shrugged and pretended to knee him, kick his kneecap and stomp on his foot.

"Good, now," he said turning her around and wrapping his arms around her from behind. "What are you going to do to get away?"

She wiggled experimentally, but he kept his grip on her. "I don't know."

"Lean forward," he said into her ear. "Shove your butt back. That'll give you some space between us."

She did that.

"Now kick my kneecap with your heel or stomp on my foot. Go through the motions."

She delivered a slow-mo mule kick to his knee.

"That move hurts. It'll make it easier for you to get away."

She twisted and broke out of his hold.

She spun around, looking surprised. "You let go."

"Nope. You incapacitated me. Let's do it again a little faster."

Excitement changed her face, made her seem younger. She didn't hesitate, turning to present her back to him.

He wrapped her in his arms again and said, "Do it."

"Sergeant," a voice barked. "Take your hands off the captain."

Con released her and was three feet away before Colonel Maximillian was finished yelling.

"This is unacceptable. No, it's reprehensible behavior," the colonel continued. "Take a seat in my office until the MPs arrive." He turned to Sophia. "Captain, I'm sure you'll want to press charges for—"

"For what?" she snarled. "Him showing me how to defend myself from an attacker who grabs me from behind?"

Max rocked back on his heels. "Say again."

"Sergeant Button wasn't assaulting me, he was demonstrating how to get away from someone grabbing me from behind."

"He wasn't…oh."

"Sergeant, can we try again?" she asked Con.

Shit, he was going to have to prove he wasn't doing

anything funny with the captain before the colonel made that call to the MPs.

"Yes, ma'am."

She gave him her back and he got a grip on her again. "Go."

She bent forward, pushing him back with her ass, straightened, rotated her arms around and was free in about three seconds.

"Excellent," he said. "Now what do you do?"

"Kick you in the testicles and run?"

"Yes, ma'am."

She turned, gave her boss a narrow-eyed look and hooked a thumb at Con. "I'm starting to like him."

"Starting?" Con asked.

At the same moment, the colonel asked, "Really?"

She looked at the two of them like they were five years old and she had caught them putting a frog down someone's shorts. "Don't let it go to your heads."

SOPHIA WAS ALREADY at her microscope when Con walked into her office at 0800 the following morning.

She'd met with Max at 0700 to discuss the more worrisome disease hot spots in their part of the world. Neither had brought up the subject of Sergeant Connor Button.

She'd woken with the decision to accept him as her partner, with conditions, but she wanted to talk to Con first.

"Morning, Sergeant," she said with a glance at him before returning her attention to the slide she was evaluating.

"Morning, Captain." He paused, then asked with audible curiosity, "What are you looking at?"

She didn't take her eyes off the slide. "A blood smear. I'm checking the morphology of the cells."

"Morphology... Size, shape, color?"

"Yes, all that and more. Normal cells look one way. Abnormal, every way else." And this was where he'd check out of the conversation like every other soldier she'd ever met.

"What can change how a cell looks?"

Wait, had that been an intelligent question?

She pulled away from the microscope to meet his surprisingly inquisitive gaze. "Everything from your diet to a virus. Sometimes the change is so specific, I can tell you which vitamin you're deficient in or which virus you have without doing any other tests."

"Huh. So." He cleared his throat. "What else do you do?"

"You tell me," she said instead of answering the question.

"I think I know the basics. You go into areas where possible biological weapons have been used, determine what agent has been released and recommend treatment and clean up procedures."

"Change the word *agent* to *pathogen*, and you've got most of it. Treatment and clean-up can be complicated depending on the pathogen."

"Understood." He gave her a masculine nod that said the conversation was finished.

He was so wrong.

"That's a nice, neat description, but in real life, there's nothing nice or neat about it. It is dangerous, messy and often disgusting work. I could be wading through dead and partially decomposed bodies for samples, or if the pathogen is nasty enough, having to watch people die before a treatment can be administered."

She'd been in those destined-to-die shoes and sometimes pitied the doctors and nurses who'd had to appear strong and upbeat, despite their belief she couldn't be saved.

She'd been one of the lucky ones. She'd lived. In a cancer hospital for children, the word *remission* had an almost mythical quality to it. A state they all attempted to achieve. Not everyone made it.

"War is never pretty and I've seen my share of gruesome."

Right, he'd been blown up. Body parts were never easy to see, and if those parts belonged to a friend... perhaps he did understand.

"Point taken." She studied him a little more. She didn't want a babysitter, a man who'd watch her like the hawk he resembled. He'd see more than he should, but refusing him without a reason Max would accept wasn't possible. She'd been bothering Max as little as six months ago to get out into the field. If she changed her mind and said she didn't want to go, Max was going to want to know why.

She wasn't ready to tell him she was too sick to go on assignment. Leukemia had taken its toll on her body, the chemo and radiation therapy leaving her with weak bones and a disorder that had plagued her on and off for years even after she was declared cancer-free. Idiopathic thrombocytopenic purpura. In the last six months her ITP had gotten much, much worse. Her bone marrow had slowed production of platelets, special blood cells that played a big role in clotting blood. Without them, a person could bleed to death from cuts received while playing with their cat.

She was taking medication that spurred the bone marrow to produce more blood cells, but her platelet count had dipped dangerously low. She was going to have to start infusing units of the tiny cells into her blood in order to maintain a normal-looking life. Unfortunately, transfused platelets didn't survive near long enough.

Her next physical was only four months away.

She wasn't going to pass.

If her ITP carried on like it was, she might not even survive. The cancer that had nearly taken her life when she was a child might kill her yet. She and Max had talked about a bone marrow transplant in theory about a year ago, when her platelet count had been hovering around the low end of normal. There was no guarantee she'd find a match. Even if she put her name into the system, she'd have to go home, and provide all the reasons for the move. It would effectively end her military career.

If she wanted to do something worthwhile, now was the time. Before it ran out. Before the little voice in the back of her head stopped whispering *hurry, hurry* and started to scream it.

It appeared her partner had the same goal. If she could keep the severity of her ITP a secret, she might… Oh, this was ridiculous. She was kidding herself. She wasn't going to be able to keep it a secret for much more than a couple of weeks. Unless she and her babysitter were deployed soon her body wouldn't have the strength or stamina to do the part of her job she craved to do. She wanted to help people. People who'd been forgotten, abandoned and abused.

Sophia stared at the broad shoulders of this soldier, so desperate to do his job he was willing to babysit the geek. Could she work with him?

It had taken only an hour to get rid of the last guy Max had tried to pair her up with. Mr. *Army way or no way* had been intelligent enough, but with all the flexibility of a piece of steel. The one before that had treated her like a china cup, fragile and delicate, rushing to do everything for her. Terrified she'd stub her toe and the damn thing would fall off.

She needed a partner, a real one.

"If I take you on, I expect to be part of the decision-making process. None of this *it's for your own good* shit. My situation is unique enough that you can't know what's good for me or not."

"I don't have a problem with that," he replied. "From what I've learned from Colonel Maximillian and Private Walsh, you're more than capable of taking care of yourself. I'm not here to give you orders, it's the other way around."

"You'll take my orders, no questions asked?"

He crossed his arms over his chest. "I'll be honest, I probably will ask a lot of questions, but not to argue. I need to understand what we're doing and why, so the next time we're in a similar situation, I'll know what to do or what not to do."

That was a pretty good answer, but she wasn't going to make this easy for him. She couldn't. The wrong man could end her career months too soon. "Got any other questions?"

"Yeah," he said. "Quite a few. You're one of the people who identify which pathogen is causing an outbreak, right?"

She nodded.

"I get how you do that here. I mean, this is a fully equipped lab, but how would you do it in the field?"

"See that large duffel bag?" She pointed around the microscope at it, parked along the wall to one side of her desk. "That's my portable level two lab-in-a-bag."

Interest sharpened his gaze. "You got one of these for level three or four?"

"Level three, yes. Level four, no. Level four requires an entirely separate air system for the lab tech and the sample. We haven't quite found a way to do that so the lab can be broken down into bags."

"What about oxygen tanks, like firefighters?"

"No. It's not just about the personnel. Level four pathogens have to be kept isolated completely. They can be airborne."

"That is a problem."

He said it like he'd found a puzzle he wanted to solve. Should she compliment him on his apparent intellect, or would he find that insulting?

He sat down on the floor next to the bag and braced on arm on his knee. "So, tell me what I need to know so I don't get in your way or irritate the hell out of you?" He gave her a crooked smile.

Holy shit. A man who could probably kill people with one hand *and* was considerate? A man who was built to protect and was smart enough to read her body language and extrapolate reasonably accurate insights about her emotions?

Not possible.

"Okay, now this is too good to be true," she said,

leaving her microscope to stand in front of him with her hands on her hips. "No man is this perfect. What's wrong with you? Did that explosion scramble your brains?"

He put his hands up like she had a gun on him. "Hey now, no need to get upset. I'm just trying to be accommodating."

"Yeah, telling me what you think I want to hear." It was an insidious kind of lie. She knew all about the lies people tell to keep a dying adolescent hopeful. It seemed like they were all she'd heard after being diagnosed with cancer. Lying to make someone happy in the short term never resulted in anything good in the long term.

He frowned and lowered his hands. "What's wrong with trying to get along with people?"

"I don't want a cardboard cutout for a partner. I want someone who's going to be honest with me about who he is. Otherwise how can I possibly anticipate what you might do in a dangerous situation?"

"You'd rather I was an asshole?" he asked, his voice rising in disbelief.

"At least assholes are honest."

He studied her for several seconds, his lips tightening. Finally, he let out a gusty breath. "Look, my job is to keep you safe, or as safe as is possible in our line of work. I have to be adaptable to do that. I'm probably going to nag you to death with questions until I wrap my head around what exactly it is that you do. I'm trying to make your life easier, not more difficult."

He didn't get it. And that was okay.

Thank God he wasn't perfect.

She opened her mouth to tell him she wanted him as he was, but he added one more comment to his explanation. "I'm trying to make my life easier too, if that helps any." He dropped his gaze to the floor and absently scratched his left shoulder.

He meant that. He was genuinely trying to fit in and not paying lip-service to his assignment. She might be able to work with that.

She slowly sat on the floor a few feet away from him. "Tell me about yourself."

He took in a breath, but she wasn't finished. "Tell me about your work. You're a Green Beret, right? I don't know much about what makes you different from other soldiers or why you'd make a better backscratcher than a marine or some other guy."

"You know more than a lot of people. They think a Special Forces soldier is the same as a marine or an Army Ranger. We're not."

She waited silently for him to continue.

"Every group of highly trained soldiers has a specialty. For Navy SEALs it's rescue and targeted attacks, Army Rangers it's advance scouting, Green Berets or Special Forces soldiers are infiltrators and trainers. Special Forces soldiers are trained in more than just fighting techniques, weapons and tactics. We're expected to learn multiple languages, understand other cultures and work within indigenous armed forces. We train other armies to use the latest weapons, adapt strategy to fit their cultural needs and environment." He stopped and tilted his head. "What your boss said is true. We're taught to throw the fucking box out and that the more creative you are, the better off you are."

"How long have you been in the Special Forces?" She'd give a little and use the name he seemed to prefer.

"Since I got out of college. Six years."

"What's your degree in?"

He gave her a hang-dog look. "You've got to swear not to laugh."

"Why? Are you planning to say something funny?"

"No, but everyone laughs anyway."

"Um, I'm not very good at that. If it's funny, I'm going to laugh." She'd been told her practice of telling people exactly what she thought was a vice rather than a virtue. Better he found out now than later.

He stared at her for a couple of seconds. "Are you always this...honest?"

She grinned at him. "Are you calling me an asshole?"

He banged his head on the wall behind him. "What did I do to deserve this?"

"You already answered that question. Answer mine."

He sighed. "French literature."

She couldn't have heard that right. "What?"

"French literature," he said louder.

"Really? Isn't that one of the most useless degrees to get, a language fine arts degree?"

"Yes," he snapped. "Yes it is. Thank you for pointing out the obvious."

He probably spoke French, and he said they liked their soldiers to speak multiple languages. "How many languages do you speak?"

"Why, so you can call me an asshole in all of them?"

She had to bite her lip to keep from laughing at his frustrated tone. "I only know English, so that's unlikely."

He muttered something under his breath then said, "I speak seven. English, French, German, Spanish, Arabic, Dari and Urdu."

He looked so irritated she couldn't help herself. "Is that all?"

He gritted his teeth and said, "I'm a Communications sergeant. I specialize in—"

"Communications?" she finished for him, coughing instead of laughing outright at his annoyance.

"I can use any gun, rifle or rocket launcher ever made. I'm a qualified sniper and I particularly enjoy setting traps to capture or kill enemy personnel. I'm an expert in combat jujitsu and I'm an instructor for the Special Operations Combatives Program. Hand-to-hand combat."

Her bodyguard was a ninja. Now *that* was interesting. She folded her legs and hopped up on her knees. The grin on her face felt...strange, but there was no stopping it. Here was an opportunity to learn something that might help her reach her goal. "So," she began, trying to keep the excitement out of her voice. "Can you teach me some more self-defense moves?"

He bared his teeth in an expression that was even scarier than his blank face. "I don't teach defense. I teach offense."

There was a difference? "Oh." Rather than feel threatened by his display, she found it...exciting.

"Why was your self-defense training omitted from your training?"

"I'm a specialist. They accelerated my intake." She shrugged. "It wasn't my idea to omit the training, but they wanted me deployed as fast as possible."

He studied her with a frown on his face then said, "Is that the only reason?"

She sighed. No avoiding a direct question. "I also have a medical condition that would have kept me from getting into the military if my skills weren't so desperately needed." She held out her hand. "I get some pretty big bruises sometimes."

He examined it, then nodded. "I can modify things so you don't accidently injure yourself."

"Awesome." When had her breathing gotten so fast and choppy? No. She wasn't... She didn't think he was good-looking, did she? He was built like a tank, which should have scared her to death, but it didn't. He didn't.

He stared at her. "This is serious, Dr. Perry. Not a game or something you use to impress people. If you do it wrong, you can kill someone."

"I'm taking it seriously, I just..." She stopped to try to find the right words. "No one has ever taken the time to show me that sort of thing. I never played sports in school because I was always years younger than my classmates. In college, I was so busy with my classes and other..." Summing up the weirdness of her adolescent years in one word was not easy. "Stuff. I never had any opportunities to learn how to do something physical." Ha. Like her parents would have allowed her to do anything that might result in an injury, no matter how slight. "My spatial orientation isn't very good, so I'd probably be terrible at martial arts, but I've always wanted to learn Tai Chi. It looks relaxing."

Con's face lost its hard edge. "I could teach you that. It would be a good place to start, especially if you're not used to a lot of physical activity." He looked her over—what he could see of her with her legs tucked underneath her, anyway.

What did he see? A normal woman of twenty-four, or could he tell she was different? Most people only ever saw the differences and never the parts of her that longed to be ordinary.

"You seem in good shape now."

She was about to tell him about being sick as a kid, which had resulted in a couple of medical oddities making any sort of physical training difficult, but Max's voice interrupted her train of thought.

"What the hell are the two of you doing on the floor? Having some kind of Girl Scout meeting?"

"I wish I'd had a chance to be Girl Scout. They learn all kinds of cool things," she said as she got up, giving Max a cool look. What was his problem? "Connor was checking out my portable lab and telling me about some of his training and skills."

"Really."

"Yes. Did you know he's a hand-to-hand combat instructor for the Special Forces? He's going to teach me how to defend myself."

Con nodded and slowly got to his feet as well, his gaze not on Max's face, but on a spot behind her boss. Was someone else there?

Max asked another question before she could check for herself. "Is that it?"

"No. He also speaks seven languages and is qualified to shoot any weapon the Army has."

"I'm a combat jujitsu instructor for the Special Forces and I'm good at it," Connor said, crossing his arms over his chest, his low voice rolling across the room like a storm. He glanced at her, but it was quick, his gaze going back to that spot just outside the door.

"I don't think that kind of advanced training is appropriate for Dr. Perry, Sergeant Button." Another man appeared from behind Max. General Stone.

Sophia had only met the general once, when she was first stationed here four months ago. He'd looked at her, nodded, and left.

She didn't like the look on his face now. Angry and impatient.

"Sir," Connor began. "She's completely deficient in her self-defense training. Why wasn't she taught fundamental hand-to-hand in basic?"

"She's a doctor, brought in under medical dispensation, that's why," the general barked. He took several steps toward her and she found herself backing up into Connor as the general invaded her personal space.

Idiot. Both men were going to think she was some kind of frightened child. She'd faced far worse things than a man with a war on his mind. She lifted her chin and was about to ask the general to step back, but Connor slid around and in front of her.

The general stopped his advance, nodded in a satisfied way and stepped back.

"I disagree, sir," Connor said, shifting to one side before she could ask. "That's exactly the reason why she should have all the fundamentals, plus some."

"You have a problem with your orders, Sergeant?"

"No, sir. My orders are to act as bodyguard, translator and Special Forces liaison for Dr. Perry. She's a high-caliber asset with unique abilities and knowledge. Self-defense skills should be required for such an asset." He glanced at Max, and Sophia was surprised to see censure in his gaze.

Max turned to her. "You want to learn self-defense?"

"Yes, I do." She managed to restrain herself from bouncing on her feet with eagerness. "Within reason, of course."

Max glared at Connor. "Do not put a single bruise on her, understand?"

"Yes, sir."

"Sergeant, as you mentioned, she's an asset we can't afford to lose," the general said. "Are you prepared to take total responsibility for her training and safety?"

Connor's face froze for a moment, then hardened. His lips twisted into a scowl. "Are you sure you want me to have that responsibility? You know I won't follow the rule book when it comes to her safety. I *will* train her. I *will* ensure that she can defend herself vigorously."

"I'm beginning to think, in Dr. Perry's case, that might be necessary."

Connor thought for a moment, then nodded once. "Yes, sir. I accept Dr. Perry as my responsibility."

"Good." General Stone bared his teeth and pointed a finger at him. "Don't fuck this up."

Max and the general left the office.

The general's warning had levels of shit to it she'd never smelled before.

Wait. Teaching her martial arts, even Tai Chi, was going to put him into close physical contact with her. He might see more of her than she wanted him to. See the big, ugly bruises that often appeared on her body even when she hadn't walked into something. See the scars on her arms where the doctors had to cut into her to search for veins damaged from IVs.

She wanted him to treat her like any other soldier, but working with him that closely might prove to him that she was anything but ordinary.

FOUR

"WHAT THE HELL was that all about?" Sophia asked.

"A test," Connor replied. "I think."

He'd been close, so close to failing that test. The general knew exactly what he was asking of him when he asked if Con would take responsibility for Sophia.

Con alone had survived the IED that blew up the vehicle half of his team had been in. Five men who'd been his brothers in every way but blood. Five men who died, leaving him behind to pick up the pieces of their lives and his own. He wanted another mission that would put him in a position to deal a little payback, and if he got killed doing it, it was a price he was willing to pay.

He'd tried to get assigned to another team, but his temper, so well controlled before the blast, hadn't lasted past the first battle simulation. He'd beat the crap out of an "enemy" soldier before recalling that it was just a simulation.

Stone was testing him all right, testing to see if what Con needed to pull himself out of shit creek was a protection mission for a woman who needed it more than anyone he'd met in a long time.

He'd be stuck like glue to her for months.

"They were both very adversarial," Sophia said staring at the door. "Almost as if they were trying to make us mad."

"No almost about it. That's exactly what they were

trying to do." Connor looked at Sophia, reined in his anger, and asked, "Bruise easily?"

She blew out a breath. "I had a childhood leukemia. The chemo and radiation therapy resulted in below normal bone density. I also have idiopathic thrombocytopenic purpura."

He was going to have to add a new language to his list: Medicine. "In English, please?"

She sighed like it was the fiftieth time she'd had to explain it. "My bones aren't as strong as they should be. And my body doesn't make enough of one of the cells in my blood that's responsible for clotting."

He couldn't keep his eyebrows from rising. "Okay, now I understand why Max was so uptight about you learning hand-to-hand. We're going to start with Tai Chi and a few escape maneuvers that aren't fancy, but are effective, and with a minimum of contact between you and an attacker."

"You can minimize contact with an attacker?"

"Yep, 'cause there's one rule and one rule only that's king in hand-to-hand."

"What's that?"

"The only person you can control without question is yourself. If you know yourself, your strengths, limitations, reactions and responses, you win the fight."

"Is that Confucius?"

He couldn't stop the smile. Did she have any idea how freaking cute she was when she got all serious? "Nope. That's Connor Button. It means I'm going to teach you how to cheat. I'm going to teach you how to fight with whatever is in the room, no matter where you find yourself."

"Cool." She hummed a little. "Okay, your turn. What

was General Stone so worried about when it comes to you?"

How much should he tell her? "I had to fight to earn my return to duty. Getting blown up and requiring months of physical therapy doesn't look good on a soldier's record."

"And?"

"And, if this assignment hadn't come along when it did, the best duty I could have gotten was full-time instructor back in the States."

"What's wrong with that?"

"Nothing, except my job here isn't done." It wouldn't be done until he'd avenged his dead. He sure as hell couldn't do that as an instructor.

"Tell me about your injuries."

Her question was a shot to the gut. The last thing he wanted to remember was the days spent lying on a hospital bed, unable to get up and walk to the can by himself. "You don't ask for much, do you?"

"I know what it's like to feel powerless." Shit, she wasn't backing down an inch. "To be inside a body that won't do what it's supposed to do. I understand pain and I understand how hard it is to rebuild strength in muscles weakened by lack of use. It's frustrating. It makes you angry. You feel a fear that's bone deep."

He might have gotten angry with her attempt to identify with him, except the expression on her face wasn't pity, it was understanding and acceptance. "I was in a hospital for a month. A bed for three weeks, a wheelchair for one and in therapy for six months," he said. "How about you?"

"I was in and out for a year. Sometimes for a day or two, sometimes for a couple of weeks at a time. Chemotherapy was hard. Painful, and I couldn't keep any food down. That all changed when I went into remission."

"How old were you?"

"Eleven when I was diagnosed with leukemia. Almost fourteen when they confirmed remission. But, I'd been doing school on my own and once I started to feel better, nothing could keep me from devouring knowledge and information like it was candy."

"Shit," he drawled. "You never had a chance to grow up normal."

She leaned back and crossed her arms over her chest. "Nope."

Touchy subject. Well, he knew how to get around that. "Neither did I."

"Oh?" she asked with a disbelieving snort.

"I have four older sisters."

Her jaw dropped open. "Four?" She burst out laughing. "I almost feel sorry for you."

He grinned and shrugged. Yup, they were just two odd peas in a pod. Max thought she was high maintenance, but she wasn't. What she was, was defensive. All that snark was her way of protecting herself. She used her words and blunt honesty to keep men at bay because she didn't know how to flirt or make chitchat. She never had time for the bullshit as a kid and she probably thought she didn't have time for it now.

"Tell me about your schedule," he said to her, getting down to business. She scrolled through a couple of pages on the tablet sitting on her desk before stopping and staring at the screen.

"Okay, I'm free after dinner tonight, unless there's an emergency where I'm needed."

He liked her professionalism. "Good. You'll get your first lesson then."

She nodded and went back to her microscope, humming under her breath. She looked...happy.

So, why did he feel guilty?

Maybe because he was hoping this assignment would give him the opportunity to kill at least one very bad guy, and probably get killed himself?

"I need to get the info on this Akbar asshole and there's probably a stack of paperwork with my name on it that needs to be signed. I'll try to make it back before dinner."

"Okay," she said, but she wasn't looking at him, absorbed by whatever was in view on the microscope.

Shaking his head, but oddly relieved at how fast she'd tuned him out, Con stopped at Max's assistant's desk. "How's my room assignment?"

"Good, sir. It turns out you were beside Dr. Perry already."

"Eugene," Connor said, leaning against his desk. "I'm not a sir. I'm a sergeant. Big difference. Plus, I owe you a couple of favors. Call me Con."

"Favors?"

"Yeah, you clued me in to the fact that all this—" he waved a hand to indicate the drab, unassuming building "—is a lot more important than it looks."

"How many hours until she decides?" Eugene asked.

"Tomorrow morning," Con answered. "What do you think my chances are?"

"I bet fifty bucks on you," the kid said.

SOPHIA FINISHED HER report on the last sample and hit Send on the computer. Usually, she felt tired and only wanted to go to bed or read a book. Tonight she was going to learn Tai Chi. Part of her was excited, the other part was irritated by that excitement.

Dinner was quick in the food court in the Freedom *souq*, and she ate with Max and Eugene like usual. What was unusual was the addition of Connor. Sitting next to Eugene, Connor looked huge. Now she understood why women called a muscular man's arms "guns." His were dangerous. Delicious.

Sophia froze, her fork halfway to her mouth. Delicious? Where had that thought come from? She shoved the fork in, chewed and glanced around the court. There were other female soldiers eating, here and there. More than one of them watched Connor's big shoulders shake as he laughed at something Eugene said.

As Sophia looked at him, her stomach felt funny in a way that had nothing to do with food.

She choked on the mouthful she'd just tried to swallow. Oh no way, she was *not* in lust with him.

She continued to cough and Max frowned at her. "Are you okay?"

She nodded and grabbed her glass of water. "Went down the wrong way," she managed to croak out. A couple of sips of water and the coughing calmed down.

Her blush didn't. Not when Connor was looking at her with concern on his face.

"What are you thinking about so hard that you forgot how to eat?" he asked.

She almost choked again, but managed to get it down this time. "Nothing."

Across the room a group of soldiers turned to look at her, one of them with a venomous expression on his face.

The asshole who wouldn't take no for an answer.

Suddenly, she wasn't hungry anymore.

The asshole's expression transformed into a sick smile as he stared at her.

She was on her feet and headed toward the dirty tray racks before she'd consciously made the decision to move. She shoved her tray into the rack and shouldered her way into the women's bathroom to prop both hands on the counter and try to figure out how to restart her breathing through the glacier her chest had turned into.

What the hell just happened?

That asshole smiled at her, and *boom* she was moving before anything else could register.

"Captain?"

Sophia turned at the sound of the female voice behind her.

Lieutenant Jones came all the way into the bathroom and let the door swing shut. "You okay?" Jones, a lab tech who often worked with Sophia, came over to the counter and washed her hands in a sink.

Sophia laughed without any humor. "The last day or so has been more interesting than I would like."

"Ah." Jones nodded sagely. "I've had one or three of those. Anything I can do to help?"

She chuckled, but she could hear the pain in it herself. "Got a pair of steel-toed boots I could borrow?"

Jones's half grin dissolved. "Someone need his ass kicked?"

"Yup." Con's face, his teeth bared when he'd told her he taught offense, not defense, appeared in her head. That fire burned away some of the ice crowding her lungs. "But I'm working on it."

"Let me know if you need any backup."

"I will, thanks." She was going back out there and she was going to walk through that food court with her head up.

She left the bathroom to find Connor outside the door, leaning against the wall. Wonderful. Not. She didn't want to need him for anything, yet seeing him waiting for her got rid of the last of the ice.

"Are you lost?" she asked him.

"No, I just thought I'd wait for you."

"Bodyguarding already?"

He shrugged. "Why wait?"

There wasn't much she could say to that.

They walked back to the lab building, passing the two checkpoints without talking. They could have been two strangers walking together except for the slight tension in his shoulders and the way he walked half a step behind her.

It made her want to tell him to stop with the secret service routine, but it was part of his job and she had to get used to it. She wasn't going to admit she kind of liked it to anyone, including herself.

Inside the office's entry there was an eight-foot empty space in front of Eugene's desk. Con looked around and nodded. "Yeah, this will do." He looked at her. "Have you ever tried Tai Chi before?"

"No, but I've seen it in passing on TV and sometimes people did it in the park at one of the hospitals I spent time in."

"Good, no bad habits to unlearn." He smiled. "First, there's more than one kind of Tai Chi. I'm not going to go into the history of it or all the details, but what I'm going to teach you is a form of Tai Chi that's used for meditation and improving health. It's one of the simpler versions that's relatively easy to remember."

"Okay." So far so good.

"What I want you to focus on is your breathing. It should come from deep in your diaphragm, balanced and not rushing. Okay?"

She nodded.

"I'm going to demonstrate how you start and then the first form. Just watch the first time."

He stood in front of her, his knees slightly bent, shoulders relaxed and face calm. When he moved it was as if she were watching water flow through the air. His movements were graceful, fluid and unhurried.

It was almost a dance.

When he stopped, a disappointed "oh" spilled out of her mouth. She could have watched him for hours and been content.

He blinked, met her gaze and smiled. "It hits a lot of people like that when they see it for the first time up close. Ready to begin?"

She nodded, afraid that if she spoke out loud she'd reveal how eager she was to learn.

He showed her the beginning stance, which she copied, then he moved and she followed him. He stopped several times to begin again, so she could practice the movements correctly. One form seemed to escape her ability to copy and he came around behind her to put his body in contact with hers.

Close contact.

She could feel him spooned up behind her so she was touching him from knees to neck and all the way down their arms.

His body heat penetrated their clothes and she found her breathing and heart rate accelerating.

Normally, if someone came in contact with her for more than a few seconds, anxiety and awkwardness would force her away from them as quickly as possible. There were very few people she trusted to touch her.

Her therapist said it was a result of too many strangers handling her when she was young and sick, some of them associated with the pain and discomfort of chemotherapy and radiation therapy. Who'd have thought that a doctor who hadn't seen a day of fighting outside of her lab would suffer from Post-Traumatic Stress Disorder.

No anxiety, but lots of excitement. Her body seemed to have no problem with Con touching her. As he moved with her, guiding with subtle pressure cues on her body, she found herself growing hyperaware of him. His nearness set off proverbial butterflies in her stomach and an aching desire to be touched.

Kissed.

She wanted to bury her nose against his skin and lick.

No matter how hard she tried to mentally classify his proximity as work—part of her job—her body wasn't believing it. She was practically panting.

Could he tell?

She'd never live it down if he was aware of her reaction to him. She let out a breath and tried to follow him, focused on the flow of each action.

"That's it," his voice rumbled in her ear. "Let your muscles loosen as you move, as you breathe."

He moved her into the starting form again and began without hesitation or hitch.

Oh, but she liked this exercise. Despite the intense

sexual arousal of being this close to him, she didn't want to stop.

She let herself fall into the movement, her eyes half-closed, and was disappointed when he stopped guiding her and backed away slowly. Startled, she asked, "Are we finished?"

His lips curved upward just a little. "Do you know how long ago we started?"

"Ten minutes?"

He shook his head. "Thirty minutes."

No way. "That can't be right, it feels like much less."

"Nope, thirty. You're a natural at this. You didn't hesitate to follow instructions and very quickly relaxed into the movements. I'm proud of you."

She was a natural at something physical? He was proud of her? No one had ever been proud of her for something that didn't involve her brain very much. Pleasure warmed her from the inside out. "Thank you."

Holy crap, was she blushing?

He stared at her face like someone had zapped him with a Taser.

Yep, she probably looked like a lovesick teen. What was wrong with her? She cleared her throat and looked away. "You're a good instructor."

God, she sounded like an idiot.

He swallowed, then gestured at the door and they left the building. "Tomorrow morning I'd like to take you to the shooting range for a couple of hours."

"I've done some shooting, but not a lot." She winced. "I'm not very good."

"That's okay," he replied with a funny smile on his face. "I'm very good."

Heat flooded her as her imagination went places it

shouldn't. With his size and muscles, he'd be good at all kinds of things. Especially if he devoted the same focus and physical prowess to sex as he did to self-defense.

She'd derive as much pleasure from touching him, exploring his wide shoulders and discovering where his personal erogenous zones were, as being touched by him.

An image filled her head of the two of them on her bed, naked. For a moment, she wanted that image to come true, come to life so bad she could almost taste him on her tongue, but reality intruded. Bringing cold reason with it. Hello...

Her hands curled into fists.

Not possible.

Not for her.

Not without a fucking miracle.

FIVE

CON ESCORTED SOPHIA to her room half afraid she was going to gush happy words all over him for showing her some Tai Chi. She'd worn a grin nearly the whole fucking time, like he'd given her something expensive or hard to find.

Her gratitude made him uncomfortable, given his body's reaction to being so close to hers. He had a plan: get back into active duty and avenge his dead. But he wasn't two days into his new assignment and his head was filled with fantasies of getting his new partner naked and under him.

Her mouth was going to drive him out of his fucking mind. He kept picturing it around his cock.

He needed to get laid. He hadn't bothered since the explosion, mostly because he'd been so focused on getting back into shape and into active duty. But other needs were making themselves known and he had no business imagining Sophia satisfying them. She wasn't some easy lay. She needed a man she could trust.

That's rich, asshole, you're planning on going Rambo and getting killed the first chance you get. She shouldn't trust you at all.

He didn't want this, not any of it. He didn't want to care about her beyond the scope of his duty, didn't want to feel something for her beyond professional friendship.

He had a plan and it didn't include him getting all cozy with Captain Sophia Perry.

Professional. Distant. Hands-off. That was going to be his motto from now on.

They reached her door and she unlocked it, then paused and turned to look at him. The smile was gone and in its place was a thoughtful expression that made her look years underage.

"Thank you," she said, her tone serious. "For keeping your word and teaching me everything you promised."

His brows went up. "People break their promises to you?" Was this why she acted so tough? Why she hadn't wanted a partner, because all the other men who'd been assigned to her had broken their word?

He hadn't known her long, but it hadn't taken him long to figure out that what she brought to the team was something unique and valuable.

She shrugged. "All the time. As soon as they find out about my ITP, they treat me like I'm unable to do anything. I've learned not to trust people to do what they say until they actually do it."

"That's really stupid. No team can function well if you can't trust someone to do what they say they're going to do. Promises matter, especially here."

She smiled at his comment. "I know, right?" She glanced away and shook her head. "There's not much I can do about it, though. It's just…irritating."

"I'll be irritating," he told her. She trusted him and for the first time since the explosion, he didn't want to let anyone down. *Her* down. "But in other ways. According to my sisters, there isn't a man alive who can go ten minutes without annoying a woman somehow."

She laughed and it washed through his battered heart in a warm wave.

He took a step back, wavering between wanting more and running away from any chance at healing the broken pieces of himself.

"I'm right next door if you need anything," he told her. "Just hammer on the wall a couple of times and I'll come running."

"Thanks. It helps that…" She paused and shook her head.

"What helps?"

"You don't just pat me on the head." She lifted her chin. "Thanks." Then, before he could say anything, she nodded at him shyly, unlocked her door and disappeared into her room.

Con went into his own room, showered and lay on his bed and stared at the ceiling for a long time. Taking on this assignment had been his only chance to avenge his dead and find peace for himself by joining them. He'd give everything he could to his new team, but he was only one of many and was easily replaced.

Sophia changed that. She challenged him to prove his worth to her, and in doing so, she'd proved herself to him.

He didn't want to like her.

He didn't want to want her.

Con punched his pillow a few times, but it didn't help at all.

What he thought he wanted didn't seem to matter anymore, and that tore him in two.

He couldn't put his dead to rest and fulfill his obligations to Sophia at the same time. He was going to have to choose. Either choice was going to kill him one way or another.

SOPHIA CLOSED THE door to her room and leaned against it.

Oh my God. That had been the most sexually intense and frustrating hour of her life. Another ten minutes with him and she would probably have done something to embarrass herself. More than she already had, anyway. He wasn't an idiot. He knew what a blush on a woman's face meant.

She had to get him out of her head before this lust for his body drove her crazy.

After a quick shower, she got into bed and pulled out the romance novel she was reading. It was a suspense, with the law enforcement hero and heroine in danger from gun-toting drug dealers. They were holed up in a remote mountain cabin, and after denying their feelings for each other through the first half of the book, had thrown caution to the wind and were about to have sex.

Brad cupped her breasts, licking his way from one to the other to tease her nipples.

Sophia kept picturing Connor in the role of the hero as he kissed, caressed and undressed the heroine. *"Like that, baby?"* he asked Jessica, *his voice fanning the naughty side of her to life.*

It was Connor's voice she heard in her head.

Sophia slammed the book shut, embarrassment heating her face.

After a moment, she opened the book.

"If I'd known your wicked tongue was this talented," Jessica said breathlessly, *"I'd have put it to better use a lot sooner."*

He grinned and slid down her body. "You ain't seen nothing yet." His wide shoulders spread her thighs apart...

Sophia slammed the book shut again, but there was no getting the image of Connor between her thighs out of her head.

She looked at the book and scowled. Was pleasure so bad a thing to want?

No. What she did in the privacy of her room was her business and no one else's, and right now she needed satisfaction like never before.

She opened the small bedside table drawer and took out a small vibrator, then closed her eyes as she began using the vibrator to stimulate her clit. She restarted the fantasy, but now it was Connor pleasuring her.

Connor's wicked, wicked tongue flicked across her clit fast then slow, hard then soft, until she thought she'd lose her mind.

"Please," she panted. *"I need you inside me."*

"Yes, ma'am," he said in that smoky tone that told her he was happy to follow this order. He positioned his cock at the entrance to her body then thrust in all the way, triggering an orgasm that made her scream.

Sophia came, too, but her orgasm wasn't nearly that satisfying. She groaned in frustration and glared at the wall separating her room and Connor's. What she needed didn't come with batteries.

She'd decided a long time ago that she was holding out for love and a man she could count on to be there even if things got tough or painful.

Her ITP had put her life on a countdown, and until now she hadn't met a man who made her want change her policy about casual sex. Connor was more than daring. He had her willing to break not only her rules, but the Army's, as well. Was it worth the risk?

He didn't really seem the sort that would let himself get attached during a deployment.

Was she really considering asking him to have sex with her?

And what if he said no?

A KNOCK AT his door woke him.

"Connor?"

Sophia.

He glanced at his clock. It was only 0500. He got up and opened the door. "What's up?"

Her eyes widened and her gaze took in his nude torso, then dipped to his underwear for a long moment before she brought it back up to his face.

Her cheeks flushed. "Sorry." She cleared her throat, her gaze bouncing over him like she didn't know where it was safe to look. "Um, I need to— Can I...?" She looked nervously down the empty hallway before gesturing toward his room.

What had her so worried?

"Come in," he said, putting a hand under her right elbow and drawing her into his room. Once she was inside, he took a look down the hall, but no one was in sight.

He closed the door and locked it, then turned to find her staring at him with eyes too wide. There was fear there, and something else he couldn't pinpoint. He found himself herding her toward his bed and urging her to sit down.

He squatted down next to her, putting his head level with hers so he wouldn't crowd her. "Something scared you."

"It's probably nothing." She gave him a weak smile. "A coincidence."

"There are no coincidences in war, only unannounced enemy action."

She tilted her head to one side. "Who said that?"

"Connor Button, though others have said something similar."

"You say some interesting things." She blew out a breath. "Well, someone called me, but didn't say anything when I answered. I could hear rustling in the background and breathing. Someone was there. They just didn't say anything. I hung up after a few seconds."

"On your cell phone?"

"No, the landline to the room."

He grunted. "Could it have been the moron I chased off that first night?"

"I don't know," she burst out. "I thought I could read people better than that, but when he put his hands on me and tried to kiss me…" She sucked in a breath. "I didn't see it coming." All the air went out of her. "I'm an idiot."

Con struggled with himself for a moment. She'd come to him at 0500 with her fear. Not Max or anyone else, *him*. He could play it safe and call in a female therapist or maybe Max to talk her through why the phone call had bothered her so much, or he could offer her the support she was looking for himself.

She'd already put herself out there by coming to him first. Could he turn her away?

"No, you just weren't prepared for the calculated tactic of a hunter."

"If you hadn't come along, I'd have been a victim." She glanced at him and blushed. "Um, maybe I should go."

He'd let her, but her hands were fisted in her lap so hard her knuckles were white. "How about you just relax for a few minutes?"

"I might be able to if you put some clothes on," she muttered as she waved her hand around in front of him. "All this nakedness isn't helping."

As much as he appreciated the comment—he did, he was a guy—he couldn't believe she'd just say it so baldly. "You're not flirting with me, are you?"

"What?" she squawked. "No. I hate that shit." She frowned and huffed. "Why can't people just say what they're thinking? Why do they have to play mind games?"

She really didn't know? With her weird history, maybe she didn't. "People play games to protect themselves," he explained after a moment. "In order to connect with someone you have to step out of your comfort zone and put your heart on the line. It can be scary." His heart had been torn apart by that IED despite the fact that it kept beating. The deaths of his teammates, his *battle buddies*, men he could trust with his life, were open, bleeding wounds in a tired heart that longed for rest. He wouldn't survive another loss, he knew it, but he had to survive long enough to put his dead to rest. He *owed* them that.

"I guess that's the part I don't get," she replied on a sigh. "Sticking my emotional neck out doesn't scare me at all. It's looking back and realizing I missed an opportunity to do something important or be with someone important to me that's scary. I don't have time to play stupid games."

Wow. That was all kinds of smart, and nothing he

could aspire to. *Wait a second.* "You mean, you didn't have time when you were a teen."

"Right." She gave herself a shake. "Sorry."

"Don't be. Your teammates are there for you to rely on. Whether it's something like this or any other problem. They've got your back and you've got theirs." He nudged her elbow. "Eugene and Max have an enormous amount of respect for you.

"I'm going to make your self-defense lessons a priority," he continued. "I want you capable of dealing with morons."

"He's the only one who—"

Con cut her off. "There are plenty of others thinking the same thing. The Army has just as many predators in it as the general population, sometimes more."

"What do you mean, others thinking the same thing?"

"Less than fourteen percent of soldiers in the Army are female. What do you think happens in a man's head when he's been out on a mission, been shot at and hasn't seen a woman in weeks?"

"I understand *that*," she said with another eye roll. "What I don't get is…" She stopped talking to suck in a breath, then stayed silent.

What the hell just went through her head? "What?"

She turned away. "Nothing. I need to think."

He could continue questioning her or he could give her some time to do that thinking. He knew which one of those options was more likely to work. "Do you want to go back to your room or wait here?"

She glanced at him, her eyes unfocused. "Oh. Would it bother you if I waited here?"

It would, but not in the way she meant. "Be my guest."

He set the water in the shower to lukewarm and got in. Sophia was mixing him all up inside and what made it worse, she had no idea she was doing it. She was so damned honest it hurt. She also seemed to hate the normal flirtation that most men and women engaged in. No, hate was wrong. She didn't know what the fuck to do with it, so she ignored it.

That didn't make it go away.

Ignoring it was dangerous, because she might not recognize another vulture like the one he interrupted the night he met her.

He was going to have to take a page out of her book, and explain with naked honesty, her situation and the dangers he saw in it.

As his partner, she deserved nothing less. This was something he *could* do for her.

He dressed and left the bathroom to find her sitting on the cot staring at the wall. "Got it figured out yet?"

"Not really." She shrugged. "There's a lot of things about people I don't get."

"Yeah, like what?"

"Like how anyone can justify any of the evils that seem so common in society."

"Theft, rape and murder, you mean?"

"For a start, yeah."

"I think you have a pretty unique view of life," he began. "You seem to see the world in absolutes. Useful, not useful. Smart, dumb. Good, bad. Most people are all over the place."

"That sounds like a psychological analysis." She glanced at him with a disbelieving expression. "Are you trying to manage me?" She shook her head and answered her own question. "Of course you are. It's a coping strategy you learned growing up with all those older sisters." She leveled a scowl at him. "I'm not them."

Thank fuck.

She wanted the truth. Fine. That's what he would give her. He crouched in front of her and met her gaze. "You've got an hourglass figure that no uniform can hide, a face that makes a man race to open doors for you, even if that door leads straight to hell, and your hair is the stuff of wet dreams. The only reason you aren't overwhelmed with offers is because you don't notice any of them. And if a man gets too pushy you shut him down so fast he doesn't even realize you've castrated him until he's standing there with his balls in his hands wondering what the fuck happened."

She blinked. "I assume you're speaking of my castrating people figuratively."

"You're so damned smart when it comes to what you do that Max describes you as a prodigy, but you are completely clueless when it comes to men."

"I know that."

"Well, wise up."

"And just how am I supposed to do that?"

He closed his eyes and wondered if prayer was the only way he was going to get through this assignment.

"I'm not," she began in a softer tone, "all that comfortable around men in a sexual connotation."

He opened his eyes and watched her head tilt to one side.

"It's not that I don't crave contact with another person, it's just that I never had time to experiment like all the other girls do when they're teenagers. So here I am, twenty-four and I don't know what to do, how to do it or when to do it."

"You," he began, his voice as soft and easy as he could make it, "are very beautiful. Just be honest with the guy you decide you want to be with. Tell him your situation. If he's any kind of decent, he'll be happy to let you experiment on any part of him you want."

Didn't he sound like the voice of reason when the last thing he was feeling with regards to her was reasonable. He *wanted* to be that man.

She swallowed. "Oh, okay."

"Yeah?" he asked, searching her face. She still looked too thoughtful, too anxious. "We're good?"

She hesitated a moment longer then nodded. "Yes. Thank you." She paused, then said, "And I've decided to give you the green light."

All Con could think of was their proximity to the bed.

"I think you're the best partner Max could have found for me anywhere."

She wasn't talking about sex, *asshole*.

He cleared his throat. "We need to report in," he managed to say in a businesslike tone. "And I need you at the shooting range for at least a couple of hours this morning."

They headed out with her asking him about which weapons he preferred for himself and in what situation would he use them. It was a safe topic and the conversation got them all the way to the lab building.

Max was waiting for them. The colonel looked Sophia up and down, and Con remembered the warning about the bruises.

"Hey, did you get any bruises last night?" he asked her.

"Just a little one here." She unbuttoned the cuff of her uniform sleeve and pushed it up to reveal a greenish-blue bruise the size of a grapefruit on her arm.

"That's little?" It looked pretty damn big to Con.

Max leaned in and looked at it. "That's not bad actually. How did you get it?"

Sophia put her hands together and demonstrated the move with her arms. "It's a way to break out of a hold if my assailant has grabbed me face to face."

Max looked at Con expectantly.

"I gave her a Tai Chi lesson and went over how to get out of the most common holds."

"Hmm." Max glanced at her then asked Con, "And today?"

"The shooting range this morning and more Tai Chi tonight."

Sophia moved away to read some paperwork Eugene gave her.

Max stepped closer to Con and lowered his voice a little. "We're getting some conflicting information out of a couple different refugee camps. I know you just got here, but I may need to send you both out with a team in less time than I'd hoped."

"I'll do my best to get her ready," Con said. "She's a good student."

"Really?"

"Yeah, took to Tai Chi like a duck to water."

"I'm glad to hear it. She's one of a kind and we're lucky to have her."

"Why did the Army need her so bad they let her skip most of Basic?"

Max took a moment to respond. "She has an unusual skill. She's able to understand, and even predict, the rapid shifts in a virus's genetic code. Those shifts make sense to her in the same way music makes sense to a composer. Some things work well together, others not. We were very lucky to have her join the team."

Sophia waved at him and headed to her office.

Eugene called Max away then, giving Con a chance to observe everyone for an hour or so. There were at least a dozen different people working in the standard lab and another eight in the airtight lab everyone called the *bubble*.

Some of the tests were the standard sort any hospital would do, others were much less standard.

The staff in the accessible lab were happy to answer his two questions: *How long have you worked here?* and *If you were a bad guy, how would you get in the building?* They all seemed to know he was Dr. Perry's soldier, like he was some sort of accessory only certain people got.

Eugene said he'd have an updated report on Akbar for him after lunch, so Con went to see if Sophia could spare some time for the shooting range.

She agreed and they left.

"What are you going to have me do?" she asked as they walked.

"We're going to keep it simple. I want you to practice as much as possible with your 9 mil. The chances of you using a rifle aren't all that great, so let's stick with your most likely weapon, okay?"

He got her set up, they both put on hearing protection, then he nodded at her to begin.

He let her take six shots before calling a halt and pulling her back from the range where they could talk. She'd hit the target, but her shots were all over the place.

"Your arms are straight with your elbows locked. When you do that, every time you shoot, the kickback moves your arms up and down, spoiling your aim for your next shot. Try keeping those elbows soft, and don't hold your arms out so far from your body. You want those elbows to absorb the kickback. Make sense?"

"Oh. Yes."

"Good, let's try it again, another six shots."

She took up a firing position, but this time Con kicked at her feet until they were shoulder-width apart and pressed down on her shoulders until her knees were slightly bent. She took aim, and he nodded at the improved stance.

She fired, giving herself a full second between shots to resettle her aim. This time her shots were all concentrated below the waist.

Con snorted at the holes in the target.

She grinned at him.

He had her reload her weapon and made more small corrections to her stance. "That's it, slow and easy." He had to shout, but it was better than pulling her out of position every time to suggest a correction. "Take your time and aim for mid-chest."

She sucked in a breath at the same time she squeezed the trigger. The shot penetrated the target's shoulder.

"Try breathing out and firing just as the air is all gone. There's a moment then when you're as still as you're going to be."

She nodded, her hair, tightly pulled back into a bun, brushing his cheek. She let the air out of her lungs and fired. It hit dead center.

She gave an excited yip, which screwed up her next

two shots before she settled down and began hitting the target mid-chest consistently again.

By the time they were done, it was lunchtime and Con was hot, bothered and bad-tempered about it.

Sophia wore a huge grin on her face and preened as they made their way to the food court. As soon as she saw Eugene and Max she rushed over to tell them about her success in the shooting range.

"You're not a sniper yet," Con told her, nudging her shoulder with his. "But with some practice I think you'll be a good shot."

Eugene gave her a high five, and while Max attempted to look repressive, he also couldn't hide his pleased smile when he said, "Excellent. Perhaps you could give Eugene and me a lesson or two as well."

Sophia snorted. "You'd need a lot more than a couple of lessons, Max." She turned to Con and said, "He doesn't even hit the target most of the time. Eugene's pretty good, though."

"Sounds like you need an intensive refresher," Con said to Max. "I'm not sure I have time for that."

"He's getting his own instructor in a few weeks," Eugene put in. "But I'd like to ask a few questions about firearms."

Yup, he was working with a bunch of geeks. And that was okay. They needed him just as much as he needed them.

"No problem, Gene. Do you want time on the range?"

"Not right now. Things are busy at the lab." The way he said it, with a quick look at his boss, told Con things were moderately shitty at the lab, and were likely to get shittier.

"We can talk shop after lunch," Con told him.

"Sounds good, Conman."

Conman. The nickname his old team had given him.

Everything he'd just eaten turned to cold stone in his stomach as he was thrown back to the last happy moment before the blast. His best buddy was telling a joke and Con had interrupted to correct the punch line.

"*Don't you believe the Conman,*" Wayne had said, laughing to everyone else.

All he remembered after that was noise, pain and darkness.

SIX

WELL, WEREN'T THEY a happy group.

Sophia walked next to Eugene, and in front of Connor and Max, both of whom looked grumpier than a couple of grizzly bears fresh out of hibernation. She understood why Eugene and Max were out of sorts. Jones had taken Eugene aside for a quick conversation about supplies, she said. From the shell-shocked expression on his face, Sophia doubted they talked about how many swabs needed to be ordered. Max had his own set of women troubles. He had an ex who could trample an entire team of Special Forces soldiers and she'd called him on his personal cell phone. Sophia didn't know what she said, but Max had looked like he wanted to kill someone. Her boss also had a female weapons and self-defense trainer who was very hard to please.

Why Con was suddenly in a crummy mood, she didn't know.

He followed her into her office, where she found a tray of blood smears waiting for her to look at, as well as a stack of reports for her to review. She glanced over her shoulder to see him glaring at her.

"You're harshing my mellow," she told him. "Why don't you talk to Eugene? I'm not going anywhere."

Con's eyebrow climbed up his forehead. "Harshing your mellow?" He shook his head. "The new age was two decades ago."

"Stop glaring at me and I might consider using a more current metaphor."

He blinked, then rubbed the back of his neck. "Shit." He muttered something else she didn't catch, then said loud enough for her to hear, "Sorry, Sophia. Something I ate isn't agreeing with me. If you have other work to do right now, maybe I'll go see what Eugene needs."

"I have to review these slides and reports. It's going to take me some time."

He nodded, still looking chastised, and left her office.

She stared after him. She'd liked the way he'd said her name. His voice, low and rough, made it sound exotic.

Stop daydreaming, idiot.

An hour later, she finished reviewing the reports and got up to take them to Eugene, who would make sure they got where they needed to go.

He wasn't at his desk, but she could hear him talking to someone in Max's office. Except she was sure Max was at a meeting with the base commander. Then she heard Con rumble a reply and she relaxed.

She was about to return to her own office when she heard Eugene say quite clearly, "I really need your help. I've never been in a situation like this before, and I've got no one else I can ask."

"Okay, okay," Con replied. "I'm not seeing the problem, though."

"Thanks, man. The thing is, I don't want a quick blow job, but how do you tell a woman no to that? She's going to think I'm crazy."

The word *blow job* froze her in place.

"How many times has she offered?"

"Just the once, but that's not what I want. I want a real relationship."

"So tell her that. And then tell her what you want to do to her." Con's voice was matter-of-fact. "In great detail."

"I don't know. I mean, I'm not so eloquent when I'm nervous, you know?"

"Gene, most women like it if you talk dirty to them."

"Um, I just, what should I do to her?"

There was a pause, then Con sighed and said, "Holy fuck, Gene, have you never fooled around?"

"I'm a geek, Con, and I've never been comfortable talking to women I don't know. If Jones hadn't made the first move I wouldn't have gotten to the point where I needed to have this conversation with anyone."

There was a long pause, then Con said, "Okay, here's what you're going to do. You tell her that it's your turn for some dessert, and then you're going to eat her out."

"Uh…"

"Oral sex, Gene. You're going to lick and suck on her clit while you finger fuck her. All you have to do is listen to her to know if you're doing it right. You're smart, you'll catch on quick."

Ohmygod.

"Oookay." Eugene sounded as gobsmacked as she felt. Who needed to breathe when the image of Con doing all that to her, *his head between her legs*, was all she could think about.

"Something tells me she'll give you very specific feedback for the whole shebang."

Sophia's breathing was much too loud, but she couldn't do a thing about it. Con's advice on how to give oral sex sounded good to her. Really good.

Movement from inside Max's office had her rushing into her own as quietly as she could. She dashed across the room and sat behind her microscope, breathing much too fast for someone who was trying to pretend she hadn't just overheard the sexiest sex advice ever.

A knock on her doorjamb jerked her gaze up.

Con stood in the doorway. "Do you mind if I bring my reports in here to read?"

He looked perfectly normal, not like a man who'd just been mentoring a younger man on how to pleasure a woman. She managed a shaky smile. "Not at all, you can use the other desk if you like."

He frowned. "Is there something wrong? You look a little shell-shocked."

She ignored the heat coming off her face and prayed he didn't notice. "I'm okay, just lost in thought when you knocked." Very lost. Who cares if she ever got found, lost.

"I'll be right back." He disappeared and Sophia finally let out the breath she was holding.

Con came back a minute later, enough time for her to put an actual slide on the microscope. She took it off after he came in and put the whole tray of slides aside to be filed.

In an effort to get sexual fantasies about Con out of her head, she pulled out a report sent to her from the CDC regarding the current incidence of a variety of infectious diseases around the world.

If people knew how many deadly infectious diseases were active on the planet, they'd be surprised—and a whole lot more paranoid about catching one.

Con swore and she glanced at him. His voice sounded tight. "What?"

He looked up from the report he was reading, anger sharpening his features. "This Akbar asshole is nuts."

"Yes, he is."

"How did he not kill himself with that anthrax he messed with?"

"We don't know. He doesn't appear to take the proper precautions to prevent infecting himself with whatever he's working with, but we could be wrong."

Con grumbled under his breath some more, then said clearly, "The problem with predicting what a madman will do is that they're unpredictable. He won't make rational decisions."

She considered that. "He has no moral compass and wants revenge. What would a man determined to kill as many people as possible do?"

Con stared at her, but she could almost hear the gears in his head turning. "He's a chemist."

She waited for him to continue his train of thought.

"Why isn't he using chemical weapons?" Con asked.

She thought it was a rhetorical question, but she answered it anyway. "Chemical weapons have a limit. Infect people with the right disease and it could end up everywhere."

"I think you're right." He gave her a sidelong look. "That's creepy."

She ignored his last remark. "It makes sense if the goal is to kill as many people as possible."

"The anthrax he used killed in hours."

"Yes, it did, but we haven't seen it pop up anywhere since. I think he's moved on to something more infectious. Something more easily transmitted from person to person."

"Like what?"

He asked the question like there was a simple answer. There wasn't. "There are many possible pathogens that fit the criteria of infectious and deadly."

Con looked startled. "*How* many?"

"Dozens. Some bacterial, some viral, some more exotic. There is a microscopic world that most people don't realize exists. Most microscopic organisms are benign, some even helpful, but there are plenty of pathogens that are primed and ready to wipe us out if the conditions are right. Or wrong."

"Something tells me," Con said slowly, running one hand through his short hair. "I'm going to learn way too many things I don't want to know on this mission."

She scooted over to him and poked his shoulder. "Lucky for you, I happen to be an excellent teacher."

DINNER THAT NIGHT was oddly entertaining.

Jones watched Eugene with covert glances while he blushed and pretended an extreme interest in his food. Max and Sophia spent the whole meal discussing which viruses and bacteria would make the best weapon in Akbar's mind. They came up with a short list of eighteen possibilities. When Con had commented that eighteen was seventeen too many, they tried to explain to him why they couldn't remove one deadly disease after another from the list. Plus, if they removed one possibility, and Akbar used it, then they wouldn't be prepared to deal with it.

He swallowed his sigh and simply nodded.

What he'd learned about Akbar sparked anger and anticipation. The guy deserved to die. He'd murdered soldiers and civilians alike, and taking him out would go a long way to put to rest Con's need to administer retribution against the extremists who killed his team.

So why was he so damned tired?

Max and Sophia were still chatting about pathogens, their voices determined, confident and full of energy. For a moment, they sounded like his teammates used to when talking about a mission plan. Identifying problems, brainstorming solutions and making inside jokes only they understood.

Loss hit him like a shot to the gut. For a moment he couldn't breathe and didn't much care to. Without his battle buddies, he was just a desperate fuck who couldn't wait to die.

"I need some air," he said, getting to his feet and trying not to look as fucked up as he felt. "Are you okay sticking with the colonel?" he asked Sophia.

She nodded.

"Yes, yes," Max said absently. "I'll watch out for her."

"I'll pick you up at your quarters for your Tai Chi lesson in a couple of hours," Con said. After he got his head back on straight.

"Okay." She waved absently at him and he almost laughed at her single-mindedness. He should thank her for it. So why was he almost disappointed by her dismissal of him?

At first he wandered, no particular destination in mind. He watched as a group of men went through a physical training routine led by a loudmouth sergeant. The drill, the personnel going about their duties, was so damned normal he found himself easing back from the emotional ledge he'd been balanced on.

Still, he could feel the abyss in the back of his head, ready and waiting to suck him under.

He'd done the standard tour of the base, but he wanted to take another look around to note every way to get in and out, whether it was marked or a route only an acrobat could manage. Construction was ongoing, with new barracks, administrative and operational buildings all going up. Lots of civilians all over the place.

That made his trigger finger twitch.

Infiltration was a possibility he couldn't ignore. The checkpoints inside the base were only an inconvenience to a determined attacker or group of attackers. If this Akbar guy was targeting Max and his group, the construction crews could be a useful cover to get inside.

The medical clinic was just as busy as the Freedom *souq* despite the time. The only area with no one on it was the ball diamond.

The deaths of his battle buddies required a response. Could he do that and fulfill his responsibilities to Sophia, as well? He hated using her like this. When he'd interviewed for this assignment, he'd felt sure that he wouldn't like some persnickety genius doctor, but now he'd gotten to know her, and she was funny, smart and more honest than any person he'd ever met before. He didn't want to feel something for her—not friendship or a gut-deep connection that was starting to invade his dreams.

Remember the motto before you become another moron.

Professional. Distant. Hands-off.

Con headed toward his room. He rounded the corner at the end of the hallway to find Sophia already outside her door, but not alone.

Two men dressed as construction workers had her crowded against the wall in the space between her door and his. One of them had her by the arm. The other had his hand over her mouth.

They were attempting to drag her away from her room while she kicked and punched like crazy.

Con's body dumped liquid rocket fuel into his bloodstream, and he was moving—silent, focused and bracing his body for the fight ahead.

He'd crossed half the distance when she bit the hand over her mouth and shouted, "Security."

Con reached them the next second and attacked the closest man from behind, breaking his arm in a precise, controlled movement. The other man let go of Sophia and reached for something on his belt. Con elbowed him in the gut, pivoted around him then swept his feet out from under him and took him to the ground. Fierce pleasure at taking an attacker to the floor surged through him and he ignored the man's yells of pain. Facedown with Con's knee on his back and his arms in Con's grip, he couldn't move.

Con looked at the first guy, expecting him to be attacking with a weapon, but he was on the floor, groaning, as tightly wrapped around his broken arm as a body could get.

The guy underneath him tried to buck him off, but Con shifted his weight along with his captive and leaned harder on his back. He stopped trying to get away and settled for just breathing.

"Are you hurt?" he asked Sophia, riding the emotionless plateau of the adrenaline high. Emotionless, but dangerous in a way few people understood. He could kill both men easily, without hesitation or remorse. *He wanted to*. They'd put their hands on her and would have taken her away and hurt her if he hadn't arrived when he did.

Sophia stared at him with big eyes for a long moment, then closed her mouth and shook her head. She straightened up and said in a shaky voice, "I'll go find security."

"No." His shout sounded rusty. Worse, his hands shook like he was an alcoholic who hadn't had a drink in a week. He needed to focus. She was his responsibility and he'd be *damned* if he let anyone else hurt her. To do that he needed her in sight, close enough that he could cover her if he needed to. "You don't leave my side." If he could see her, and know she was okay, he'd keep it together. Otherwise… "Give another shout, but this time yell *fire*."

She blinked, then hollered it twice.

Down the hall, a couple of guys stumbled sleepily out of their rooms. They looked at Con and the men on the floor.

"Call the MPs," Con ordered. They were probably officers, but he didn't give a shit. "These men were assaulting an officer."

The attacker with the broken arm tried to get up and run, but Con kicked his feet out from under him. He fell, landing on his side.

That had to hurt.

One of the two guys they'd woken up ran down the hall while the other approached carefully.

"Can I help?" he asked.

Help? Con opened his mouth to tell the useless fuck to go back into his room and not come out until he'd found his balls.

Sophia put her hand on Con's shoulder and stroked him as she asked, "Can I borrow your handcuffs, Roger?"

Con hadn't believed anything could disarm his fury, until Sophia did it with one completely serious question.

Roger looked scandalized.

Con actually felt sorry for him.

"Ah, no," Roger replied, rubbing his face and giving her a brief, stiff smile. "Someone borrowed them. What happened?"

"Those two guys tried to grab me," Sophia said.

Broken Arm tried to run again. This time Sophia tripped him. It wasn't smooth or coordinated, but it worked.

This time the guy landed on his broken arm with a crack that was very audible.

Con gave her a grim smile. Good. She hadn't hesitated to take action.

"Looks like I'll be busy." Roger glanced at Con. "I'm a surgeon and that is an arm I'm going to have to put together like a puzzle."

"He's lucky I didn't break his neck."

Roger took a wary step back.

"Con," Sophia said, staring at the guy he had pinned to the floor. "Can he breathe?"

Con glanced down and let up on the pressure a little. The guy beneath him sucked in a couple of frantic breaths before yakking away in Arabic, telling his partner to get up and get out.

Con leaned down and said in the same language, "His arm is in pieces. He's not going anywhere. You attacked an American soldier inside an American military hotel. You're not going anywhere either. Except prison for the rest of your worthless life."

The guy on the floor stopped talking.

Right about then, the MPs arrived.

It took a couple of hours for Sophia to give her version of events, and Con his, for the reports to be written and signed and everyone dismissed. He never let her out of his sight the entire time. At one point, the psychologist on duty tried to talk to Sophia in private, but Con nixed that idea, pulling the *I'm the bodyguard* card. Sophia had backed him up, thank God, and after giving Con a searching look, the psychologist had compromised by talking with Sophia where they could be seen, but not heard.

The possibility of not being able to see her had him fighting the need to pace. If they noticed, he might be reassigned or removed from active duty. He expected the psychologist to want to talk to him privately after she talked to Sophia, but instead she allowed Sophia to remain while she questioned Con.

Con went through the takedown in an even tone, answered the shrink's questions as succinctly as possible and said nothing more than he had to.

Max made an appearance and seemed surprised at how easily Con had taken down the two men. It was the psychologist who smiled and said that most Special Forces soldiers were quite capable of taking down several adversaries.

It was almost midnight before Con walked Sophia to her quarters. They hadn't spoken to each other since Max scowled at them and told them to get lost.

Sophia unlocked her door and turned to look up at him. "Thanks for doing your ninja thing."

"Ninja?" Had she watched too many movies or what?

"You came out of nowhere."

He angled his thumb over his shoulder. "Down the hall actually."

She didn't follow his gesture, her gaze unfocused. "I couldn't believe anyone would try to kidnap me in the middle of the Navy hotel."

"If they timed it right, it would be no more difficult than taking you off the street."

He should have never left her alone.

Maybe he shouldn't have said it so matter-of-factly, because her face lost all its color.

"Oh." She swallowed hard and looked at the floor. A couple of seconds later, she met his gaze wearing a pasted-on smile and the saddest eyes he'd ever seen. "Still…not very nice of them. Thanks for interrupting their plans. Good night." She turned away, unlocked her door and slipped inside.

Oh no you don't. Pretending it hadn't happened wasn't going to make things better. She needed to vent, the sooner the better. He'd learned that the hard way.

Con stuck his foot in the door before she could close it. "We need to talk."

"Oh." She hesitated, her gaze darting down the hall.

She was afraid and was trying to tough it out all on her own. He knew how fucking useless it would be and that was unacceptable. A soldier needed his battle buddies to get him through the shit. The loss of his had damn near killed him.

"I get it," he said with a sigh. "You're probably scared, angry and fifty other emotions no one likes to deal with, but you and I, we're a team, and I need to make sure you're okay. That includes checking your room and talking about this shit."

She stared at him for a long moment, then backed up and let him by. "Okay." She closed the door behind him and locked it. As soon as the door was closed she let out a huge pent-up breath and her tense shoulders came down.

Yup, she was scared. But not of him.

Something wound tight inside his chest relaxed a little. He wanted to hold her for as long as it took to get that lost expression off her face.

He made himself turn away to inspect at her quarters.

Her room was a bit bigger than his, but not by much. Where his was OCD neat, hers looked like a tornado had hit it. A tornado full of books.

Textbooks, biographies, romance novels, even some graphic novels were stacked all over the room. There had to be a few *hundred* books lying around.

"Sorry about the mess," she said with a dismayed look on her face. "I tend to forget to tidy things."

"You really hate reading, don't you?"

She snorted, but controlled her response almost immediately. "Well, yeah. I guess I really, really hate reading. I mean, almost as much as you must hate martial arts."

"Touché." He looked down at the pile closest to him and discovered a biography of General Pershing on top and below it one about Erwin Rommel. Was she studying military tactics and strategy? He'd never really understood how smart could be sexy until Sophia. "You'll like the book on Rommel. He was another person who didn't like boxes."

"He seems interesting, not like most of Hitler's generals."

"I think Hitler disgusted him."

"Do I disgust you?" she asked in a small voice.

Con's head turned to look at her so fast whiplash might be a concern. "What?"

Her eyes and mouth drooped, but she wasn't looking at him, she was staring at the floor again. "I didn't do anything but stand there like a frightened little girl. They were going to take me somewhere and probably hurt me, but did I fight back? No, I froze." She glanced at him finally, her lips pressing into a tight white line. "I promise to do better next time."

"Whoa, stop with the self-flagellation." She thought he was unhappy with *her*? "I'm disgusted with security at this place and with Max for not making sure you were properly trained in *some* self-defense before now, but I'm not disgusted with you."

She frowned. "Why not me?"

"Because you *did* do something. You bit that guy and gave yourself a chance to yell for help." He moved some books out of the way and sat on the edge of her bed. She sat next to him, then leaned her head on his shoulder.

Not exactly his normal method of helping a teammate decompress—usually that had involved throwing darts with Wayne or boxing with Patterson—but he could handle this. When he put his arm around her, she sighed happily and nuzzled a little closer. Her breast brushed his side and his dick started to take notice. *Asshole.* Hadn't been interested in sex for months, and now he was perving on his vulnerable partner.

He cleared his throat, gave her what he hoped was a friendly nudge. It was time to get off the bed and put a little space between them before he did something to fuck this up. "I'm really proud of what you did today. You took the training I gave you and used it exactly the way you were supposed to. You're a good soldier, Doc."

He stood, trying to inconspicuously adjust his pants as he took a few steps away from her. There. Crisis averted. No inappropriate reactions here.

"I want to have sex with you."

He couldn't have heard that right. His dick was trying to convince his brain of something that wasn't possible. "What?"

She stood and stepped up close. Way too close. "I want to have sex with you."

He sucked in a breath as heat flashed through him like a lightning strike, and suddenly the room wasn't near big enough. "Come on, we're going to the hospital."

"Why?" she asked as he took her by the arm.

"Because you obviously hit your head or something."

She resisted, trying to twist out of his hold. "I'm fine. A request for sex does not equal diminished mental capacity. Besides, I decided I wanted sex with you earlier today."

He let go of her arm and stared at her, his brain unable to connect any fucking dots. "Why?" He couldn't think of a thing he'd done to inspire this good girl to ask him to get dirty with her.

"Your sexual advice to Eugene sounded really good." She blushed and stared at his mouth.

A groan came out of him at the knowledge she'd been listening in.

"Look, I'm not some kind of sex guru, I'm your teammate. We can't...do that."

"Why not?"

He stared at her, unable to think of one reason.

"If you're worried about me becoming attached to you, like a girlfriend, don't worry. I know this is just for now. No strings. Isn't that what people say?"

"No *strings*?" He couldn't believe it. He ran his hands over his face. He couldn't fucking believe it.

"Just listen to me, please." She closed her eyes for a moment, then looked at him with a determined expression on her face.

He'd seen that expression on her face. It meant she wasn't going to back down.

"I've always been too sick, young or busy to even imagine becoming intimate with someone. But you..." She paused, obviously searching for words. "You wouldn't laugh at me if I say or do the wrong thing. You don't treat me like I'm so fragile you can't touch me, and I know you won't act like you've done me a favor afterward."

She smiled and glanced at his crotch. "I'm not an idiot, I saw your erection earlier. I think you want me, too."

"You have no idea what I want." For a moment he wanted nothing more than to show her. Kiss her and pet her until she was drunk, then strip her bare and show her that sex wasn't rational. It was hot, messy and uncontrolled.

The angry, wounded part of him wanted to take what she was offering, wanted to drown himself in her in the worst way.

He'd feel something other than guilt and despair.

"You're right, I don't know." She threw up her hands. "But I'd really, really like to find out." She huffed. "I've never felt this way about any man before. I'm so, so..."

"Horny?"

"Yes," she barked at him, frustration a visible thing in her clenched fists and teeth.

He snatched her close and kissed her. He couldn't stop himself.

She melted against him and moaned, and her immediate surrender gave him back a measure of control. He gentled his grip and his kiss.

"No" she muttered after a moment, pulling back to look at him. "I want everything. No holding back."

His lips were on hers again and she let him in with a needy sigh. He eased her closer, one hand behind her head, the other on the small of her back, and tried to keep things gentle.

Her arms encircled him, her hands pressing against him, and she raised herself on tiptoe to kiss him harder.

She might not know what she was doing, but her eagerness was contagious.

One of her hands slid down his back. A second later, she was cupping his cock through his pants.

Oh holy fuck. He pushed her up against the wall, trapping her there with the weight of his body. Her curves pressed against his body, and the tits he'd admired felt fucking awesome against his chest. He wanted them in his hands and under his tongue.

Her lips parted under his assault and his tongue fucked her mouth, while one hand slid down to learn the perfect curve of her ass and the other cupped one of those gorgeous breasts.

She moaned and clutched him tighter, following his lead, tangling her tongue with his. Her hands were busy everywhere, stroking his shoulders, chest and cock. She couldn't seem to stop stroking his fucking cock.

She lit him up with raw electricity. Her untutored touches and moans robbed him of all his civilized veneer. He couldn't remember ever feeling this scorching hot for any woman ever. He groaned and dropped all pretense of restraint, taking her mouth the way he wanted to take her body. Her under him in a full-on, no-holds-barred possession.

She followed his lead without hesitation, adding fuel to his fire. *She wanted him as much as he wanted her.* He slid his hand up her body to cup her other breast. And her response was to try to climb his body. She got as far as riding his thigh, then couldn't seem to make herself move any further.

Hot damn, she *liked* that.

When he caught her nipple between his thumb and index finger, pinching and rolling it through her clothes, she pulled her head away.

She stared at him, not hiding her lust or frustration in any way, her chest heaving with breaths that couldn't seem to find enough air. "I want…"

"What?" he asked, rubbing his thumb over her nipple again.

Her teeth clenched together. "An orgasm, one I don't give myself." She ground herself down on his thigh.

He grinned and leaned down to suck at her earlobe, then whispered in her ear. "How do you do it? Do you fuck yourself with your fingers or do you have a toy?"

"Both," she hissed as she rubbed herself against his thigh. "But it's not enough. I want you, but I don't have any condoms."

He wanted her—fuck, he craved her—but if he took her, could he let her go? He couldn't just take her and then leave. She trusted him. He had to draw the line somewhere, no matter how much it was going to kill him. He gave her breast more attention and she arched into his hand. "You don't need to have intercourse to have an orgasm."

She frowned at him. "I really want...penetration."

That one word had him ready to show her how it was done, but he couldn't do it, not when he was lying to her about why he really wanted on her team. He was an asshole, but he wasn't a complete douche. He could still give her what she wanted, though maybe not the way she expected. He turned them so it was his back against the wall, then he spun her around so her back was plastered his front. He played with one breast, molding it and teasing the nipple. "Rock your ass back and give my cock a taste of you."

She didn't answer with words, just followed his order and moaned as that beautiful, plump ass pressed and stroked against the biggest boner he'd ever had in his life.

"Open your pants," he whispered in her ear.

As she did it, he kept teasing her breasts, first one, then the other, while his other hand spanned her lower belly. "Are you sure you want this?"

"Yes," she moaned, rubbing her ass over his erection. Her hands reached behind her to touch him. There was no finesse, just fingers seeking him out, her palms massaging his hips.

"Hold on." He stopped her as she went for his dick, even though he seriously didn't want to. "Let's focus on you for right now."

"I don't want to stop." Her voice shook and she rocked back harder. "Please. Tell me what to do."

She was killing him. He was going to die, right here.

He ground his dick against her ass one last time before putting his palm over her mound and stroking her through her underwear until she whimpered and pushed back. He dropped another kiss on her neck before whispering, "Put my hand down your panties."

SEVEN

SOPHIA COULDN'T BREATHE, couldn't think, couldn't do anything but imagine what he might do. Her whole body shivered and if he hadn't been holding her up, she'd have collapsed at his feet. His order incited an explicit fantasy in her head and she had to know if this could be as good as what she was imagining. She took him by the wrist and pulled his hand downward.

She tugged his hand down until his fingers grazed her clitoris. His touch triggered a cascade of sensation, pleasure like she'd never known and a need that continued to build.

He took over, exploring her. His fingers slipped between the folds of her sex easily, and she jumped when he circled her clitoris with one finger.

Wow.

She bucked and writhed against him. Oh *so* good.

He rocked his hips against her ass and kept circling the stiff nub, winding something deep in her core tighter and tighter.

"Con?" She'd meant to order, but his name came out as a plea. She was going to come apart at the seams if he didn't do something soon.

Maybe she could speed things up.

She reached back, found his erection and, using her hands and her ass, stroked him through his clothing.

"Holy shit," he muttered, his fingers moving faster,

surer over her clit. His hips ground his long, hard penis into her hands and butt. "Harder, sweetheart," he growled into her ear.

She did as commanded and was rewarded with him thrusting one finger up into her.

He tilted her head back so he could kiss her, then added another finger, fucking her with them both.

Intense pleasure and the desperate climb toward an orgasm the likes of which she'd never experienced before made breathing almost impossible.

"Oh my *God*, Con," she cried out. "*Please.*"

He flicked her clit rapidly and pressed down with the heel of his hand against her mound as he fucked her hard with his fingers. "Come for me."

Her body seized, unable to process the extreme pleasure rocketing through it.

She screamed into his mouth.

Sophia didn't know where she was, when she was or who she was, and she didn't care. She'd never felt anything like it before in her life.

She wasn't sure how long they stood there with his hand between her legs. It could have been a few minutes or an hour, but eventually, her higher brain functions began to bring her down to earth.

She'd just orgasmed with all her clothes on. He couldn't have gotten much out of the exchange. That wasn't right. Fair was fair.

She lifted her head and looked up at him. His face was flushed and he stared at her as if he wanted more. She'd put that expression on his face. Her. A geeky doctor who never in a million years thought she'd ever be in this sort of situation with a man who was even more dangerous than he was smart.

She put her hand on his crotch and sucked in a breath. The fabric beneath her hands was damp, his penis semi-rigid under her questing fingers. Though it did seem to be growing longer and harder.

He pulled her hand away and put it on his neck.

"You had an orgasm?"

"Oh yeah." He traced one large finger down her face and bit down on his bottom lip. "I haven't come in my pants since I was about seventeen."

She swallowed down her need to kiss him again. "I... I don't know what I'm supposed to do next."

He traced her ear. "What do you want to do?"

She shivered. "I want to kiss you. I want you to touch me. I want to touch you. I want—"

He put a finger over her lips, his expression changing from lazy and sated man to something harder. The soldier was looking out of his eyes. And she was his target. "Slow down a little. We need to get a couple things straight." He leaned his forehead against hers. "I'm here to keep you alive and safe." For as long as he could.

"I know, but can't we...?" She let out a frustrated huff. "I'm going to say this all wrong, so take it like I mean it and not how I say it."

He started to laugh.

She punched him on the shoulder. "I want you. Jerk. I know it's against the rules and probably not the smartest thing to do, have a sexual relationship with my bodyguard, but..."

He closed his eyes and let his head fall back for a moment. "I could get transferred at any time. You and I can't have a relationship." He put air quotes around the last word. "All we can have is an understanding that what we do together during our off-hours is recreational."

He was right. With her projected life span, she couldn't have a relationship with anyone. But if she could, it would be with him. "So, no emotional attachment?"

"Yes."

She was missing something, she knew she was. His expression was too conflicted. He should have looked satisfied and focused, but now he looked sad and angry.

"You want me?" she asked, uncertain.

"Yeah. You're gorgeous, inside and out."

"Smart is sexy, and I like your muscles." She gazed at him and licked her lips. She still hadn't found out what his skin tasted like.

"Oh yeah, which ones?"

"Your pectoralis major, trapezius and deltoid muscles." She stroked each pair of muscles as she spoke their names. "Are amazingly well defined. I could fondle you for hours." She wanted to tell him to take his shirt off, but the grin on his face convinced her to wait for his response.

He opened his mouth to say something, but there was a knock at her door. He eased her away from him and he nodded at her to answer.

"Hello? Who's there?"

"Doctor," said a male voice, "I have a message for you from Colonel Maximillian."

Sophia looked at Con and shook her head. If Max wanted to tell her something at this time of night, he'd tell her himself or have Eugene deliver a message. Whoever was at the door was *not* Eugene.

Con signaled her to keep talking while he snuck across the room to stand next to the door.

"Just a moment, I need to put my uniform on." She zipped up her pants and tucked her shirt back in.

"No problem, ma'am," said the voice.

Con put his hand up, palm out for three or four seconds, then nodded at her to approach the door. He had her stop a few feet away, then opened the door swiftly, grabbing the man who waited on the other side.

Con threw him past Sophia and into a pile of books. Two strides and Con had his arm behind his back.

It was the idiot who'd tried to kiss her.

Con gave him a grim smile. "What the fuck?"

Moron stared at Con like he was the boogie man. "Sorry, man, I got the wrong room or something."

"No," Con told him, yanking him up by his collar. "You got the right room, you just didn't expect her to have security *in* the room."

"Are you brain damaged?" Sophia asked, examining the idiot like he was a cockroach. "I said no and you ignored me. You *hurt* me." She showed him her bruised hand, which was now a sickly greenish, yellow color.

The idiot started babbling. "I'm sorry, I'm sorry. I really am. I was just…just…"

Sophia paused and looked at Con.

He tightened his grip on idiot's arms and asked in a low, deadly voice, "Just out for a stroll and thought you'd indulge yourself and assault an officer?"

"No! No, no, no. I got lost and…and knocked on the wrong door."

"You used my CO's name," Sophia reminded him. "You said you had a message for me from him. How does that equal the wrong door?"

Idiot stared at her, horror in his eyes, and said nothing.

What did he think they were going to do, kill him?

She glanced at Con, who did sort of look like he wanted to kill someone, and decided enough was enough. She was tired, physically and emotionally, and she didn't want to spend another two hours with the MPs explaining how another person out to attack her got his arms broken. Or a leg. Or his neck.

Having a partner was more work than it looked.

She picked up her cell phone and called her boss.

"Max," he barked into the phone after one ring. "You think of something to add to your report, Sophia?"

"No," she sighed. "I have to write a new report, though. Connor is currently restraining an American soldier who thought he could gain entry to my room by saying he had a message from you."

"*What?*"

"Luckily, Connor was still here…" Saying they'd created a *sticky situation* together would probably be a bad idea. "…debriefing me on the earlier incident when this idiot knocked on my door."

"I'll be right there with a couple of MPs." Max's growl practically vibrated her phone.

Oh, he was pissed. "Very good, sir." She ended the call and slipped her phone back in her pocket.

Idiot, who had been so tense his entire body vibrated, relaxed, closed his eyes and let out a huge breath.

"You shouldn't look so relieved," she told him. "Colonel Maximillian doesn't take anyone screwing with his staff lightly."

"But I didn't do anything," Idiot said so fast he nearly tripped over his own tongue.

She couldn't understand the stupidity of his actions. "Only because I have a bodyguard."

"You're so fucking weird," he hissed. "I thought he was to keep you from tripping over your books." He squawked then, a pain-filled sound.

Con had tightened his grip and was bending Idiot's shoulders back in a move that would eventually dislocate them.

She shook her head at Con, then gave Idiot a smack on the head. "I'd rather be weird than stupid, Stupid."

The sound of several booted feet marching closer had her moving to the door. She was about to open it, but turned to look at Con. When he gave her a slight nod, she went ahead and opened the door.

Max was just stepping up to knock and she got out of the way so he could come in along with two MPs.

The look he gave the guy Con had by the arms could have frozen him stiff. "Do you have any idea how much trouble you're in?"

"Sir, I was mistaken about the room."

Max's expression went glacial. "Shut the door," he said softly to the two MPs.

They did, then stood at parade rest waiting for orders.

"Do you have any knowledge of the two men who attempted to abduct Captain Perry earlier tonight?" Max asked, carefully enunciating every word.

Surprise rounded the idiot's eyes for a second. "What?"

"Did you provide information, maps or schedules relating to this base and its operation to the two men who attempted to abduct Captain Perry?"

"What men?" He looked wildly from her face to Max's. "Someone tried to *kidnap* her?"

"This is the last time I will ask. After that, you won't have an opportunity to speak until your legal counsel has been brought in. By that time, every soldier on this base will believe you're a traitor and a terrorist."

"I'm no traitor!" His breathing was frantic. "I was going to… I mean she's not bad looking and—"

"Your intent was sexual assault?"

The idiot's mouth opened and closed, then finally he just nodded.

Sophia had to breathe through her mouth to keep from kicking him in the testicles.

Max glanced at the MPs, his face tight with disgust. "Take him away."

Con released the idiot to the two MPs. The three of them watched silently as he was handcuffed and taken out of the room.

Max closed the door behind them and turned to face her and Con. "I'll post a guard outside your door."

Sophia's stomach knotted. "Sir, I'm not…that is, I don't feel…" God, how did she explain the mixed-up muddle of her emotions?

"Safe?" Con offered the word tentatively.

"Yes, that. Could I bunk with Connor for the rest of the night and worry about my room tomorrow?"

Max stared at her like she'd spoken a foreign language. "You said he was here debriefing you?" Max asked in a deceptively soft voice. He looked at Con with a tight expression.

Con didn't flinch or fidget. "You know as well as I do that venting to a buddy is important after something like this."

"So you're *buddies* now?" Max asked in a tone that said he didn't believe it.

"Yes," Sophia answered. "I trust him. He…" How did she explain? "He doesn't treat me like I'm twelve or disabled."

"You only met him a few days ago," Max said, his voice rising.

"So what?" she demanded. "He's kept his word to me, Max." She stared at her boss and mentor, and begged him with her eyes to believe her. "I feel safe with him." She held out her hands. "Isn't that what you wanted?"

Max looked at Con again and opened his mouth a couple of times before anything came out. "Fine. We'll discuss this further in the morning."

"Yes, sir," she and Con said simultaneously.

Max shook his head and said, "Grab what you need for tonight. I'll meet you two in his room with a cot." Max didn't wait for their answer. He slammed the door on his way out.

"That was weird," Sophia said after a moment. And scary and infuriating.

"Can you be specific?" Con asked. "A lot of weirdness has happened in the last few hours."

"All of it."

"Yeah," he sighed. "I need a shower."

She glanced at his crotch and noted that the wet spot had dried enough that it wasn't noticeable. "I'm uncertain of the protocol. Do I apologize, because getting undressed is probably going to be an even *stickier situation* than it was earlier?"

He looked at her with a frown that turned his eyebrows into one long straight line. "Seriously? You're going to ask me that out loud?"

"How else am I supposed to ask? Charades?" She spun on her heel and went to grab her go bag.

"Whoa." Con took her by the shoulders and turned her around to meet her gaze. "You only apologize if you're sorry you did it. Are you?"

That cooled her frazzled nerves. "No. Are you?"

"I don't think it was the smartest thing either of us has done, but I'm not sorry either." His face was somber. What had him looking so sad?

"Okay," she said, trying to smile. After all that had happened in the last few hours, it probably looked more like a wince.

He watched her for another moment. "I scared you. When I took down those two assholes. Didn't I?" He looked like he regretted what he did.

For the first time since she met him, Sophia was tempted to lie.

EIGHT

SHE HAD BEEN SCARED, but for the two men who attacked her. Con had looked both capable and willing to kill them. "No, I wasn't scared of you. I was scared you were going to do something you'd get in trouble for." She paused. "Though I admit I did have a hard time not kicking them both in the face. I really wanted to do that."

He grunted, and Sophia followed him out her door and into his room. No one else was around, which was probably a good thing. Rumors didn't take long to make their rounds on the base and if anyone saw her going into Connor's room, it would be all over the base by morning that they were sleeping together.

Connor locked the door behind her.

She took three steps in and came to a stop. Aside from the bed, much too narrow and probably too short for a man Connor's size, there was a duffel bag on the floor. That was it.

"Max said something about a cot, didn't he?" she asked.

"Yeah." Con moved around her to crouch down next to his duffel. His shoulders were hunched over and he wasn't looking at her at all.

"What's wrong?"

"Nothing." But he still didn't look at her.

"Don't lie to me." She hadn't meant to say it so hard,

but despite her normally excellent coping skills, after the events of the last few hours she was discovering she had very little control of her emotions.

He glanced up at that with a fierce frown. "I'm not."

"Then why are you acting so strange?"

"Strange? How long have we known each other? Three days tops and you think in that time you've got me all figured out?" He shook his head and went back to his duffel.

"I know your job is the most important thing in your life." She took a step toward him. "I know you hate feeling weak or out of control." Another step. "I know that when you saw those two men attacking me in the hallway you were willing to do anything it took to save me." One more step. "I know that if you were injured during that fight, you wouldn't tell me because you don't ever want to step foot in another hospital again."

He stood, staring down at her with an unreadable expression. "I'm not injured."

"Prove it."

He stood, unbuttoned his shirt and shrugged it off, letting it fall to the floor.

She visually examined every inch of his chest, then took one wrist and rotated his arm to see if she'd missed a cut or a slice. Nothing. She repeated the inspection of the other arm.

God he smelled good. Like pine and earth and strength.

"Turn around."

He followed her order without comment and she found no injury of any kind.

He turned around and pulled his shirt on, though he didn't bother with buttoning it up. "Believe me now?"

"Yes. But, I still think you're acting strange."

He let out a gust of breath and said, "You want to know what's bugging me? Fine, I'll tell you." He pointed at the bed and growled, "All I can think about is sleeping with you on that bed, knowing I won't get any sleep at all."

She snorted. "Of course we wouldn't get any sleep. All you'd have to do is turn over once and you'd squish me."

Connor covered his face with one hand for a moment. When he dropped it, he was laughing. Hard.

He moved over to sit on the bed and continued to laugh. "You never say, do or think in a way I can predict." He shook his head. "You are the most frustrating woman I've ever met."

"Ha." She walked over and poked him in the chest. "I am a *constant* fucking delight."

He looked at her, his face alight with amusement, his eyes burning with what she now recognized as desire, and said, "Yes, you are."

A soft knock at the door and Con was up and heading toward it before she even realized what was going on. Gone was the amused man. In his place was the deadly soldier. He pointed at her to hide in the corner where someone in the doorway couldn't see her, then opened it.

No words were exchanged, but Max came in with a cot and a sleeping bag.

As soon as the door was closed, Max turned on Connor and asked, "Why the hell is your shirt undone?"

"Sophia thought I might have gotten injured when I took down those two goons earlier."

"He's got an irrational fear of hospitals," she said wryly to Max, coming out of the corner.

"My dislike of hospitals is based on very rational reasons, thank you very much. Most of which involve pain, boredom and pain."

"You said *pain* twice."

"It hurt," he told her. "A lot."

She raised an eyebrow. "Baby."

"Bossy."

"Shut up, both of you." Max sounded fed up and looked it, too. "Here's your cot, Sophia." He dropped it on the floor. "In light of tonight's events, you and your bodyguard can report in at 0900."

"Whoopee, we get to sleep in a whole two hours."

"Hey," Con said. "Two hours of sleep is two hours of sleep. Don't knock our benefactor."

Sophia rolled her eyes.

"This is a terrible idea," Max muttered as he shook his head and left. "They're too much alike."

Con locked the door and smiled at her. "That was awesome."

She blinked. "I didn't plan on being so irritating, it just sort of happened."

"I know, that's what makes it so awesome." He held out his fist toward her.

She glanced at it for a second, then very slowly bumped it with her own fist. "We're starting to think like a team?" she guessed.

"Yeah." For a moment he looked like someone had hit him in the back of the head with a bat. He turned away, picked up her cot and began assembling it.

It only took him twenty seconds or so to have the

cot ready. He put it against the wall leaving a space between his bed and her cot to walk.

Too much space, and she was starting to shiver. When had she gotten so cold?

"Connor?"

He pulled the sleeping bag out of its sleeve and unrolled it on the cot. "What?" he asked without looking at her.

"Can I sleep a little closer to you?"

She hadn't even finished talking and his gaze was on her face. Whatever he saw made him approach her and cup her cheeks.

"You're starting to feel the effects, aren't you?"

"If you mean shaking, nausea and dizziness, then yes." She wasn't sure when it had started, probably sometime after they arrived in Connor's room, but it was getting progressively worse as the seconds went by.

It was like her whole body was going haywire. Something short-circuited somewhere.

Connor coaxed her to sit on his bed, then he pulled her cot right over so there was no space between their sleeping areas.

The shaking got worse and she began to have trouble breathing. An invisible weight sat on her chest and she couldn't seem to breathe around it.

Connor sat down beside her, then pulled her right on to his lap and wrapped his long arms around her. He crooned into her ear, "I've got you, you're okay. You're safe now." Over and over.

She turned her face into his chest and began to cry. "What's wrong with me?"

He rocked her a little and said, "It's your body coming down off the adrenaline high and the stress reaction to the ugliness of what you experienced all wrapped up in one nasty package."

"But, I wasn't hu…hurt."

"The threat is often more than enough." He sighed into her hair and kissed her temple.

"You must think me a pretty po…poor partner, to fa…fall apart like this."

"Hey, none of that now," he said in a stern tone. "Something similar happened to me during my first year of training."

"You cried?"

"Like a fucking baby."

She lifted her head to study his face, but there was nothing closed about it. He looked at her, his eyes and mouth drooping with sadness.

"And my battle buddy…" His voice died. After a hard swallow, he cleared his throat, then continued, "held me while I blew snot nuggets into his shirt."

It should be physiologically impossible to laugh and cry at the same time. It kind of hurt in a hiccupy, sneezy sort of way.

It did help to calm her down, and she was able to stop after a few more minutes. She wiped her nose on his shirt and eased off his lap. "Thanks."

He looked askance at his shirt. "Anytime, partner."

"You said you were going to have a shower anyway," she said, wincing.

"You going to be okay if I have that shower?"

"Yeah, I think I'm done blubbering all over you." Now that she was calm, exhaustion made her limbs feel like they weighed ten times what they normally did. "I'm kind of sleepy."

He nodded. "I'll only be a few minutes. Don't open

the door to anyone. As far as the rest of the world is concerned, you're not here."

She yawned. "I understand." Sophia stretched out on the edge of his bed, intending to move to her cot in a second or two. "Go. Get clean."

He made little noise as he grabbed his toiletry kit and towel. She barely heard the door close behind him.

CON WOULD HAVE liked to have someone he could pound on, but a shower in the hottest water he could stand was all he had time for. He was finished and checking on her in three minutes. Clean and wearing only the towel around his waist.

Sophia was fast asleep on his bed.

One little push would have rolled her into her cot, but he found he didn't want her even that far away. He put a pair of boxers on, then pulled on a pair of sleep pants. He slid in behind Sophia, spooned up against her, put an arm around her and fell into a deep dreamless sleep.

A NUMBER OF booted feet marching down the hall created enough noise to wake the dead. Con discovered himself held down in the most awesome manner possible. Sophia had rolled over in her sleep and somehow draped herself over his chest. One of her legs was thrown over both of his, effectively holding him down.

He checked his watch. 0845. "Hey," he said, giving Sophia a small shake. "Wake up."

"Why?" she mumbled.

"Because we have to report for duty in fifteen minutes."

She groaned and sat up. She looked around, took in

her position and his and asked, "Did I sleep with you on this plank all night?"

"Yes, and it's not a plank, it's a bed."

"It's barely a bed."

"It's the same as yours."

"Ha," she snorted. "I added another mattress to mine because it felt like I was sleeping on a *plank*."

"And you snore."

"I do not."

"It's kind of like a purring snore. Cute."

"I'm going to cute you in the mouth," she grumbled. "I need a shower."

Connor considered her for a moment. She seemed okay. "Sure, go ahead."

She got to her feet and took a step before he saw them.

Bruises.

"Sophia?" He was up and next to her before she got all the way around.

"What?"

He lifted one of her arms and took a good look at the bruise pattern on the skin of her biceps. A hand.

She followed his gaze and sighed. "That's not bad, actually."

He touched her face, stroked one finger along her jaw. "You have more here." The sight of them made him want to beat the shit out of the two assholes who'd put their hands on her all over again.

She shrugged. "I get new ones every day."

He could see them, the old bruises, some dark, some pale yellow and green. Her uniform would cover most of them up, keep them out of sight. Was anyone aware of how many she carried on her body?

Was he responsible for any of them?

"It looks worse than it is," she said, a crooked smile on her face. She shrugged again and went into the bathroom.

He stood there for a whole minute, thinking. Trying to figure out a way he could keep her safe.

Safe. That was one state of being no soldier counted on.

FIFTEEN MINUTES LATER, they reported for duty only two minutes late. As soon as she said hello to Eugene, Max was in the doorway to his office.

"Sophia."

"Yes, sir?"

He didn't reply, just looked at her for a moment, then went back inside. Wonderful, he was in a mood.

She followed.

Connor touched her arm and asked in a low voice, "You okay?"

He asked her that now instead of when they woke up? Or was his complete avoidance of their sexual encounter his way of reinforcing the *no relationship* part of their relationship? "Of course, it's just Max."

"If you need anything, you call me. Got it?"

"What, like a cup of coffee and a muffin?"

One eyebrow rose. "Funny."

Oddly, needling him made her feel better, almost normal.

She went into Max's office. He was reading something on his computer and didn't look up when he said, "Close the door."

She closed it then sat down in the chair in front of Max's desk. Good God her back hurt. Connor was wrong. That thing he slept in wasn't just a bed, it was a bed of nails.

Max turned away from the computer to examine her as if she were an interesting new disease. "How are you?"

How are you? or *how did this happen?* The questions Max often began within his informational fishing expeditions. If she answered honestly, she'd probably be in therapy the rest of her deployment.

"Tired and irritated."

Her answer seemed to surprise him. "Irritated?"

"You'd understand if you had a six-foot-something guardian Green Beret watching your every move for signs of injury, distress or even worse, a paper cut."

Max grunted. "Good. The lone man who tried to gain entry to your room leaves on a flight later today."

"Good." They stared at each other for another moment. Then Sophia said, "Anything else?"

"Send Button in."

She nodded and left. "Max wants to see you," she said to Connor. "I'm going to my office."

"See you there."

She kept walking, but Connor didn't move. He was still watching her when she glanced back as she opened her door.

Paranoid much?

She flipped on the lights, made her way to her desk and logged in to her computer. After looking at all the lab results for all the tests completed this morning, she began reviewing blood smears.

Everything about the day was normal, so why did shivers rack her body every few minutes?

Connor stuck his head through the doorway. "Everything okay?"

"Yes." She looked him over. "You appear..." *Perfectly lickable.* "Undamaged."

He grinned. "Max is a professional. Roughing me up would hurt his reputation. I've got to pick up some additional gear. I should only be gone for a bit."

"I'm not your mom, you can go wherever you like."

He lost his smile and came all the way into the room, not stopping until he was crouched next to her. He put a hand on her knee and it felt so shockingly warm she jerked.

His expression was so neutral she knew it was a lie.

"When I get back," he said in an easy tone. "You're going to get another Tai Chi lesson."

"I don't have time."

"It's only going to take ten minutes."

"That doesn't seem worth it."

"It'll help with the shakes."

She wanted to tell him he was imagining things, but that would be a blatant untruth. She just nodded.

He left and she managed to work another ten minutes before the nervous energy in her body forced her to get up and walk around. Might as well go to the bathroom.

Jones was in there and she looked Sophia over. "How are you? It's all over the base what happened last night."

"I'm okay. Kind of sick of everyone asking though."

Jones smiled. "Got it. Most of the women on the base will be showing some solidarity by sitting with you at meals today. Wave at me when you're ready to go to lunch."

"That's not necessary."

"You're tougher than most people, Dr. Perry, but we need to do it for all of us."

"Okay."

A minute later, she and Jones exited the bathroom.

When they reached Eugene's desk, Jones said to Sophia, "See you at lunch." Then she turned and smiled at Eugene. "Hi, Gene, having a good morning so far?"

"It's okay," he said, his gaze darting between Sophia and Jones. "Got a lot of extra paperwork to do thanks to those assholes last night." He focused his attention on Jones, looking her square in the eyes despite a blush heating his cheeks. "You're being safe, right? Traveling in groups?"

"Yes." Jones's smile deepened. "I knew there was a reason why I liked you. Catch you later, Gene." She winked at Sophia and left.

"She likes you," Sophia told him as they both watched the woman walk away.

"She likes me?" Eugene asked incredulously.

"That's what she told me," Sophia said, then winced. "Was I supposed to tell you that?"

Eugene threw his hands up in the air. "I do *not* understand women. That one least of all."

"I think she likes smart and you've got more brains than most of the men on this base."

"Thanks," Eugene said dryly. "But I'm small fry compared to Sergeant Button. The guy could give lessons in interrogation."

"He interrogated you?"

"Yeah, about you, Max and the whole team."

A cold ball of uneasiness settled into the pit of her stomach. "What did you tell him?"

"About you? That you like solving puzzles that involve really small things and you want to make a difference." He paused. "Should I have kept my mouth shut?"

"I doubt he would have let you." Sophia looked away for a moment, then said, "Thanks, Gene."

"Anytime. Oh, I almost forgot, Colonel Maximillian wants to see you again. General Stone and Connor are in there, too."

That can't be good. "Okay."

Last night was a jumbled mess in her head. She'd been frightened, then almost overwhelmed with lust, then ridiculously angry. The only constant in all of it was a man who couldn't let go of his ghosts.

Now she had to face him, as well as her mentor and a general who could put an end to her partnership with Connor anytime he wanted.

She slipped her focused physician mask over her, let it settle into place and prepared to deal with the coming interrogation.

NINE

"I'LL TALK TO Max first, thanks." Sophia gave Eugene what she hoped was a businesslike nod and walked toward the colonel's office. The door was closed, so she knocked.

"Enter."

She found Max, General Stone and Connor in the room. Max and the general were seated, Connor was standing at parade rest.

All three men wore grim expressions.

Sophia stepped inside then closed the door before asking, "What's wrong?"

General Stone spoke. "We've interrogated the two men who accosted you outside your quarters last night. They're part of the construction crew, and were already on the base when a man approached them and offered several thousand American dollars to grab any female American soldiers who have white-blond hair and deliver them to a truck waiting outside."

Her stomach turned and twisted. "How many women on the base have my hair color?"

"Two. The other woman is one of our telecommunication techs and was on duty last night. They never could have reached her."

All three men stared at her, but only Connor's mouth looked angry. Max and the general appeared more resigned than anything else. Or tired.

"It was your idea to sleep in Sergeant Button's quarters last night?" General Stone asked, one corner of his mouth tightening briefly in disapproval.

"Yes, sir."

"Why?"

"I trust him, sir."

This time the general allowed disapproval to take up residence on his face. "Just like that?"

"He was there when I needed him and he let me cry on his shoulder afterward without making me feel like I was being a wuss. I slept in his room and he didn't try anything remotely inappropriate."

Stone stood and said to Max, "I'm not in favor of this because it sets a bad example, but we've got an information leak, and I can admit that the situation is a unique one." He turned his attention to Connor. "Are you keeping your head in the game?"

"Yes, sir," Connor promised in his deep baritone.

General Stone stared at him for a couple more seconds, then looked at her again and angled his thumb at Connor. "Rumors will, without a doubt, go around. Can you deal with that?"

"I can deal with that better than getting kidnapped."

Stone sighed. "Max, I thought you were being paranoid, but last night has changed my mind. I'm going to ask for help profiling Akbar, see if we can figure out what he's going to do next, or at least come up with a short list of possibilities. We have to get ahead of this maniac before he starts World War Three." He nodded at everyone and left the office.

Max waited until the door was closed again before saying, "I need you both to write a report for that second event last night. Then I need you two to prepare for a last-minute departure."

"Are you thinking of sending me somewhere safer?" Sophia asked, stomach churning at the idea of being taken out of the field.

"No, I think we're going to have one, if not multiple, outbreaks. I think Akbar is planning to use another biological weapon soon, and he's behind the attempt to grab you last night."

"To stop us from responding to an outbreak?"

"Yes."

Sophia's stomach twisted harder. "It makes sense in a sociopath sort of way."

Connor snorted, but didn't comment otherwise.

She fixed her gaze on her boss. "I don't want to go through another night like last night, Max."

"Agreed." He looked at Connor with one eyebrow raised.

"I won't let her out of my sight."

He sounded so uptight Sophia couldn't help but say, "Why don't you microchip me while you're at it?"

"Good idea," Connor said with a toothy grin.

She rolled her eyes.

"No. Really." Connor was talking to Max now. "It *is* a good idea. If she gets nabbed we can find her."

"What's to stop the bad guys from using such a chip to find me too?"

"How are they going to know?" Max asked.

"How did they know where *my* room was last night?"

Connor stared at her with an expression that made her shiver with dread. "Where are they getting their info from?"

"You're suggesting that we have a traitor on base providing information to Akbar?" Max asked.

"Money makes people do all sorts of things they normally wouldn't. Then there's the possibility that some radicalized kid has joined the American military so that they can cause havoc, sabotage equipment, people and information."

"We've considered that," Max told her with a grim look. "It's why we're going to be changing how things are done in this part of the base. Changing things without informing anyone who doesn't need to know."

"I don't know if that's going to be enough," Sophia said.

"It probably won't," Connor put in. "I'd like to make a request."

"By all means," Max said.

"I'd like to bring in a couple other Berets to help. If you're right and we do get deployed to investigate an outbreak, I want men I can trust working with me to protect Sophia."

"You have specific men in mind?"

"Yes. Both are currently training Afghan troops and could be pulled for that duty no problem."

"Give their names and particulars to Eugene. He'll get it done."

"Thank you, sir." Connor nodded and left the office, giving her a nod as well on his way out.

Sophia looked at her commanding officer and noted the dark bags under his eyes. "Things just got a lot harder."

"We can't let that stop us from doing what we must."

"It won't, but the danger to everyone is greater now.

Not just to me, but you, too. What are you doing to protect yourself, Max?"

His mouth tightened. "General Stone has decided to assign me a bodyguard, too."

"Another Special Forces soldier?"

"Not exactly." It was the way he said it, the stiffness in his shoulders and in his crossed arms, that told her who it was.

"Oh. *Sergeant* Stone."

"Exactly."

"I thought you liked her."

"I do like her. That's the problem."

She thought about Connor and how she felt about him, every confusing thing, and what it would do to her if he got hurt protecting her or took a bullet meant for her.

The thought was enough to make her stomach twist so hard it made breathing difficult.

"I understand. I've only known Connor for a few days, yet the length of time doesn't seem to matter. He's the first soldier who didn't dismiss me as irrelevant the moment he met me."

"Like I said, these guys…soldiers don't even know where the damn box is that most people spend their lives in."

"She doesn't know where the box is either, Max. She's one of the people who makes sure *they* don't."

"Unfortunately, the box isn't the only thing she doesn't see." He dropped his arms and gave her a patient look. "Your report?"

As much as she wanted to help him, this was something he had figure out on his own. Like how she had to create a working relationship with a man she wanted for something other than work. "Can I write it in my office?"

"Of course, tell Button to write his, too."

"Yes, sir." Sophia left Max's office, relief, anxiety and anticipation making her muscles shake and her head dizzy.

She wasn't sure how her sexual encounter with Connor was going to impact their ability to work together. Would it change the way he treated her during their working hours?

She couldn't stop thinking about it, but Max and General Stone were keeping such a close watch on them, Con wouldn't want to risk getting caught with his pants down. Or his hand down her pants. Whichever.

A large part of her wanted more. The rest of her was uncertain and a little afraid of the way she'd lost total control with him.

Connor was standing next to Eugene's desk talking with the young soldier. Both of them had determined expressions on their faces.

"Are you good?" Connor asked her.

No, I'm not good. I'm terrified, turned on and two seconds away from throwing up. She couldn't tell him all that in front of Eugene, so she found herself lifting her chin. "I'm going to write my report in my office. You're supposed to come with me. You can use Dr. Samuels's computer to write yours."

He nodded, then said to Eugene, "Let me know if you have any problems."

"Of course, but I don't expect any. Colonel Maximillian's team is high on everyone's priority list."

Connor walked with her to her office and for the first time since she met him, his height and size made her feel…awkward. "Was that about the extra men you want on my security detail?"

"Yeah. I've asked to for two specific guys. Demolitions and Engineering Sergeant Lyle Smoke and Medic Walter River."

"I know Smoke. He was assigned to Dr. Samuels for a short time when she was here recovering from getting blown up and infected with anthrax." She paused. "I didn't know his name was Lyle."

"Don't use his first name. Ever."

"I know. He told me when I asked him if Smoke was his first or last name."

Connor glanced at her, his brows raised. "He talked to you?"

"A little. He gave me a nickname."

Con's eyes widened. "This I can't wait to hear."

"Ghost. You know, because I'm so white." She pointed at her hair, then turned on Dr. Samuels's computer, entered the password and waved at Connor to sit. "I don't know the other man. What's he like?"

"River is an interesting guy. He has an eidetic memory."

Sophia paused in the process of entering her password on her computer. "Really? I'm not sure if that's a blessing or a curse."

Connor tilted his head. "Most people get excited and start imagining all the ways River can use his memory to their benefit."

"My memory may not be eidetic, but it's pretty good, and there are plenty of things I wish I couldn't remember. Not being able to forget would be torturous." She met Connor's somber gaze. She wasn't the only one who wished they could forget. "How does he cope with the bad stuff?"

"You'll have to ask him."

"When will they be here?"

"A day, two at most."

"Good." She blew out a breath and concentrated on writing her report. The faster the better. All the assholes from last night weren't going to get any more air time inside her head than they already had. She was done. *Done* with being scared.

One fact stood out, however.

They'd been waiting for her outside her door.

She'd been their target.

"Connor?" she asked, attempting to come up with alternate places where she could sleep and be secure. "How safe is the lab?" She glanced at him to see if she had his attention. She did. He was watching her with an eagle's interest in prey. "I mean, in your professional opinion, is the lab secure?"

"Security, safety, whatever you want to call it, is mostly a myth." He shrugged. "With the right intel and planning, any area could be breached." He thought about that for a second. "I'll talk to Max about moving your hotel room around every few days."

"What about you?"

He gave her a strange smile. "Whenever I say *you,* I mean *me,* too."

"Oh. Right, we're a team." Having him that close all the time might prove inconvenient when she needed to give herself a transfusion of platelets. How was she going to explain an IV sticking out of her arm? She should probably give herself one today or tomorrow.

Could she get away with locking herself in the bath-room for a couple of hours?

Or would that cause a whole new set of problems?

TEN

CONNOR CORRECTED SOPHIA'S grip on the Beretta slightly, and had to make himself take a long step back and resist touching her for too long. His body language was going to give him away to even a casual observer if he didn't watch it. "Again."

She nodded. Sighted down the weapon, took in a deep breath, let it out and fired. Once, twice, three times.

Instead of putting his hands on her to show his approval, Connor brought the target toward them. All three shots and the three before them had hit the human-shaped target somewhere. Not perfect, but plenty good enough to kill. If the bad guy was ten yards away or less. Her proficiency at hitting the target dropped to seventy percent at twenty-five yards, and rapidly lower outside of that.

Practice would improve her confidence and aim.

"That's it for today," he said, finally allowing himself to touch her on the shoulder and angle his head toward the rest of the world.

"Okay!" Sophia smiled and continued yelling, "I did good, right?"

Con reached out and took her ear protection off. "Not bad," he told her at a normal volume. "You rate a not-bad, which means you get to practice every day."

"Oh." Her smile dimmed a little. "Not a surprise. My depth perception isn't great."

"Your depth perception, your spatial orientation... Have you considered glasses?" They left the range and headed across the base toward the lab.

"My vision is twenty-twenty. I don't need glasses, I just don't have ten-twenty vision. I'm not a pilot or a sniper, Connor. I'm a doctor and when I need to look at little things I use a microscope."

"Am I catching some attitude from my student?"

"No, I'm simply explaining why my eyesight is normal and not superhero abnormal."

He shook his head and exaggerated his sigh. "Yep. I'm getting attitude."

He liked it. Too much.

"Button." A shout from behind them caught Con's attention.

Two men were walking toward them. Both in Army Special Forces uniforms. "Hey, if it isn't the cavalry." Con turned to Sophia. "Here's your backup."

"Our backup," she said, frowning at him.

"Right, sure." Con held his hand out to Smoke, who shook it once. River did the same. "You two wasted no time in getting here. What did they do, get you onto transport as soon as Colonel Maximillian made the request?"

"Yeah," said River. His voice was oddly high-pitched for a grown man. He had a slight build, about five ten and maybe one seventy-five, but he was all muscle and bone, with not an ounce of fat on him. He was also one deadly son of a bitch. When River and Smoke did advance recon, no one ever knew they were there. If they did, they were dead.

Smoke, on the other hand, was a big, broad-boned man, who stood over six feet and had a face that never seemed to show any emotion at all. He was Navajo, but had pale blue eyes. He also never talked unless he had to.

"Is this Dr. Perry?" River asked.

"Yes, I am." She stepped forward to shake his hand, then nodded at Smoke. "It's good to see you, Smoke."

"Who's trying to kill you, Ghost?" Smoke asked.

Got to like a man who got straight to the point.

"Come on," Con said. "Let's get you two settled and we'll fill you in on all the fun we've been having."

"How are you doing, Con?" River asked as they continued on to the lab. "Back to full strength?"

"Yeah. I have to keep physically fit, but that's nothing new."

"There is absolutely nothing wrong with his reflexes or his fighting skills," Sophia added.

The silence following that was a little uncomfortable. Both men stared at him.

"Who did you kill?" Smoke asked.

"No one," Sophia said before Con could. "Why would you assume he killed someone?" She waved away any answer Smoke might have given, though he didn't look like he was going to anyway. "He broke one guy's collarbone and the other guy's arm." She sucked in a breath. "Then I broke the guy's arm again." She stopped and said in a whisper, "It took the orthopedic surgeon several hours to get it all put back together."

Con had to rein in his irritation and their chatter in a public place. "Come on, you bunch of old ladies, let's get inside and somewhere we can have a real conversation."

"Why are you so grumpy?" Sophia asked, frowning at him.

"I don't know, maybe because last night was a little busy?"

"Well, you would have gotten a better sleep on that plank you call a bed if you had put me in my cot." She started walking away. "You'd have had room to turn over at least."

As soon as she was out of earshot, Smoke punched Con on the shoulder. "You slept with her?"

"*Slept*, slept. For fuck's sake, her safety is my responsibility and she fell asleep on my bed when I was having a shower. I decided to let her sleep." He shrugged. "She's a good kid." *Liar, liar.* "A little weird sometimes, but in an interesting way."

"You realize that's how most people talk about us," River said. "Until they find out we're Special Forces, then they figure we're weird 'cause we're trained to notice shit most people wouldn't see with a magnifying glass."

"No," Smoke intoned. "Because we're trained to kill."

"I've got to go with Smoke on that one," Con said as they caught up with Sophia at the first checkpoint. He was going to have to really watch how he acted around her, so Smoke and River didn't catch on to the fact that he'd already crossed the sexual line with Sophia.

Having the other two guys around to watch out for her was a relief, but it also made him tense, which surprised the fuck out of him.

For months all he could think about was getting back on active duty and into a place where he might be able to kick some ass. Permanently. Today, he'd woken up and all those plans had taken second place inside his head behind protecting Sophia.

Having Smoke and River around would help him with that, but prevent him from following through on his goal to get revenge.

He'd just screwed himself royally.

Con got them checked in with Eugene and introduced River to Max while Sophia went to her office. Then he took the two men there. She was waiting for them.

"I have a job for you guys," she said far too happily.

Smoke sighed loudly.

"Are we going to like this job?" Con asked.

Sophia thought about that for a second. "Do you like tents?"

Con looked at Smoke, who shrugged.

"Tents are okay," River said.

"Good, because if I get called out to investigate an outbreak, which Max is certain of happening, we all have to be extra-prepared—"

"You have a tent you want us to construct?" Con interrupted. He didn't need to know the whys and wherefores, he just needed orders.

No, what he really needed was space and time to get his shit together.

"Yeah, the level three tent." She pointed at three large duffel bags.

"Where can we build this tent?"

She deflated fast. "Oh. I don't know."

"Do you want it kept a secret?"

"Sort of."

"Okay, what are the dimensions of the tent?"

She winced. "Um, it's not really that simple."

Con was rapidly running out of patience. The presence of the other two men was making him edgy. He should be happy to have them as a buffer between Sophia and himself. Instead he was irritated and resentful. "Does Eugene have the specs on this tent?"

"Yes."

"How about we figure out where to construct it and you do your thing here?" There, that ought to get everyone doing something productive, and him away from temptation.

She stood and stared at him for a moment, all her earlier enthusiasm gone. "Sure. See you."

As she turned her back on them and went back to her microscope, he wanted to take her by the shoulders, turn her around and kiss her until she was demanding another orgasm from him.

That he shouldn't want it made him that much angrier.

SOPHIA STARED AT the closed door, barely keeping her anger from boiling over. Connor had dismissed her, like she wasn't of any use or interest. Like she was a problem that needed fixing.

"I'm going to fix his wagon," she grumbled as she grabbed a new slide and put it on the stage of her microscope. She was ridiculously behind in checking blood smears for any unusual morphology.

Morphology of blood cells was an early indicator of all kinds of health problems. Infections, both bacterial and viral, cancer, and immune responses were only a few.

It was interesting work, but her thoughts kept going in circles, always starting and ending with Connor.

She couldn't get the intense, deadly expression of his

face when he'd fought her two kidnappers out of her mind. Then there was the expression of satisfaction he wore after their sexual encounter. The concern when he tried to explain human nature to her. His laughter after surprising him.

Why was he so upset today?

She couldn't remember doing or saying anything too awkward. She'd worked hard not to seem like a girlfriend.

She sighed.

Throwing him out of her head wasn't working.

She examined a dozen of slides then grabbed the handful of Complete Blood Count reports one of the techs dropped off. The one on the top was flagged with a red sticker.

The name on the report was her own. She looked at the platelet count. Low. Really low.

Shit.

Shit. Shit. *Shit*.

This was the second test with a much too low platelet count. One more like this and she was done. Sent home for medical treatment. A medical discharge almost guaranteed.

She'd taken medication that should have raised her cell count, but it hadn't done the job. Her bone marrow wasn't responding. If she was going to stay on the job, be of any help at all to Max and the team, she was going to have to up her dosage or try another medication. Or both.

Her bruises were going to get worse. If she started bleeding spontaneously, Max would send her home immediately.

She left her office and went to Eugene. "I need to go

to the Dispensary and don't want to piss off my baby-sitter. Would you go with me?"

"Sure," he said. "Just let me let the boss know."

Eugene called Max, got the go-ahead and they left.

The Dispensary wasn't far, just two buildings over, and the pharmacist didn't even blink when Sophia handed him a new script for the medication she took to keep her ITP in check.

She and Eugene returned to the lab without talking. Eugene seemed intent on watching for threats and she let him. Right now, talking wasn't high on her list of things to do.

As soon as she got into her office, she took another dose of her medication, then attempted to go back to work.

Her brain wouldn't let her.

Ten years. She'd had ten years since she'd gone into remission, worked so hard, become a doctor, all with the hope of making a difference in people's lives, only to get sick again.

She wanted to make a difference. Wanted to help people. She'd worked so hard, yet her body was betraying her again. It didn't matter how tired she got, she wasn't going to give up her dream until it was done.

A sob caught her unawares and she slapped a hand over her mouth. No. If someone heard her crying, they'd investigate. She breathed deep, through her nose and out through her mouth.

She had time yet.

Time before she had to tell Max.

Time to make a difference. She'd figure out a way to contribute. She would.

Connor. What was she going to do about him? He

was going to notice if she started showing more physical symptoms. He noticed everything.

She'd told him about her funny platelets. Maybe she could blame them for the bruising and nosebleeds that might occur.

She nodded to herself, wiped her face and was cleaning the morning's work away when her door opened.

Connor, Smoke and River walked in.

"Hi, Doctor," Connor said. "Miss us?"

ELEVEN

"WHERE'S MY TENT?" Sophia asked, looking at their empty hands.

"Set up in an empty staging area," Connor explained. "Which won't be empty for much longer. Eugene said that the base is expecting a bunch of electronics, parts and body armor from the States sometime later today. So, if you want to check out how we did and make any changes, now is the time."

"Good idea. I can come now." She walked toward them and made to go around, but Connor caught her arm and pulled her to a stop. "I'm sorry for being an ass earlier."

"It's fine." She tried to pull away, but he wasn't letting go.

"It's not fine. What's going on?" He studied her face so hard she was afraid he'd see everything. "You don't look so good."

She sighed and glanced at Smoke and River. They had the same expression on their faces as Connor did. Concerned. "After you guys left," she said, feeling her way through the words, hoping she didn't say the wrong ones, "I tried to keep my mind on work, but found it difficult, and I had a little bit of a cry." She straightened her shoulders. "I'm okay now, though."

Connor raised one eyebrow.

She crossed her arms over her chest. "I said okay, not great."

"You should talk to someone," Connor said.

He was right. The events of last night would probably rate a few conversations with someone. Friends were acceptable if the soldier decided to talk to them.

"Could we talk? Later?"

"Sure, my therapy rates are very reasonable," he said with a smile. "All it'll cost is an hour or two at the shooting range."

He was trying to be funny, but she just couldn't find the energy to be more than sarcastic. "I keep telling you, shooting paper people isn't therapy."

"It is if you shoot enough of them."

She stared at him. Was that supposed to be funny?

"I prefer explosives," Smoke said after an awkward second of silence. "Boom."

"I'm a knife man, myself," River said.

"You guys are nuts," she told them. "Now take me to my tent."

"Yes, ma'am." Connor led the way. Inside the large storage area was the level three tent. She walked all the way around it, inspecting every seam, grommet and pole. Then she went inside and inspected it again.

It wasn't round or square or oblong. Rather, it was shaped more like a star, with several narrow working areas that could be enclosed and isolated from the rest of the tent. The tent itself was composed of a tough canvas covered in a non-breathable plastic-like material that was stretchy, resisted tears and had some limited ability to reseal even if cut.

The initial idea for the material had come from studying spiderweb silk.

She checked the internal room separators, zipping them up to see if there were any places on the tent that were too tight or too loose. There were special holes in each working area so power and air purification connections could be made from the outside. Each hole had to be sealable and resistant to air movement even when something was in them.

She couldn't find a single thing she'd change or adjust. They'd done a perfect job.

How long would she have to do her job before her misfiring body took it all away from her?

Took *everything* from her.

Despair hit her with a sledgehammer to her gut and she had to bend over to breathe through it.

She wiped her face again and made herself stand up straight. She couldn't let her thoughts dwell on the negative. She'd never get anything done that way.

She pinned a smile, a small one, on her face and exited the tent. "Great job, guys," she said to the three men waiting for her assessment. "It looks and functions as it should. Would it be possible for you to write up a short report on the assembly procedure?"

"There were a few steps where more details might make things less confusing," Connor said, staring at her with a frown. "The shape is a pain in the ass to figure out at first."

"So far, that's the biggest problem we have with the design."

Connor walked up to her, his gaze never leaving her face. "Crying again?" he asked softly.

"You can tell?" Did she have a neon sign on her forehead?

"You have tear tracks on your face."

"Damn it." She wiped her face again, but it probably didn't help. "I didn't want to bother you with it."

Connor turned to Smoke and River. "You two dismantle the tent and bring it back to Sophia's office. I'm taking her for a little therapy."

"Shooting? Really?" she asked.

He looked at her with one side of his mouth turned up. "A hot shower and something to eat."

"Meet you in the food court," River said as he and Smoke walked past them to the tent.

Connor put a hand on the small of her back and urged her toward the door. As soon as they were outside, the sun hot on her face, he said quietly, "Are you sure you don't want to talk to someone, you know, official?"

He said the word *official* like it tasted bad.

She grunted. "No. That just creates a ton of paperwork and usually results in the Army sticking its nose somewhere it doesn't belong."

"Don't I know it," he said, his gaze roving the area like he expected an attack.

"What did you do after your...you were blown up? Did you talk to a psychologist?"

"Yeah, I didn't have a choice."

"Will I have a choice?"

"You're the doctor, what do you think?"

"I'm not that kind of doctor."

"A doctor is a doctor. Don't you all go through the same training for the first few years?"

"Yes, but I was never very good with people."

"Makes sense I suppose. You seem to like your tiny things a lot."

"Not everything I like is tiny." She said it under her breath.

Connor stopped walking. "You did not just say what I thought you said." He shook his head.

"What? You're unhappy because I like the size of your—"

"Do *not* say the next word."

"Hands."

TWELVE

Sitting on his bed listening to Sophia shower wasn't where Con wanted to be. Nope, he wanted to be in there with her. Holding her so she could let go of all the crap circling inside her head, the fear and horror of what might have been.

He thought she'd been okay this morning, but something had happened to derail her while he, Smoke and River had wrestled with her tent. She'd have told him if someone bothered her, right?

Of course, she'd be naked and he'd be naked and he'd do a lot more than just hold her. He'd do his best to wipe last night right off her mental map. It'd take only a half-dozen orgasms or so. Maybe.

The bathroom door opened and Sophia came out brushing her hair. She was wearing cozy pajamas made of a fabric that looked soft and touchable. There was nothing sexy about it, except for the woman wearing it.

Right now, that woman was wearing a hesitant expression.

"What's wrong?" he asked. When she ducked her head, he moved closer until he could tilt her chin up.

She made eye contact and what he saw in her gaze made his stomach clench. She was *hurting*. "Sophia?"

"I need you." The pain in her voice stabbed him in the gut.

"What's wrong with that?" He was happy to give her whatever she needed. More than happy.

"I don't know any of the rules. I thought we'd talk about it this morning, but there wasn't time, and now I'm scared I'm going to mess things up."

"First off, the only rules there are, are the ones we agree on. What happens between us in private is just that, private." He kissed her, a slow slide that had him hungry for more. He gazed down into her big eyes and asked, "What do you want?"

"My brain won't shut off, and it's driving me crazy." She looked at him like he was the only man who mattered in her world. "You fried my circuits last night. Do it again?"

Holy fuck.

He wanted to give her what she wanted, sex, hot, sweaty, dirty sex, but she was a fucking *virgin.* Despite their no-strings agreement she deserved a man who'd be there for her. Not a guy who wanted to walk into the first righteous battle he could find and never walk out.

There were other ways to blow her mind besides full-on sex.

"When you listened to me and Eugene talking about oral sex, did you like what you heard?"

She licked her lips and nodded. "All I could think about was your head between my legs and what your mouth would feel like on m—"

Her bald confession lit him up and he was kissing her before she finished saying the last word.

Settle down, asshole, you're going to scare her.

Eager hands wrapped around his shoulders as she leaned into him and moaned.

Or not.

He hauled her closer, one hand at the base of her back, so he could rub his erection against her belly.

She shuddered and groaned into his mouth, kissing him back just as fiercely.

He moved the hand cradling the back of her neck down. All he felt beneath her pajama top was skin.

"I want your nipples in my mouth," he said, hardly recognizing the ragged voice coming out of him as his own.

The noise that came out of her was sharp, urgent and needy.

"I'm going to strip your top off you and suck your nipples until you scream."

"Connor," she moaned. "Stop talking and do it."

He kissed her again, his hands pushing her top up and over her breasts. God they were pretty, with berry-red nipples he couldn't wait to taste.

Bruises were scattered across her torso and arms, making him pause. No, he wasn't going to let what those assholes did sour this for her.

He cupped her with both hands and they filled his palm and then some.

She gasped and stumbled back.

He caught her with one arm, the other hand molding the breast it cradled. Her top got in the way, so he pulled it over her head and off.

He couldn't take his eyes off the swell of her flesh, the dusky areolas or her nipples, hardened with arousal.

"Connor?" Her question sounded frustrated and impatient.

He dragged his gaze up to her face. "How's your brain? Still thinking?"

Her brow furrowed. "What?"

He petted her, letting his fingers massage and stroke the sensitive skin around her breasts. "Do you have any idea how beautiful you are?"

She hung in his arms, her breathing fast and shallow, her eyes dilated until the rim of blue was just a ring around the black. "No one has ever seen…" Her voice trailed off into nothing as he put his hand on her breast and flicked his thumb over the nipple. He rolled it between thumb and forefinger next and her eyes fluttered shut.

No man has ever seen her like this. The thought made him harder than stone and greedier than King Midas. *No man has ever touched her.*

She clutched at him and ran her hands over his chest, abdomen and shoulders. "I want to touch all your muscles." Her untutored hands had him shaking with the need to fuck her, but this wasn't about him, it was all about her.

He continued to torment her nipple as he leaned down to kiss her softly, gently. He wanted her with him every step of the way. "Gorgeous," he whispered. "So fucking gorgeous." He trailed kisses, stopping every so often to nip and suck down her neck. "Still thinking, sweetheart?"

She moaned, but nothing intelligible.

Getting closer.

"Let's find out if you can orgasm just from this." He bent her back and nibbled his way to her nipple. He sucked it in and she bucked and bit the heel of one of her hands.

He laved it with his tongue and sucked it, over and over.

She gasped and shook.

She was nearly there.

He sent one hand down her body and massaged her clit through her clothes.

She screamed into her hand, her knees buckled, and he scooped her up, laying her on his narrow bed. Her eyes were squeezed shut. "Sophia?"

THE SOUND OF her name coming from his throat made it a demand, an entreaty. She forced her eyes open to stare up at Con, the marauder, the thief who'd stolen her breath, her will. He'd given her something in return.

Pleasure.

Pleasure was something she'd felt little of in her life, and what she'd experienced was mainly intellectual satisfaction. Not physical, primitive, sensual satisfaction.

Now that she knew what it was and felt it, she craved it. And she found she loved seeing him like this, hot, hard and hungry for her.

"Do you want me to stop?" he asked, hovering over her breasts like a great beast. Yet, she knew he was putting her own sexual needs before his own.

"No," she breathed. "Never stop."

He growled and took her mouth in a rush, kissing her like she was as necessary for him to continue breathing as air.

When he lifted his head, he slowly looked down her body until he reached the juncture of her thighs. "I'm going to take these off you and make you come again." His voice sounded like it had been ground up by gravel.

She made a shocked sound at the back of her throat. Oh, how she wanted that. "Yes."

He smiled at her and it promised so much sin, she shivered.

He lowered his head and began sucking on her breasts, while his hands worked her pajama bottoms and panties down and off. His gaze flicked up to meet hers as his mouth moved lower and he left kisses on her abdomen and navel.

Why did everywhere he touched feel like an erogenous zone?

She panted, unsure what to do. This position left her so exposed. A whimper escaped her lips.

"Easy, sweetheart," he whispered as he moved up to kiss one breast then the other. "I've got you."

He began to lick and suck one of her nipples while he circled her clitoris with one thumb.

The sensations were electric and were winding her up even tighter than before.

When he replaced his thumb with one finger and began shallowly penetrating her she thought she was going to come off the bed. "Oh *God*, that feels so good."

He hummed, sucked hard on her nipple while fucking her with his index finger.

"*Oh God, oh God, oh God.*" He had her wavering on the edge of an explosion she wasn't sure she was going to survive.

He hooked his finger inside her, rubbing a spot that might as well have *blast off* written all over it.

She stuffed her hand in her mouth and screamed as the pleasure rocketed through her in waves lighting up every nerve ending and neuron. It seemed to last forever, but finally her body calmed and she opened her eyes.

Connor was leisurely playing with her breasts, toying with one with his fingers while his mouth continued to drive her a little crazy on the other.

She looked down his body toward his crotch and found an impressive erection. "Connor," she breathed.

"Feel better, sweetheart?"

"Yes." She arched her back to press her breasts up and into his hold.

"So responsive," he whispered.

He seemed occupied, so she sent one hand toward the bulge in his pants, cupping him, learning his shape and size.

He hissed and thrust himself into her palm.

She tried to undo his pants, but he grabbed her hands and pinned them to the bed. "Not yet, sweetheart. We'll get there."

She smiled and pulled out something she'd read about in one of her books and always wanted to try. "What about my breasts? You like them, don't you? Wouldn't you like to fuck them?"

His gaze dropped to her breasts and he groaned, "Holy fucking shit."

"Please?" she asked. "I want you to."

"So do I." He gritted his teeth and let go of her. "Don't move."

She nodded and watched as he pulled away to remove his pants and underwear.

His cock was big. Bigger than she thought it might be. Thick with veins running down the side and bottom of it. It curved up, pointing toward the ceiling.

He grabbed something from the bathroom and returned with a bottle of something he squirted on his hands.

Then he was rubbing the lotion down the center of her chest. His gaze met her curious one. "Are you sure you want—"

She grabbed his cock again in a gentle grip. "Yes, I want." She stroked him.

"*Fuck.*" He pulled her hand away then grabbed the other hand and set them on either side of her breasts, showing her how hard to push them together. Then he fit his cock in the space between her breasts and pumped once, twice. "Fuck me, sweetheart."

She watched his cock slide between her breasts and found she received pleasure from this, too. She pressed her breasts together a little harder and was rewarded with a low groan from Connor.

He slid his penis back and forth in a slow, leisurely pace that made her hungry for more speed. But maybe she could taste pleasure a different way. As his cock thrust upward toward her face, she flicked out with her tongue and swiped the crest of his penis.

He groaned, so she did it again. And again. He began thrusting faster and she found herself mesmerized as his arms began to shake, and he threw his head back as he came.

His head fell forward and his eyes opened to stare at her like he wasn't sure what just happened.

"Could I give you a blow job next time?" she asked. Bringing him to orgasm was a heady experience. There was an equally intense pleasure in seeing him lose himself to orgasm as there was when he brought her to her peak.

He shook his head and glanced down at her chest. "Every time I think I have you figured out, you go and change the rules on me."

"You have four sisters. How is this a surprise?"

He pulled away and she made a move to sit up. He put a hand on her shoulder to keep her lying flat. "Stay there, I'll be right back." He eased off the bed and went into the bathroom. When he came out he had a wet washcloth, which he used to clean the semen off her.

She got her pajama top and was about to put it back on, when he said, "You don't...have to wear that if you don't want to."

She looked at him and realized from the slumberous expression that he liked the thought of being able to fondle her breasts during the night.

She loved having his hands on her, so that was a win-win. "Okay."

Sophia went to the bathroom, brushed her teeth then went out to find Connor on his side on his narrow bed, the blanket swept back for her.

She got in and he covered her with the blanket and his arm, pulling her close and spooning her from behind.

His lips teased one ear and he whispered, "Blow job next time."

THIRTEEN

HEAT WOKE SOPHIA. A hot male body wrapped around her, her back to his front. One of his big hands cradled her hip, the other a breast. She loved it. Loved the intimacy of sleeping with someone she could trust.

There was just one problem.

Did he have to throw off so much heat?

She shifted her legs. He had a knee in between hers, and the hair on his legs tickled a little. The sensation added to the ache deep inside her vagina. She rocked her hips, pressing her ass against the rapidly hardening penis nestled between the cheeks of her butt.

The hand on her breast began to massage it and tease the nipple.

"Go back to sleep." Connor's voice rumbled against her ear as he pinched her nipple.

She gasped as pleasure whipped through her, and she tried to turn over to face him, but he wouldn't let her.

"Con," she moaned as his other hand slipped between her legs to tantalize her clitoris. "You're not helping."

He dipped his long middle finger into her. "I have an idea," he whispered.

"Does it involve your penis in my vagina?"

"Time for a vocabulary lesson." She could feel his lips smile as he kissed the back of her neck. "It involves your lips wrapped around my cock."

"What's wrong with 'penis'?" she asked, wiggling against that very long, hard part of his anatomy.

"'Penis' is for pansies and hospitals. Cock is what you say in bed with a beautiful woman. This—" he cupped her vagina "—is a pussy. And these," he said, finally allowing her to turn onto her back and capturing her breasts in his hands, "are the finest tits I've ever fucked."

She stared up at him, panting and so damned needy she was afraid she was going to self-combust. "I want that."

He played with her breasts, his fingers stroking her nipples. "Hmm? What do you want?"

"To get…" She'd use his word. "…fucked."

His gaze, which had been glued to what he was doing to her, jerked up to meet hers. One corner of his mouth slanted upward. "No."

She was beginning to recognize that expression on his face. Devious. He already knew what he was going to do. He had a plan, and when Connor had a plan, he didn't deviate from it. "What then?"

He slid down her body, pushed her thighs apart and stared at her…pussy.

She propped herself up on her elbows to get a better look, and because she felt so exposed. "Are you going to eat me out?" she asked breathlessly.

He grinned. "Does thinking about that make you hot?"

So hot, but… "I…what if you don't like how I taste?"

He closed his eyes and inhaled. "You smell like sunshine, summer and a spice that's yours alone." His eyes opened and the desire on his face made her breath catch.

"I can't wait to taste you." He didn't move, seemed to be waiting. "Okay?"

He was waiting. Waiting for her to be ready.

With him, she was ready for everything. "Yes."

"Good."

He lowered his face and licked.

She had no idea what to expect, but it certainly wasn't what she got.

Pleasure. Languorous, yet it built quickly as he used his tongue to stimulate her clitoris.

"Oh," she breathed. "That's…"

"What, sweetheart? Tell me."

"Very arousing."

"It's about to get a lot more than that."

He continued to lick and suck at her clitoris, but he also added a finger, which felt huge. The dual stimulation built up the pleasure leading toward an orgasm she couldn't wait to experience again.

When he added a second finger, she damn near came off the bed. The stretch from two fingers threw her from first gear into fifth and she stuffed the heel of her hand in her mouth to keep from screaming. The other hand speared into Con's short hair and held his head against her. She had to come now.

He changed the angle of his fingers penetrating her and she detonated. The pleasure radiated out in a wave that sucked her under, making everything else, the whole world, inconsequential. Unfortunately, the wave eventually ebbed and she came back to the reality to find Connor watching her with a self-satisfied grin on his face.

"See," she said, still out of breath, "I like penetration."

"Let's see if you like it another way."

There were only two possibilities she could think of. "Blow job?"

He nodded.

She wanted that too. Now.

She sat up and pushed him with both hands until he was on his back.

His hands landed on her hips, but he didn't stop her, he steadied her. "Hold on, slow down."

"To quote you, *no*. I've wanted to get my hands on your…cock since I noticed how big your hands were."

He laughed silently. "How soon after meeting me was that?"

"About two minutes." She studied him. His penis was erect, impressively so. "As I suspected you're larger than average."

"And you know that how?"

"The question of penis size came up during a study session during medical school," she said absently.

His grin was almost as wide as the Grand Canyon. "You can touch me anytime."

She scooted down his legs to get a better look, then decided there was only one way to go from here. His erection didn't feel anything like she expected. A hard shaft covered in silky skin that had its own scent. One that made her crazy to taste.

She held him at the base of his…cock and ran her tongue up one side of it.

Con gasped, his mouth falling open.

He tasted good.

Con started to say something, but it was her turn to give him an orgasm. She opened her mouth and managed to swallow about half of him.

Con's reaction was immediate. His body arched and one of his hands threaded through her hair. His face was a mask of pleasure and it looked like it had taken a great deal of self-control for him not to shout.

She pulled back, letting her lips form a seal, so he would feel a strong negative pressure, and from his shaking body and rapid breathing, he enjoyed it. She repeated the act again and again, watching his face and body to learn what he liked and didn't like.

He kept trying to say something, but every time he managed a word or two, usually her name and *stop*, she'd swallowed him down again.

It didn't take long for him reach his climax, but it didn't go quite according to plan, as he pulled her off him a second before he erupted all over her neck and chest. Again.

Con stared at her with wild eyes while he panted, then asked as soon as his vocal cords appeared to work correctly again, "Where did you learn to do that?"

"Jones gave me a few pointers."

"Jones?" His voice strangled the woman's name. "I kept trying to tell you to stop so I could put on a condom. Did she forget that piece of advice?"

"No, she mentioned it. I'm the one who decided you didn't need it."

"*You* decided *I* didn't need it?" His voice rose and a red flush made its way up his neck.

"You're clean and so am I."

"How do you know... You looked me up?"

"I'm a doctor, of course I looked you up. Besides, I didn't want a barrier between me and you this first time."

His nostrils flared. "That decision wasn't yours to make alone. We should have talked about it."

"Are you saying you didn't want a blow job?" she asked as he got off the bed and strode to the bathroom.

He came back into view only a few seconds later with a wet cloth. "No, I'm saying I would have preferred to wear a condom."

"Why would you want to do that when it reduces sensation for you?"

He wiped his semen off her skin then he cleaned himself. "Because it's *safer*." The last word was little more than an angry growl.

He wanted a physical barrier between them. A barrier that probably made it easier for him to emotionally distance himself from the woman he was with.

Which was exactly what she had wanted, and what she promised him, no-fuss sex. She had always been good at compartmentalizing her emotions and keeping people at bay, but Con had gotten inside. She didn't know what to do about that.

"I'm sorry, I won't do it again," she said, her face oddly stiff. She could barely move her mouth.

He glared at her. "What did I say about apologies?"

"But, you're upset and I *am* sorry." How could she possibly know what to say when he changed his mind about what was acceptable or not whenever he felt like it?

He held up a finger. "Just stop talking and go back to sleep." He stomped off into the bathroom.

Sophia pulled her panties and sleep pants up then grabbed her sleep shirt off the floor and put it on.

Her cot was pushed against the far wall. She was

pulling the blankets back when he came out of the bathroom. He scowled. "What are you doing?"

She scowled right back, "Going to sleep, as ordered."

"Nope," he said after a moment of complete stillness. "Not there." He motioned with his hand for her
to lie down on his bed.

"No more growling at me?"

He sighed and shook his head.

She still wasn't sure. "You need to work on your
communication skills. Next time, tell me all the things
I shouldn't do before I have my hands on your cock."

He stared at her like he didn't understand English for
a moment, then wiped his face with one hand. "Yeah,
I was a moron."

She waited for him to go on, but he just gestured for
her to lie down again.

She got into his bed and he spooned up behind her.
If he asked her to take off her shirt, she was going to
tell him to fuck off.

He didn't ask.

SMOKE, ACRID ENOUGH to make her eyes water, woke Sophia. For a moment she was disoriented and unsure of
where she was. Something was on fire, but there was
no alarm blaring.

A moment after that thought, the alarm began its toll,
an ear-splitting sound loud enough to hurt. She turned
to wake Connor, but he wasn't in bed with her.

She jumped out of bed to turn on the light, but nothing happened when she flipped the switch. Damn it.

She made her way back to the bed and her pile of
stuff just in front of it and fumbled around for a couple
of seconds for the tiny flashlight she had in her uni-

form pants. Flicking it on, she quickly got dressed and was tying her combat boots when the door to the room opened. Someone slipped inside silently and closed the door.

She froze. Waiting.

"Sophia?" Connor's voice.

Something terrified and wound tight inside her relaxed a little. "Yes, I'm here. I'm dressed. How big is the fire?"

"Not too big. It's at the front of the building, so we're going to have to leave via one of the side doors."

She stood. "I'm ready. Are you dressed?"

"Yeah. Smoke called and woke me about five minutes ago. Said there was some kind of dust-up at the front desk. I don't think this fire was an accident."

"Someone started it on purpose?" That was akin to playing Russian roulette with people's lives.

"I want you to wear this," he said grabbing something from his go bag. It was a black cap, the kind soldiers wear for night missions. "Make sure you get all your hair under cover."

"Are you saying this fire is another kidnapping attempt?" Suddenly the fire made horrible, insane sense. Whoever wanted her had failed on their first try. This was attempt number two.

"Oh my God." She grabbed her go bag and moved toward the door.

Connor grabbed her arm and pulled her to a stop.

"We have to get out—"

"I know, but I want you to have this." He thrust the butt of a gun into her right hand. "Hang on to it."

"Okay."

"Here." He had a holster for it and quickly got the

straps wrapped to her right thigh. She slid the weapon into the holster while he slung his backpack on and grabbed his SCAR rifle. "Grab the back strap on my pack and don't let go of it. Okay?"

She grabbed it. "Got it."

"If we get separated, I want you to go the base and directly to the lab, get inside the level three containment area if you can and stay there."

"Why there?"

"Because you can lock yourself inside if you need to."

"What if someone isn't just after me? What if they're after what we're working on?"

Connor stared at her for one full second. "We can worry about that if we don't get roasted alive. Ready?"

She nodded.

He bent low and opened the door.

She followed as he headed down the hallway. Smoke flowed across the ceiling like a murky, muddy flood.

He moved quickly, but not faster than she could manage. They stopped at an intersection, he looked both ways, then turned left. As they made their way down the hall, the smoke grew thicker and thicker. She began coughing and tried to tuck her face into the collar of her shirt.

Someone bumped her from behind and three people—she couldn't see well enough to tell if they were men or women—rushed past. They pushed her against the wall and she found herself struggling to maintain her hold on Connor's pack.

She sucked in a breath to yell at him, but all she breathed in was smoke. She thought she was going to lose her grip when Connor stumbled back and into her.

She looked past him and saw more people yelling and waving their hands, but none of it seemed intelligible to her.

Connor got himself right side up and yelled into her ear, "Hang on!"

She made sure she had a good grip then nodded.

Connor surged forward, shoulder checking one man out of the way better than any hockey-playing enforcer. He continued moving, almost dragging her along with him past another couple of people.

Something got in between her legs, tripping her, and she went down. Sophia tried to hang on to Connor, but she was knocked to one side, effectively ripped away from him.

Smoke was billowing throughout the hallway, cutting visibility down to zero, three feet above the floor. All she could see were legs. Most of them were dressed in off-base clothing and no one looked like Connor, Smoke or River.

Get out, get to the lab.

Sophia got on her hands and knees and crawled, trying to avoid all the booted feet dancing around in the smoke. A man fell to the floor right in front of her, his face only inches from her own. He stared at her for a partial second, then yelled something at her in a language she didn't understand and grabbed the collar of her shirt.

She tried to jerk herself out of his hold, but he wouldn't let go.

That's when she remembered she had a gun. She pulled it out and raised it, pointing it in his face.

He let go this time, rolling away into the smoke.

Sophia didn't hesitate—she scrambled for the door.

Just before she reached it, there was another knot of
people, some obviously shoving others in an effort to
get out. She watched them for a few seconds and discovered something disheartening. Two pairs of booted
feet appeared to take an interest in those leaving, but
didn't leave themselves.

Either they were assisting everyone in getting out
of the building, or they were looking for someone in
particular.

She pressed herself against the wall as more people
thundered past her, then jumped in at the back of the
pack, not crawling anymore, but crouching very low
with her gun tucked in close to her right side, chest high
and pointed straight ahead.

Just as she was about to come abreast with the doorway, another person rushed past. Something about the
gait caught her attention. Smooth, yet precise.

It reminded her of the way Connor walked when he
led her out of their room.

She grabbed one of the person's legs, wrapped herself around it and brought whoever it was to the ground.

Smoke.

He was already halfway on his back, probably turning while he fell, and pointing his gun at her. When he
saw her, he dropped the muzzle of his weapon, grabbed
her collar and yanked her close.

"Stay low."

No shit.

He got to his feet and rose up into the smoke, but kept
his grip on her shirt as he mostly dragged her through
the doorway. His hand disappeared and he turned as if
facing someone on the right.

The feet on the left moved toward his back.

Nope. Not happening. Sophia kicked out at the man approaching Smoke's back as hard as she could in the knee.

The man went down, grabbing the joint.

The man in front of Smoke went down, too.

They both saw her and one of them reached out, so she pointed her gun at him. A second later Smoke grabbed her by the collar again and hauled her to her feet. The man on the right lunged at Smoke, who lost his grip again.

"Run," he shouted.

She ran.

The struggle, the smoke and the fire alarm had left her disoriented. She ran almost blindly for a minute before slowing down to take a better look around her.

Wonderful. She'd gone the wrong way.

She headed back toward the base, but stopped cold at the sound of gunfire. She recognized the coughing *pop, pop, pop* of a SCAR and her stomach dropped. What had happened to Connor? Was Smoke all right?

She started jogging toward the nearest gate to enter the base. They were going to look for her at the lab, so that's where she needed to get to. It took a couple of minutes before the gate came into view. There were a lot of people clustered around it, most of them in uniform with weapons of some sort.

She could ask for help from one of the American soldiers, but she wasn't entirely sure whom she should trust. The knot of people in front of the gate grew and she decided now was the time to try to get through.

Sophia dodged and danced around the swirling mass of soldiers and civilians trying to get into the base, and found herself standing right in front of the bar between her and where she needed to go. A soldier in an

American uniform saw her and yanked on the arm of the man standing next to him who was turned away, scanning the crowd.

River.

He immediately stepped over her to grab her arm and pulled her under the bar. Then he frog marched her into the base. As they walked he said something into his radio.

"What happened?" he asked her when he was done talking.

"There was a fire. Connor tried to get me out, but we got separated. I found Smoke and he tried to get me out, but two guys jumped us and *we* got separated. Then I found you."

"There is some weird shit going on," River said. "I'm to get you to the lab as soon as fucking possible."

"Are Connor and Smoke okay?"

River didn't answer right away.

She pulled him to a stop. "Are they okay?"

"Lost contact with Connor about fifteen minutes ago. Smoke called in about ten minutes ago, said he'd found you and lost you."

Sophia looked behind her at the flickering light the fire cast into the night. She could still see the tips of some of the flames, which meant the entire hotel must be involved. She stopped and took a step back. Connor could be back there, still looking for her. She didn't want to lose him when they'd barely gotten to know each other. He was the most fascinating, infuriating and sexy man she'd ever met. He made her feel things in a way she didn't know was possible. She wasn't going to leave him behind.

They were a team.

River stopped a few feet in front of her. "Dr. Perry, we need to keep moving."

She glanced at him with an agreeable smile. "Yes, of course."

As soon as he turned and started walking again, she sprinted for the gate and the hotel.

She heard her name shouted behind her, but she didn't stop or even slow down. If Connor was still in the hotel, he was probably incapacitated by smoke. Maybe he'd been knocked out by all the people trying to get out. She didn't know what happened, she didn't know what she could do, but she couldn't let him die.

River was gaining on her when a shadow emerged from the dark to grab her around the middle. It knocked the wind out of her, but that didn't stop her from wriggling in the stranger's grasp.

"Sophia."

She knew that voice.

"Connor?"

He set her on her feet and she grabbed his face so she could look at him. He was covered in soot and smelled faintly of burnt hair, but it was him.

She threw her arms around his neck. "I thought you might still be in the hotel," she said in his ear.

He squeezed her. "Is that where you were running to? Because you sure as hell weren't going in the direction you were supposed to."

She let go so she could smack him. "Yes, that's where I was going. I thought you might be incapacitated or dead."

"So, what, you were running to my rescue?"

"Yes."

He bent down so they were nose to nose and snarled, "Wrong answer."

She sucked in a breath to tell him to fuck off, but he grabbed her by the arm and dragged her along with him as he followed River toward the lab building.

River kept looking over his shoulder at them.

"What?" Connor barked after the third glance.

"Are you okay? You look like you're hanging on to her pretty hard."

Connor eased off on his grip a little. "I'm fine. As soon as we're past the first checkpoint, go look for Smoke."

River nodded, but still looked uneasy as he glanced from Connor to Sophia.

People were running toward them and past, hopefully to fight the fire. Connor and River assessed everyone moving in their direction, obviously looking for threats. She wondered what they were looking for, what they saw.

Was it a specific posture, or tilt to a person's head that said, "I'm not an American"?

"Your hair is coming loose," Connor said to her, his tone calmer than before, though there was still a thread of violence that made her shiver.

She quickly tried to stuff it all back into the cap she wore, but as many strands as she tucked in, that many slipped out. Finally she held the stray strands in her left hand at the back of her head.

They reached the first checkpoint.

River turned and looked at Connor. "I'm going after Smoke. See you inside. Stay frosty."

Connor's teeth flashed white in the darkness. "Yeah, it's getting hot." Then River was gone and Con was tugging her toward the second checkpoint.

"Why are we in such a rush?" she asked him.

"Because you're not safe yet." He tugged her a little harder.

"You're going to rip my arm off."

He stopped and deliberately released her.

They arrived at the second checkpoint and passed through. There were extra guards at this one.

They entered the lab building, passed by Eugene's desk, which was empty, and went straight into Sophia's office. He shut the door, locked it, then pulled off her cap and began checking her over for injuries with fast hands.

She tried to shove his hands away. "I'm fine."

"Shut up," he growled at her.

His order made her so mad she put both hands on his chest, pushed, then snapped, "You shut up."

He growled at her, snatched her close and kissed her hard. His lips forced hers open and his tongue surged into her mouth like he was desperate to taste her. His hands slid around her, pulling her body into full contact with his, and he groaned into the kiss.

When he finally let her suck in some air he whispered in her ear, "I thought I'd lost you." Panic and worry gave his voice a brittle quality she never thought she'd hear from a man who'd survived what he had. He'd seemed so strong, so self-contained.

Pleasure at his obvious worry—*he cared about her*—warred with concern that he'd care too much. Maybe she was being selfish.

She was going to *die*. She had no business pursuing a relationship of any kind.

Stupid, *stupid* girl.

FOURTEEN

UNFORTUNATELY, HER HEART wasn't listening to her head. "I thought I'd lost you too." Her voice quivered.

He pulled back to look into her eyes, took her shoulders in his hands and gave her a little shake. "Don't you ever do that again."

Shock made her sputter, "Excuse me?" Had he lost his mind?

His grip on her tightened and he snarled, "You promised you'd go straight to the lab if we got separated."

"River was with me, sort of, so that changed the circumstances."

"The hell it did."

"I was safe!"

"Safe?" he asked incredulously. "You're the most dangerous woman I know."

"What does that—"

She couldn't finish because he was kissing her again.

She kissed him back just as fiercely, anger burning away the last of the cold chill of the thought of Con caught in the fire.

Someone pounded on the door.

Connor wrenched his head away and yelled, "What?"

"Smoke is back and he's got a story to tell," said a voice through the door.

River.

Connor stared into her eyes with a fierce expression. "We're not done talking."

"We did very little talking in the first place," she muttered.

He sent her one last glare then opened the door and stalked down the hall toward Eugene's desk.

Sophia trailed along behind, rubbing her arm where he'd held on to her. She wasn't sure she wanted to see the size of the bruise growing there.

Eugene, River, Smoke and Colonel Maximillian came in. All four were armed. Smoke had a blood trail down the left side of his face from his temple to his chin.

"Are you both uninjured?" the colonel asked, though his gaze was on Sophia.

"We're fine," Connor replied.

Sophia frowned at him. "Yes, we're okay."

Connor clenched his jaw so tightly she was surprised his teeth hadn't cracked.

"What happened?" Max asked in a tone so cold, so rigid, he had both her attention and Connor's immediately.

"Smoke woke me with a radio call, saying there was smoke coming from the lobby," Con said. "I stepped out to check and confirmed smoke, but the fire alarm wasn't ringing yet. It should have been. I went back into the room. The power was off, but Sophia had woken and we both grabbed our go bags and armed ourselves before leaving.

"She stuck with me most of the way to the north exit, but we got separated by a large group of people running for the way out. From there I tried to find Sophia, but was unsuccessful. She'd agreed to head to the lab if we got separated, so I worked my way out of the building on the east side. I headed straight for the gate and found Sophia and River inside the base." Connor turned and nodded at her.

She started with, "After Connor and I got separated I continued toward the exit, but I sort of crawled along the floor mostly, so I could only see people's feet. A man went by who moved like Connor, so I grabbed him. It was Smoke. He dragged me to the door, but two men were waiting there and one attacked Smoke. The other was moving in, at least that's what it looked like from three feet off the floor, so I kicked that guy's kneecap as hard as I could. Smoke grabbed me up and told me to run, so I did." She stopped to catch her breath for a moment, then continued.

"I got to the gate, where River found me, and we headed toward the lab." She was going to leave out the part where she tried to go back through the gate to look for Connor. She hadn't gotten very far, after all. "Connor met up with us and we came here." She looked at Smoke. "What happened to you?"

"Knife fight. I won."

"That's an awfully short story?"

"Stupid man offered a lot of money for you, Ghost."

"He thought you were a local?" Con asked.

Smoke nodded.

"Why didn't you just shoot him?"

"Dead men can't answer questions."

"How much?" Connor asked.

"Ten thousand."

The men all looked grim.

Sophia frowned. "That's all?"

River chuckled, then coughed to cover it when Max glared at him. "It's not funny."

"It sort of is," River said.

"I'm insulted. I'm worth more than that. Right?"

"This is the second attempt, Colonel," Connor said. "They started a fire this time."

"Did anyone get hurt?" Sophia asked.

"No casualties reported yet," Max told her. "But I'll be surprised if the answer is no."

"Why do they want me?" She couldn't understand it. She wasn't the world's authority on viruses or doing advanced research. She was smart and educated, but so were many other doctors.

Max considered her with a long look. "You're a creative thinker with viruses, a fact that's well known in our corner of the medical community. Perhaps that's it. Regardless, the way things are going, there won't be a base left if they try for you again."

"Akbar," Smoke said in his deep drawl, "likes to play games."

"Agreed," Max said. "So, what game is he playing now?"

"Doesn't matter," Connor said, a smirk tilting one side of his mouth up. "We play our own game, and let him catch up."

"What do you have in mind?" Max asked.

"Bait and switch."

Max's eyebrows went up. "How do you propose to do that?"

"Sofia will need to get a makeover, dye her hair. We take another female soldier and bleach her hair, then send her off as if she were Sophia to Germany or back to the States. Then we wait to see what happens."

"That might draw out whoever is supplying Akbar with intel on this base."

"The fewer who know about this, the better," Sophia said. "But I think it might work."

"Who is going to play you?" Eugene asked.

"One of the techs, Jones, is about my height and weight," Sophia said. "She's got dark hair, so she'll have to dye it. Mine too, I guess." She turned to Eugene and added, "If you go with her when she's playing me, it would make sense."

"Excellent idea." Max nodded. "You can pretend to be his replacement. We'll have to make up a name for you."

"I'd rather just pretend to be a lab tech or something."

"We should do this soon. Tonight," Connor said. "In response to this fire."

"Who wants to go find Jones?" Max asked.

"Go find her, Eugene. And see if she knows where to get some hair dye for Sophia and herself."

"Yes, sir," Eugene saluted, then jogged away.

"The rest of you are in sorry shape," Max said. "Clean up as best you can in the washrooms."

He didn't have to tell her twice. Sophia led the charge to the bathrooms, going into the ladies' room with a sigh of relief. Connor was behaving like he was the officer, ordering her around and getting all snarly in her face.

She washed her hands and face, then unbuttoned her uniform shirt to reveal her bra and a multitude of bruises around her neck, arms and sides. She gave herself a bit of wash all over her torso, then contemplated the bruises. None of them looked too bad. Though the only time she'd seen worse was before she went into remission.

"Holy fuck."

Connor stood behind her. He must have come in

while she'd been examining herself, but she hadn't even heard him.

She spun around and tried to pull her shirt back on, but he was there, taking it from her, putting his hands on her wrists to keep her arms from covering up what she could.

He looked at one bruise in particular on her upper arm, the shape of fingers very clearly marking her skin. He put his hand over the mark. A perfect fit.

"I did this to you?" Connor's horrified gaze met her own. "Why didn't you tell me I was hurting you?"

"Because it didn't hurt...much. Remember, I told you, I have funny platelets. I get bruises."

"I didn't think it would get this bad," he said incredulously. "Is it like this a lot?"

"Well, no. It's not usually this bad, but I've been manhandled quite a bit in the last few days." Her sarcasm was lost on him. He was too busy staring at her black-and-blue body.

"This isn't normal." He traced a bruise circling her neck. "How did you get this one?"

"A guy grabbed me by the collar and tried to drag me off, but I pointed my gun in his face and he let go."

Connor's gaze turned dangerous. "Where and when did this happen?"

"While I was still in the hotel, during the fire."

"What did he look like?"

"Like any other local. He yelled at me in a language I didn't understand."

Connor's mouth tightened, but his hand was gentle on her neck. "I'm sorry I hurt you."

"*You* didn't."

The door behind Connor opened and Smoke and River walked in.

"I'm pretty sure," Sophia said wryly, "the sign on the door says *women*."

"Who ran you over?" River asked, staring at her.

Smoke didn't say anything, but he looked very, very angry.

"A whole bunch of people," she snapped. "Now get out, all of you." She glanced at Connor to include him in the order.

He left, but there was something in his expression telling her she hadn't heard the last from him about her bruises.

Stupid terrorists. They'd already made her reconsider her sexual explorations with Connor. If they screwed up her plans to accomplish something worth dying for she was going to shoot someone.

CONNOR'S STOMACH WASN'T happy. Hell, he was fucking furious with himself. Sophia was covered in bruises. Deep, large, black ones indicating substantial bleeding.

"What. The. Fuck?" River said to him.

"She says she has some kind of clotting problem, but that is…"

"Sick," Smoke said.

"That's one way to put it."

"No. She's sick."

Con stared at him. "She said it was under control."

Smoke shrugged.

"Would she tell you if she wasn't?" River asked.

Sophia came out of the bathroom. "What wouldn't I tell you?"

Con sighed. "If you were sick."

She rolled her eyes. "I am not sick. I'm special, but I'm not sick."

"What the fuck does that mean?"

"I told you, my platelets are screwed up, so I get bruises. Sometimes they're pretty scary looking, but they'll go away eventually."

"What the hell is taking you so long?" Max yelled.

Sophia walked away.

Con watched her and couldn't help feeling he'd just been lied to.

Max was on the phone when Con, Smoke and River got back to Eugene's desk. As he was talking, Eugene came back with Jones in tow.

She looked around at all the men, weapons and Sophia then said, "You weren't shitting me, were you, Gene?"

"No."

Con looked at Eugene. "Hair dye?"

Jones held up the bag in her hand.

"Did Eugene explain everything?"

"No," the man said. "I thought I'd let someone with some authority do that."

"The short version," Connor said, "is that you're going to become Sophia, and we're going to stick you on a plane heading back to the States with Eugene."

Jones looked at Sophia. "What did you do?"

"Nothing, I mean, Max thinks someone is trying to kidnap me for my, what did you call it?" she asked Max, but he was on the phone. "Creativity in working with viruses."

Max nodded.

"So," Jones said. "Shit's going down?"

"That's what we think," Max said as he hung up the phone. "Are you prepared to take on Sophia's identity and act as a decoy?"

"Yes, sir," Jones replied.

"Good. Time for your makeover. Your plane leaves in three hours."

"I'm going to need your uniform, Doc."

"We can change in the bathroom." Sophia led the way.

Con waited until the two women were inside the bathroom before speaking to Max. "Sir, Sophia looks like a train hit her."

"What does that mean?" Max asked.

"She's badly bruised all over her body."

"You saw her entire body?" Max asked in a dangerous tone.

Sophia wasn't the only one who didn't always know how to talk to people. "No, sir. I saw her arms and torso. She says it's her medical condition that's to blame, but the last time I saw someone bruised that badly, they'd been beaten half to death."

Max looked thoughtful. "I'll speak to her."

"Thank you, sir."

"In the meantime, get prepped to leave. There are two separate outbreaks I want investigated. At this point I don't know if either is the result of a possible biological weapon, but the speed and mortality rate of both has me nervous. One is in Northern Iraq, the other is in a refugee camp just outside Syria. I'm sending Sophia and you three to the refugee camp."

"That might be the best thing to do, but I have a concern," Connor said.

"Oh?"

"How the hell is Akbar getting his intel?" For him to know what he did, he had to have someone helping him from the inside.

FIFTEEN

"THAT IS A question I'd like answered as well. We don't know. We've done security checks on every contractor on base, as well as every person who comes on base. We found a couple of questionable people and threw them out, but tonight's events make it clear that we have a bigger problem than we realized."

"Sounds like you need to go deeper."

Max was silent for a long moment. "Bruises, huh?"

"Yes, sir."

It was several seconds before Max spoke again. "Did you lose any gear in the fire?"

"Yes, sir."

"Eugene, get them emergency replacements for whatever they need. I want them ready to go in two hours."

"Yes, sir."

Max nodded at Con and walked down the hall toward the washrooms.

"How do you want to play this?" River asked Connor.

"Very carefully, gentlemen. Sophia isn't going to meekly follow instructions, especially if they're for her own safety."

"That could be a problem," River said.

"I think it's guaranteed."

Smoke grunted. "Make it about our safety."

A grin relaxed Con's face. "Now that is an excellent idea."

With a plan in place to deal with Sophia's resistance to being babysat, Con was able to focus on their preparations for this new mission. In addition to some replacement gear, they also picked up four marines for additional security. A refugee camp could be a lawless place and the likelihood of needing a few extra people with firepower was almost guaranteed.

They'd also need help with moving the supplies, Sophia's fancy lab tent, her lab-in-a-bag, and solar rechargeable batteries to power her analyzing equipment. Not to mention food, water and additional medical supplies.

By the time he, Smoke, River and their security team returned to the lab the sun was up. As they walked smoke hung in the air, clinging to their clothing and hair.

"Anyone know if there were casualties?" Con asked the marines.

"Yes, sir," their unit leader, Farrell, said. "At least six, but several others are missing, so the count will probably go up."

"Son of a bitch," River said.

Max was on the phone again when they walked in, but Eugene and Jones were there, standing in the middle of a sea of duffel bags.

"You're taking all this with you?" Con asked.

"Nope," Eugene replied. "You're taking all this with *you*."

There was enough gear to supply an entire Forward Operating Base. "We'll be lucky to get it all in the helicopter."

"You'll be in a Super Stallion so you'll be okay. We're sending some additional food for the refugees,"

Eugene explained. "You can also request food drops if things are dire in the camp. No one wants a riot." Eugene glanced at Max's back.

"Makes sense." Con looked around. "Where's our Sophia?"

"She's in Max's office getting a unit of blood plasma."

"Thanks." Con glanced at the men with him. "Let's get this shit to the helipad."

"You got it," River said.

Con knocked on Max's office door then went inside.

Sophia was lying on a cot, a bag of straw-colored fluid dripping into her arm. Her newly dyed brown hair looked out of place.

"Hey, this stuff going to stop the bruises?"

She glanced at him only briefly, like he was a minor irritation. "Hopefully."

"Are you ready to go?"

"Yep."

Shit, she sounded pissed.

"Are you going to give me more than a one-word answer today?"

"Don't know yet."

"You're angry...at me."

"No shit, Sherlock."

"I already told your boss, I'm no Sherlock Holmes. You're going to have to explain what I did wrong, so I don't do it again." He crossed his arms over his chest. "Use small words."

"You told Max about my bruises." Her flared nostrils and pronounced frown told him she wasn't angry. She was furious.

"In my place, you'd have done the same thing."

Her glare nearly stripped a layer of skin off his face. "I was going to tell him."

The look of betrayal on her face gutted him, but forced himself to appear unaffected, and shrugged. "You took too long and we don't have time to spare."

She pressed her lips together. "Asshole."

"We've already established that."

"I'm a big girl, you know. I can take care of myself."

"Doesn't matter. I won't compromise when it comes to your safety."

She stared at the ceiling for a few seconds, like she was counting to ten in her head, then asked in a calmer tone, "The fire?"

"Six dead so far."

She gritted her teeth. "If I get my hands on Akbar, I'm going to rip him a new one."

"Cool, but only if I can help."

This time when she looked at him, worry had painted lines where there shouldn't have been any on a face as young as hers. "What we're going into, it could kill us."

"So can a bullet or a bomb, but that's what we do—the shit no one else will, because it has to be done."

"There have been hundreds of deaths in the camp we're going to in the last forty-eight hours. I suspect there will be hundreds more before we're done."

Con looked at her, really looked. She appeared fragile, like a piece of spun glass, a masterpiece, until someone dropped and destroyed it.

"What the hell is Akbar planning?" he asked under his breath.

"Creating a weapon of mass infection?"

"Yeah, but what if the answer isn't that simple? The guy's wacko. We could be wrong."

"Max thinks he wants revenge."

"On who?"

"The American military."

"A big target."

"But he's already created a biological weapon. His anthrax strain could kill hundreds or thousands. If creating a biological weapon is his goal, I'm superfluous."

"There are two instances where you, one individual, would matter." Con ticked them off on his fingers. "You're part of the problem, or you're part of the solution."

The color drained from her face. If she'd been standing up, she would have passed out. "How could I be part of either?"

"You're the youngest doctor to have two doctorates."

"So what?"

"Did you do any groundbreaking research?"

"Not on anthrax. I spent most of my time on rabies and the flu, investigating genetic drift and mutation rates."

"What was your thesis on?"

"Rabies. How it's transmitted from animals to humans, its effect on the brain and what makes it so deadly."

"Deadly?"

She gave him a look. "Rabies is nothing like anthrax. It's difficult to work with and it can take weeks to kill. There's usually plenty of time to administer treatment for it if you know you've been infected, but once symptoms appear nothing can save you. You're dead." She released a pent-up breath. "What if he's picked me because I'm young, a woman and a doctor? What if his intent is to demoralize and get the American military to withdraw to a certain degree?"

"He could be trying to encourage the American military to send its specialists back to the States. You are a valuable and finite resource."

"Or reduce our numbers to the point where we're ineffective."

"So when he does release a biological weapon on a mass of people, we can't stop it."

"That makes way too much sense."

"If he's anything like General Rommel, he's got a plan within a plan."

"Yeah," Con said, standing. "That's what I'm afraid of." He looked at the bag hanging above the bed. "How much longer?"

"A few minutes."

"I'll meet you at Eugene's desk." He turned and headed for the door.

"Connor?"

He turned. "Yeah?"

"I haven't forgiven you."

He grinned at her. "That doesn't surprise me."

SOPHIA WANTED TO kiss the smug smile off his face. Or cry. Or scream the rage out of her body. There were too many emotions churning inside her, all of them looking for an exit, only there wasn't one.

Her unit of blood plasma was finished infusing. Time to go.

Only there wasn't much time left for her to do anything. No time left to make her mark or enjoy the full sexual experience with the aggravating, amazing man who'd just left.

Perhaps she should tell Max about her low cell counts, let him really send her home. But if she did that she really would leave him with too few specialists to do the work he and the Army needed to do.

The door to Max's office opened and Max walked in, shutting the door behind himself. He didn't say anything as he came over and began the process of removing the intravenous line.

"I think you should request more specialists," she said to him. "You don't have enough teams."

"Getting more teams put together is going to take time."

"Then take the time." She put her hand on his arm, bringing him to a stop as he was putting a Band-Aid on the back of her hand. "Akbar is only one man, but the threat only begins with him."

He frowned at her. "What do you mean?"

"We're fighting terrorists. They're going to use every weapon they can to inflict damage and terror to anyone who doesn't bow down to them. Biological weapons are the perfect terror weapon. Killing slowly, horribly and without mercy."

"I requested more staff and specialists two months ago, but there's a shortage of everyone."

"Is that why you're not sending me home for real?"

Surprise made his eyes widen momentarily before he laughed and shrugged. "Yes." He gestured at the bag of plasma. "You shouldn't need this, Sophia."

"I've never been within normal ranges in anything."

"No, you haven't." He paused, then continued with, "I trust you to look after yourself while on this mission, because the men going with you need you."

"You think the threat is real?"

"I do. Akbar is playing a lethal game. I need you to use that brain of yours to out-think him."

"He's willing to die, Max. He might even want to die. He'll take risks no sane person would, and I think that might make the difference between winning and losing."

"How do you know that?"

"Because I've been there. If you accept that death is inevitable, there is an intellectual freedom in it. No risk is too great to prevent the necessary job from getting done." She knew she was already risking her life.

"Where have I heard that line before?"

"Brigadier General, retired, Chuck Yeager." Connor walked all the way into the office and shut the door. "You two were taking too long."

Max grunted. "I suppose a test pilot needs to have accepted the inevitability of death in order to take the risks he does." He turned to Connor. "What do you think?"

"I think she has a point. We've got to assume he's going to do crazy suicidal shit."

"There's an advantage to being prepared for whatever horror he enacts on the world. Nothing is precious to him anymore." Sophia looked at Connor. "Nothing matters but revenge."

He flinched, but the expression was only on his face for a fraction of a second. If she hadn't been watching him she'd have missed it. "Is she well enough for the mission?"

Sophia answered before Max could. "That's an unanswerable question. I've been asked to out-think a madman. No one is well enough for that."

What had made him flinch? She thought back over

what she'd said and realized Connor hadn't reacted until the last word she'd said. *Revenge.*

"She's fit for duty," Max told Connor. "Though I agree, no one is well enough for what might be necessary on this mission." He turned to her, and hesitated only a second before saying, "Be ready to leave in thirty minutes."

"Yes, sir."

Max left, but Connor didn't move.

"Are you going to bring some more of that stuff?" he asked with a nod at the empty bag of plasma.

"Yes, one."

He tilted his head to one side. "What causes your platelets to stop working?"

"They work, mostly. Problem is, there aren't enough of them." She got up from the cot and disposed of the IV tubing and bags. "Stress, infection, sleep deprivation, any number of things can trigger ITP or make it worse."

There was a pause of two or three seconds before he said, "I'm sorry I haven't had time to teach you many self-defense tricks."

She stopped and glanced at him. He stood in the center of the office, his face serious, almost glum. "Why are you apologizing? It's not your fault an insane man chose to target me. If it weren't for you, I'd probably be not enjoying said wacko's lack of hospitality."

He shook his head.

"Or is this your way of sucking up?"

"I fully intend to teach you those tricks," Connor said.

He was watching her face so closely he probably knew how many eyelashes she had. The man was a champion worrier.

Was he also contemplating something else, like revenge?

She knew she was going to die. She'd have to make sure he didn't join her.

She grabbed a duffel bag that had been sitting on the floor next to Max's desk and stopped in front of him. "Shall we?"

She made it sound like they were going on a routine trip to somewhere safe.

Where they were going was about as unsafe as it got.

SIXTEEN

It went against Con's every instinct to allow Sophia on a mission this dangerous, but there was nothing he could do to stop it. She was the subject expert.

He led her out of the office. Max was waiting with Smoke, River and their marines.

Max had his hands wrapped around a file folder so tight his knuckles were white. "More details have come in. We received some blood samples from one of the Western aid groups based out of the UK. But the description of the illness doesn't match anthrax."

Connor considered what he knew of Max. "How many sick?"

"The information we received wasn't clear. The number was either five hundred or five thousand."

"Where in Syria? Is it a location we can realistically get to without drawing the attention of extremists?"

"It's just outside Syria, a refugee camp in northern Lebanon. It sprang up about six months ago and currently has between two and five thousand people living there. We don't have a lot of intel from the camp, just an emergency request for medical support from the aid group. They arrived a week ago with food, water and medical supplies, but there's some kind of outbreak."

"What about security? Is there any?"

"Nothing official."

"Unofficially?"

"One of the doctors in the aid group has a rich uncle. The doctor has a bodyguard who may or may not be former Special Forces. We wouldn't be sending anyone into this camp if it weren't for the threat from Akbar," Max explained. "This is an isolated group of people. It's the perfect place to test and refine a lethal biological weapon."

"Using a bunch of women, kids and old people as lab rats," Con said with a snarl.

"Which brings me to my next bit of news," Max announced. "You'll all be getting additional vaccination and antibiotic shots."

"Yeah, better safe than sorry," Connor said with a sigh. "Now my ass really is going to be sore for a week."

"Better than dead," River said with crooked grin.

Sophia led them to a small room where the laboratory staff drew blood samples from people. There was a tray with a bunch of tiny bottles of fluid and several small injection needles.

Yep, sore ass.

Con took a good look at her as she prepared the first shot, about as friendly as a porcupine. "What's bugging you now?"

She paused for a moment, then gave him a look that was clearly meant to size him up. "Roll up your sleeve."

"Nope," he said getting to his feet and turning around. He lowered his pants enough to show some cheek. "Give it to me, baby."

When nothing happened, he glanced over his shoulder to find her staring at his butt. River and Smoke had slipped out of the room. "Is there something wrong with it?"

Her gaze jerked away from where she'd been staring to meet his. "I'm surprised to find no boot prints on it."

She blushed a beautiful red.

He grinned.

She narrowed her eyes and jabbed him with the needle.

"Ow."

"Now who's the baby?" Something cool rubbed the spot where she'd poked him. "Are you sure you want all your shots in your ass?"

"Yes, ma'am. Better than having sore arms any day."

She sighed and messed around with the tray. "Just about ready with the next one."

"Dr. Perry, do you have…" Eugene's voice trailed off. "Holy shit, I'm…wow. I'll just go—"

Connor started to laugh. The view the kid must have at the moment.

"Gene, we're not doing anything kinky," Sophia told him in a patient tone. "I'm giving the sergeant several vaccinations. See?" She moved aside.

Connor got himself under control long enough to see the expression on Eugene's face. The kid looked ready to pass out and Con couldn't help the snort that came out of him.

Sophia took that moment to jab him with the second needle.

"Ah!" When Connor glanced back at the door, Eugene was gone. "Where'd he go?"

"To either throw up or get a camera. Not sure which." She got another needle ready. "Personally, I'm hoping for the camera." And she jabbed him again.

What the *fuck*? "Why are you so grumpy?"

"You have to ask?"

Duh, moron, you did just present her with your ass.
"Shit. I'm sor—"

"I saw how you reacted to the word *revenge* a few minutes ago," she said as she prepared the next shot. "I'm going to need you where we're going."

"You think I'd abandon you out there?" he asked, jerking his head to indicate the world outside the base.

"I think a guy like you might have more than one objective," Sophia replied, sticking yet another needle in his butt.

Shit, if she kept stabbing him like that he wasn't going to be able to sit down for days. "How many more needles?"

"That was the last one."

Connor pulled up his pants and got his fly zipped just as River appeared in the doorway.

He took one look at Connor and Sophia and smirked. "Huh, I thought the kid was hallucinating. Sorry to interrupt." He waved and disappeared.

Sophia glared at the empty doorway. "I hate people." Her gaze moved to him. "I hate you."

"But you like me too," he said with his best little-boy smile. "Or you wouldn't have given me shit."

"Shut up before I jab you someplace that will hurt a lot more than your butt."

He chuckled. He liked her all toothy and snarly, it made her mean. He turned his attention to the mission. "I'll get Smoke and River."

"Let them know I'm not giving any more ass shots."

Damned straight she wasn't. "I'll tell them."

The two men were lounging against the wall outside the room.

"Finished already?" River asked with a smirk.

It was obvious what River was thinking, and it triggered a cold burn in the pit of Con's stomach. "I was getting her mind off the fire."

"Oh yeah?" River's smile got even wider. "'Cause it looked like more than that."

Con took a step toward River and let some of the rage he'd been hiding the last year peer out of his eyes. "If you show her your ass, *I'm* going to give you the shots."

River lost the grin and became very still. "Well, that wouldn't be nearly as much fun."

"I guarantee it."

Smoke stood there with all the responsiveness of a piece of granite.

"What about you?" Con asked him, ready to pound anyone who might hurt Sophia in any way.

"She's too young."

Con didn't bother pretending he didn't know that Smoke was commenting on her age relative to Con's. "She's twenty-four."

Smoke shrugged and went into the room. River followed, leaving Con to calm himself down, but calm didn't come easy anymore. Con listened to Sophia explain about the shots, and let her no-nonsense professional tone wash away some of the anger. The problem was, there was always more building, like a volcano on the verge of erupting.

He'd always been the joker, the easygoing guy on his team, the one who deflected the bullshit. But now, he kept seeing his buddies' faces right before the explosion, relaxed and happy, then after, what was left of them. The ringing in his ears was as loud and insistent as the sobs of Wayne's wife when Con called her from the hospital to say her sexy love letters wouldn't be among Wayne's effects because he'd always kept them in his pockets.

Now, only the anger was easy.

After giving them the shots, she came out with the two soldiers behind her.

"What are you bringing for weapons?" he asked her.

"Weapons?"

When she looked at him blankly, he added, "A sidearm, a steak knife, anything?"

"I've got my Beretta."

The woman was wicked literal. "We'll keep practicing if we get a chance."

"Only if it doesn't interfere with my work."

Right then, he decided to add extra ammunition and a second back-up weapon, another Beretta, holstered in the small of his back. It was a custom add-on to his body armor from a buddy of his who would have fought him for the assignment of looking out for Sophia. Fred had an eye for the ladies, the more fragile the better. Sophia might be smart and direct, but she was also the most physically fragile person he'd ever met in an Army uniform.

She was the most physically fragile person he'd ever met period.

How the hell was he going to keep her safe in an incredibly unsafe location?

Usually he could trust his partner to do his part to get the job done in as safe and logical a way as possible, but Sophia didn't follow anyone's rules, including those put in place for her security.

Fuck, he was going to need eyes in the back of his head to keep track of her and everything around them.

THE HELICOPTER WAS so full of emergency food and medical supplies there wasn't much room left over for its living passengers. Sophia tried to find a comfortable way to sit, but she was squished by the men seated on either side of her. Connor on one side, Smoke on the other and River across from her. Their marines, Henry, Macler, Stalls and Norton, were sitting behind her, though she couldn't see much of them with all their supplies, packs and weapons between them.

Colonel Maximillian assigned these particular marines because they'd all had at least one rotation in Afghanistan and all had expressed an interest in becoming Special Forces soldiers.

He'd given them one order, keep her alive.

The marines stared at her like she was some kind of cockroach. They didn't ask any questions or offer any introductions. No thanks. She'd had enough people stare at her blankly with no idea what to do with her when she'd been a kid.

She'd been ready to tell them all to get lost, but Connor ordered them to help him with the supplies.

She could have kissed him for getting their hired muscle out of her way.

Thing was, next time she saw those marines, as they were all getting on the helicopter, their attitude had changed, and they'd treated her like she was part of the team.

She didn't know what the hell Connor had told them, but it had worked like a charm.

As soon as the bird was in the air, Connor kept dropping off into sleep. Every time she moved though, he woke up, so she was concentrating on keeping still. That, of course, made it harder and harder to do.

They were flying over Syria now and that didn't help Sophia's restlessness. They'd been shot at when they crossed the border, so now any time the aircraft shuddered, she tensed up, expecting the whole machine to blow up.

She normally didn't mind flying, but this trip might give her a phobia.

To keep her overactive brain busy, she went over the list of things she had to do once they arrived.

Set up the tent for her lab.

Ensure there was a safe water supply, using purification tablets and the water filters they'd crammed into the helicopter if necessary.

Examine the sick.

Examine the dead.

Test samples from the living and the dead to determine the pathogen causing illness and death.

Create a treatment plan and carry it out.

And somewhere in there she might have to add maintaining the peace in a camp full of hundreds of people likely to be in a state of panic.

Oh yeah, and sleep. Maybe. Hopefully.

At least they knew they weren't dealing with anthrax. All of the test results for bacterial infection had come back negative, so they were likely dealing with a virus.

Not better, just different.

Could even be worse.

She'd read the report of the symptoms so many times it was engraved on the inside of her eyelids.

Fever, headache and confusion lasting six to ten hours. Progressing to generalized pain throughout the body, continued high fever accompanied by increased agitation and hallucinations, swelling of the oral mucosa with many people choking to death on their tongues. Death occurring within twenty-four hours of onset of symptoms.

The most likely cause, as far as Sophia was concerned, was viral meningitis. To confirm that diagnosis, she'd need to test cerebral spinal fluid from a recent corpse and from a living patient showing the symptoms of the illness.

Max wondered if it was meningococcal disease, caused by the *Neisseria meningitidis* bacteria. The symptoms certainly fit, and the situation in the refugee camp was a perfect place for meningococcal disease to run rampant, but the tests of the few samples that had been sent ahead had been negative.

If she was right, there was little they could do besides support the patient's health with an IV to keep them hydrated and proper sanitation so they didn't get sick with a secondary virus or bacteria.

If it turned out that Max was right after all, they would need massive amounts of antibiotics and the meningococcal vaccine to give everyone in the camp, sick or not. They'd still lose a lot of people, but there was a treatment.

Treatment. Something not available for her.

Now was her moment. She was finally going to be in the right place to put her skills to the best use possible. She might not be able to save herself, but she was going to save everyone else she could.

SEVENTEEN

THE CONSTANT HUM and vibration of the helicopter's engines changed, lowering in pitch and speed.

Connor went from asleep to awake from one moment to the next.

There was movement from the cockpit of the aircraft. Connor shouted something at someone up there and her stomach flipped as they rapidly descended.

He turned to her and gave her a thumbs-up, but didn't wait for any kind of a reply.

Okay, things must be going the way he wanted them to go.

She strained to see out, but there was no way to get a good view with all the equipment and supplies in the way.

A minute or two later the helicopter touched down. The doors rolled open, but all she could see was a cloud of sand whirling around in cornea-burning sunlight.

Connor took her by the arm and helped her out of the aircraft. He ran with her until they were outside the radius of the rotor blades then yelled in her ear, "Stay here with Private Henry while we offload the bird. These supplies are worth more than gold here, so keep your sidearm in your hand and be ready to deter any potential looters."

She nodded and removed her Beretta from its holster strapped to her right thigh. Henry positioned himself on her left and slightly in front of her. She made brief eye contact with him, then faced away from the helicopter and watched the crowd quickly gathering around their landing site. Men, women and children, though the men were mostly older.

Connor and the marines began piling things around her. Bags containing the portable level three lab, more bags containing medical supplies, her fancy tent, and her level two lab—brought along at Max's insistence— and bags of rice.

The crowd shifted and a man dressed in quasi-military gear and armed with the same weapon Connor carried walked toward her.

She pointed her gun at him and he came to a stop and took his hands off his weapon, leaving it dangling from his neck by the strap.

A hand touched her back, then slid around her shoulder and pushed her extended arms down. "He's a good guy."

She made eye contact with Connor and nodded. There was still too much sand in the air for her to want to open her mouth to talk.

Connor flashed a hand signal at Henry, who lowered his weapon a fraction also.

The man she'd stopped came forward and gave her a salute as he went past. She glanced behind her to see him join the men unloading the helicopter with Connor. When she returned her attention to the crowd, she sucked in a breath at how quickly it had grown, and took an unconscious step toward Henry.

One Beretta and one semi-automatic weapon was never going to be enough to hold these people off.

The crowd surged again, but this time a half-dozen

men came forward and toward her. They weren't wearing uniforms or body armor, but they were wearing identical shirts with the logo for the medical aid group she knew was working here.

This time she didn't point her gun at them.

Behind her, the helicopter took off, finally allowing the sand to settle. Too bad it wasn't going to last.

Connor patted her shoulder. "If we try to move the food we're going to get mobbed, so the aid group is going to distribute it from here."

"What about our stuff?"

"We'll take it to their makeshift hospital while the food is being handed out."

That sounded like a very smart idea. "Okay." She grabbed up the smaller, portable level two lab bag, while Connor took the larger two bags with the level three lab components. Smoke, River and the marines all grabbed up the other medical supplies, and Connor's friend led the way into the camp.

She almost had to run to keep up with them, but didn't complain. Something in her primitive hindbrain told her that there were predators all around, waiting for an opportunity to take what they were carrying, even if it wouldn't do anyone else any good.

They traveled along a beaten path in the sand, but from underneath a cobblestone road or trail occasionally poked through. There were rough stone walls and buildings on either side of the path at first, but after a few minutes, only tents were lined up several rows deep.

Ahead, she could see a larger tent with a large red cross painted low enough on the canvas that it could be seen from the ground or air. They entered a space between the medical tent and the ones clearly meant for individual families. There were few people here, at least fewer walking around. A large mound on the left looked oddly out of place.

Sophia came to a stop. She'd seen something like this before and really hoped she was wrong about what it was. "Is this a mass grave?" It wasn't until the words were out that she realized she'd spoken out loud.

In front of her, their guide stopped for a moment to look at her. "Yes," he said, without inflection. "We'll need to dig another one soon."

"How many bodies are in there?"

He shrugged and continued until just short of the tent, but in the shade.

Sophia looked at the mound for another second or two then followed at a slower pace. Connor didn't say anything at all, but he, Smoke and River seemed to be looking all over. Same with the marines. Searching for threats?

The temperature dropped enough in the shade to be noticeable. There were rows and rows of cots, more than she'd ever seen before. Most of those cots were occupied. Other than that, there wasn't much inside the tent.

No IVs dripping fluid into the veins of the sick.

No food visible.

Very little water.

Not enough nurses or anyone ambulatory to care for all these people.

"We didn't bring enough of anything," Sophia said in a soft voice to Connor.

"Agreed." Connor sounded as horrified as she felt. "I'm going to go back to the landing area and see if I can grab a couple of bags of rice. I've got one of the water filters and some purification tablets, so we're okay there."

"Can you ask for more food to be flown in? Rice, flour, MREs. Anything?"

"You're the ranking officer here, you can make the request."

"Oh. Right, sorry, I forgot."

Their guide snorted and looked away.

"Speaking of forgetting, Captain Sophia Perry, this is Len Zobel, former Snake Eater who now works for himself." From the grin on Connor's face, they must be friends.

"I sure as shit earn enough to live on now," the other man said with a playful grin. Then he gave Sophia a thorough once-over and offered his hand. "I wouldn't have minded looking out for you, Captain. You're a whole lot easier on the eyes than any assignment I ever had in the Army."

She shook it once, then pulled her hand away despite his momentary tightening of his grasp. *Jerk.* "Charmed."

Both men blinked, then started laughing.

"Hot damn, ma'am," Connor's friend said, saluting her. "I haven't been put in my place that well since General Stone did it last, two years ago. I'd be pleased if you called me Len."

"You can call me Dr. Perry."

"Oh," Len said with mock fear to Connor. "Is she always this prickly?"

Connor smiled. "You should see her with a syringe. My ass is going to be sore for a long time."

Wonderful, now he was making it sound like they'd

done something sexual and saying it to a guy she didn't know.

"You can tell me all about it later," Len said with a wink to Connor. "We'll be right back, Dr. Perry. I promise."

She ignored him and stared at Connor. Was this some kind of male bonding bullshit? Sometimes men were so weird.

"Why don't you start sorting out your equipment and decide where you want your lab set up?" he said, glancing at Smoke and the marines. "If you pick out a spot before I get back, these guys can get it started. River, you're with me."

"Fine." She looked around, trying to find someone who looked like they were in charge, but all she saw were sick people. There had to be hundreds of them. "I need to talk to a doctor to find out what's going on." How on earth was she going to help this many people?

"Are you good, Sophia?" Connor asked. The smile was gone, replaced by a frown.

"Yeah, shoo." She swallowed hard and forced herself to focus on what she could do, not what she couldn't. "The sooner you go the sooner you get back."

Connor took one last look around, nodded at her and followed Len out.

Sophia stood, duffel bags behind her, sick people in front of her, with one Green Beret and four marines who looked like they were holding on to their cookies by the skin of their teeth.

"Um, hello?" a diffident voice asked from behind her.

She turned to see a man in his late twenties to early thirties with brownish hair hanging in dreadlocks and a full beard. His blue eyes and fair, sunburnt skin told her he probably wasn't a native of the area. His surgical mask, gloved hands and clear plastic rain poncho told her he was with the medical aid group.

"Are you, by chance, the doctor we were promised?" he asked even more diffidently. "I'm Dr. Nigel Blairmore."

"Dr. Sophia Perry, Captain, US Army, Biological Response Team." She gave him a professional nod.

Dr. Blairmore glanced at the bags around her. "I see you've brought some supplies. I was rather hoping you'd brought more."

"One of my escorts and your Len have gone back to bring some of the food supplies here for your patients." She pointed at the bags. "Most of this is my portable lab and other medical equipment. Now that we're here, I'm going to make a list of the most urgently needed items and request more be brought as soon as possible."

Dr. Blairmore seemed to wilt with relief. "Thank God. We've been without proper food or clean water for several days now."

"We brought filtration units and purification tablets." She grabbed the right bag and opened it so he could see.

"We can put that into use straight away." One of the men hovering around their conversation gave her a brilliant smile, picked up the filtration unit and pointed at a large plastic tank that sat about twenty feet away from the medical tent, inside a tent of its own. The tank was about half full and wouldn't be enough to keep a large number of people alive for long.

"Where does your water come from?"

"There's a well in the older part of the camp," Dr. Blairmore answered.

"Everyone in the camp drinks the same water?"

"It's the only source." When she continued to stare at the water, he added, "It's been tested for parasites and bacteria. Other than a high iron content, the water was safe enough to drink short term. Your filter will definitely improve the quality."

One possible infection source removed, Sophia turned her attention to the interior of the tent. "Where can I set up my lab?"

"Well, we're a little cramped for space. We've had thirty-three new cases in the last hour and we're running out of cots, as well as space."

"And everything else, it seems."

"Yes. There's probably a tent you can use. Are you a trauma doc or...?"

"I have a dual specialty in hematology and virology."

Dr. Blairmore blinked at her. "You're not a people doctor, are you?"

"I'm here to determine the cause of all of these people becoming sick and—" she glanced out at the mound, easily visible from the hospital tent "—dead."

"We need that, absolutely, but we also need front-line health care workers. Nurses, doctors, anyone who can help."

"I'll make the request, but your isolation here makes getting even the most basic of items, like food, difficult. The Army may choose to do a series of air-drops."

"Will that include nurses?"

"I don't know." She shrugged. "I guess we'll find out." She crouched down among the bags and pulled out her satellite phone.

Max answered on the first ring. "Colonel Maximillian."

"Sir, it's Dr. Perry. We're on the ground and I'm at

the camp's hospital. Food, medical supplies and trained hands to help with the sick are desperately needed."

"Orders have come down, food and supplies can be air-dropped, but until you determine what's causing so many people to sicken and die, no one new is going in. Identify the pathogen. That's your only priority, Sophia. It needs to be done fast."

"Understood, sir."

"Check in with me every four hours. Good luck."

"Thank you, sir." She hung up and tucked the phone into a holster on her belt. When she stood Dr. Blairmore looked at her expectantly.

"They're going to start supply drops from the air, but won't send more human assistance until after I determine the pathogen responsible for this outbreak."

There was no hiding the disappointment on his face, but he nodded amiably enough. "Do you need help setting up your lab?"

"No." She pointed at Smoke and the marines. "I have all the help I need."

"We'll all feel better knowing what we're dealing with." He turned and said a few things to the people waiting with him. They reacted with smiles, then frowns, but all dispersed with relatively neutral body language and tones to their voices. One man came back with a banker's box. "Our records, so far. I'm sorry some of the patient documentation is missing. We've had so many people we sometimes don't even get a name before they're too far gone to talk to us."

"Thank you. I'll read them here." She quickly went through the box, scanning the forms for symptoms, treatment and results.

A couple of people pointed, then ran out of the tent.

Sophia glanced after them. Connor, River and his buddy were laden with sacks of rice.

Smiles graced the faces of everyone not wearing a surgical mask as the men came closer to the tent with the sacks. A woman came over and directed them to another tent about fifty feet away. Probably where they did the food preparation for the sick.

Connor glanced at Sophia as he passed her. "I'll be right back."

She nodded and set the box aside. There wasn't anything in view for miles, only desert. Casting her gaze over the camp only revealed that every available spot within eyesight with any shelter or older building was already in use.

Connor came back within a minute. "You still here? Where are we setting up?"

"I thought I'd let you choose the spot."

"Really?" His expression said he didn't quite believe it.

She sighed. "To be honest, I'm not sure where to go. Nothing is closed off or easily defendable, so..."

He looked around. There wasn't much to see. The tent was open until about five or six feet above the ground so air could circulate. Anyone could see in and out of the structure.

Connor's mouth pressed into a grim line. "No privacy or protection."

"Privacy isn't a huge concern," she told him. "Safety is another matter."

"I can't promise you one hundred percent safety," Connor said, looking unhappy about it.

Little did he know, he couldn't protect her from the deadliest enemy she had.

Her own body.

EIGHTEEN

THERE WAS A small rise to the northwest of the hospital tent. It wasn't much, but it was better than flat terrain. "Let's pitch your tent over there," Connor said, thrusting his chin in the direction of the hill. "Close enough for easy access to the hospital, far enough to see trouble coming." He, Smoke, River and the marines grabbed up most of the bags, leaving just two for Sophia.

She made enough noise behind him that he didn't have to look to know she was back there.

Once he reached the spot he liked, he dropped his bags, nodded at the men and took hers from her.

They set up the lab tent first. It took him and the boys less time to get the structure up than the first time they'd done it, but it took longer to anchor it to the sandy ground. They had to pound anchor pins several feet deep.

Sophia wasn't idle while they played construction crew. She pulled out the segmented furniture that unfolded into barstool-tall surfaces she called *benches*. Only these benches weren't for sitting, they were for the pint-sized lab equipment she was going to use to determine the pathogen causing all the sickness and death.

By the time the tent was anchored, she was setting up her equipment.

He left her to it and took Smoke, River and the marines aside. "I want you on a two on, two off rotation," he said to the marines. "Your job is to defend Dr. Perry and her equipment. If things go FUBAR, *she* is top priority. Got it?"

"What will you and Sergeants Smoke and River be doing, sir?" Henry asked.

"She's my responsibility. I go where ever she goes. Smoke and River are going to go where they're needed. You might be coming with us or you could be staying with the equipment. It's going to depend on what's happening at the time. Right now, I want two of you to patrol the area. Look for places where an attack might come from. The other two can set up a tent, which we will all use for sleeping."

"Yes, sir," the marines said in unison. They didn't talk to each other, but Henry and Stalls got to work on the tent while Macler and Norton began their patrol.

They were already a team. That was a very good thing since their situation was one where no one knew what the outcome might be.

Con walked over to Sophia and crouched next to her. She was sorting through a bunch of power cords and chargers. "What do you plug all this in to?" he asked.

"Everything runs on batteries, like the ones in a laptop computer. See those black boxes?" She pointed at a row of four sitting in one of the open bags on the ground. "Those are the backup battery chargers. Between them and the batteries in the analyzers, I've got enough power here for about twenty-four hours of continuous use. After that, I'll need to charge the batteries with a generator."

He had to admit he couldn't see anything he'd change with the setup. "That's pretty slick."

"It took a while to develop the technology for us to

do this. But, there's a strong market for this kind of thing in several industries. From communications to search and rescue."

"You sound like a commercial."

She sighed. "Max made me talk in front of one of those Senate committees in order to get the funds to pay for it. I hated every second."

"I don't doubt it. Not many politicians have a good grasp of what's a good investment these days."

"Max said my being young and pretty helped more than my testimony did." Her voice dripped disgust and anger.

A strong reaction. "Did anyone come on to you? Those bastards can be pretty handsy."

"No. I just talked with big words and they eventually went away."

"You scared them away with big words? *Seriously?*" How stupid had the political population gotten?

"It works surprisingly well," she said in a chipper voice that told him she was happy to have this little defense mechanism. "I've done it before."

"It's good to know that you do that to people who irritate you. Gives me something to look out for."

She paused in her work, tilted her head to one side then said, "Yes. If I start talking with really long, complicated vocabulary, you can assume I'm unhappy or irritated."

"Cool. Let's set up a couple other secret codes."

Her response was a semi-happy shrug.

"How about if you want to warn me about something dangerous," he said. "Let's decide on specific words or maybe a sentence. What would you say?"

"Okay," she said with a small smile. "Dangerous situation equals bad allergies acting up."

"Good one," Connor said. "My turn. For an urgent message, we'll say it's time for your medication."

She laughed. "I like that. What about an enemy that's pretending to be a good guy, or a good guy pretending to be an enemy?"

"How about, I could really use an ice water with a twist of lemon."

She glanced at him, a full blown smile on her face. "You've been watching too many James Bond movies."

"Hey, I loved those as a kid. I watched them with my dad. His movie heroes were John Wayne, Clint Eastwood and Sean Connery."

"My dad loved John Wayne, too."

Connor lowered his voice and adopted a drawl. "We're burning daylight."

She laughed and her happiness hit him between the eyes like someone had shot him point blank.

He couldn't remember the last time he'd made someone happy.

"What's going on over here?" Len Zobel asked as he walked up to the tent. "You two *enjoying* yourselves?"

Con was watching Sophia's face when Len stressed the word *enjoying* a little too much. Her nostrils flared and her eyes narrowed, but she didn't miss a beat. She looked down her nose at him, hard to do when she couldn't be taller than five foot two, and said in a tone that could have done a high school math teacher proud, "A little frivolity lowers blood pressure and cortisol levels, and boosts the immune system. Something every individual in this camp could use, don't you think?"

Len blinked, opened his mouth, then frowned and closed it. "Uh, yeah, I guess."

"Excellent. Why don't you take that advice and relay it to Dr. Blairmore."

There might have been a *why* at the beginning of her last sentence, but it was nothing less than an order.

"Sure," Len said slowly. He looked at Con. "Can I talk to you for a minute?"

He nodded and they walked a few feet away.

"What the fuck is her problem?" Len asked.

Con didn't see the point in hiding the answer. "You are."

"What did I do?"

"You weren't very nice when you accused us of enjoying ourselves, and she isn't much of a people-person in the first place, so..."

"So...?"

"So." Con shrugged. "Don't be an ass."

Len grinned at him. "You're doing her, aren't you?"

Not as much as I want to. Fuck, he couldn't say that. "Do I look stupid to you?"

Len glanced over his shoulder at Sophia as she unpacked her stuff. "So, if I apologize really nice, I've still got a chance?"

"Not a chance in hell."

"But—"

He meant to say *she's my responsibility.* What came out was a quiet, certain, "She's mine."

"I thought you said you weren't sleeping with her?"

"Only a moron sleeps with a superior officer while deployed with the officer." *Yep, he was a moron.*

"You're waiting until this little mission is over?" Len watched him for a moment, glanced at Sophia again, then shrugged and nodded. "Don't blame you, Con. She's something else to look at."

If that's all Len saw, he was an idiot. "She's got more going for her *inside* her head."

"I hope you're right, because the shit that's going on in this camp is fucking scary."

Interesting. Con angled his head at Sophia and Len followed him into their lab's tent.

"Dr. Perry, Len isn't a doctor, but he is a good observer. I thought you might want to hear his take on what's been happening here the last few days."

She put down the gadget she was unpacking and grabbed a notepad and pen out of a pocket. "When did you notice the first problems? Were you here before the outbreak started?"

"Yes, ma'am. I've been shadowing Dr. Blairmore since he and his group arrived about four weeks ago. We've had a steady stream of refugees coming in from Syria, but nothing surprising until about four days ago."

"What kinds of things were being treated prior to four days ago?"

"Bullet wounds, cuts, sunburn, broken bones, we had a couple of babies delivered here. All the normal things I guess."

She wrote a few things down in the notebook. "And after that?"

"We had seven or eight kids brought in with high fevers. Then a couple of hours later, a few more. That night, the ones that came in earlier in the day got worse. The doctors gave a bunch of them fluids, but it didn't seem to do much good. They started dying the next day. Then it wasn't just kids, it was men, women, kids, old people. Everybody."

Len stopped to swallow hard and take a breath, but Con had seen Len strung out on stress before and that guy was as silent and cold as a glacier. This guy, he was milking his story for everything he could get out of it. Even though Con had already told him Sophia wasn't available.

"They ran out of IVs yesterday," Len continued. "Which means the sick started dying faster. Some of them seemed to go crazy. They thrashed around, some had seizures, quite a few choked on their tongues. I helped dig the first burial pit and it almost killed me to see all those little bodies going into the ground." Len turned away and wiped his eyes.

The ham.

"I didn't mean to get snippy with you earlier, Dr. Perry. I'm really, really tired of taking dead bodies out of that tent over there."

Oh, for fuck's sake.

Con shifted his weight from one leg to the other and had to stop himself from knocking Len on his ass.

Sophia glanced at Con, then examined Len's face and calmly said, "Apology accepted, but if he doesn't believe your sob story—" she pointed right at Con "—neither do I. Don't try to get into my good books with that shit again."

Len's jaw dropped then he started laughing. "You two are quite the team, and look at me, I'm *laughing*." He walked away, shaking his head, disappearing into the hospital tent.

Sophia sighed. "What a pain in the ass."

"I've got to agree with you there. I don't think leaving the Army has done him all that much good."

She gave him her complete attention for a moment. "Thank you."

"For what?"

She arched a brow at him, then turned to get back to work.

Trust.

A chill settled over him despite the desert heat.

He hadn't questioned her ability to read him or give Len an appropriate answer.

Trust bound people together. He could already feel the invisible bonds between them squeezing his diaphragm.

He cleared his throat. "Is there anything I can do to help?"

"Sure. Could you ask Dr. Blairmore if it would be possible for me to take some fresh blood samples from some of the sick?"

"How many do you want?"

"Three. Based on ages. So, one from a child under twelve, one from an otherwise healthy adult and one from someone older than sixty. Wait." She opened another bag and pulled out disposable masks and gloves. "Wear a mask at all times and gloves if you think you might have to touch something over there. Coughing doesn't seem to be an issue, but it's better to be proactive. Can you give our guys some of these as well?" She looked around. "Where are Smoke and River?"

"They're looking over the entire camp." Con made sure all four of their security detail had a couple of masks and sets of gloves each before he put on his own mask and gloves.

He took a good look around on the short walk to the hospital tent. Things had quieted down now and few people seemed to be moving about. The other side of the tent was another story.

There was a line-up of people waiting to get in, with a couple of aid workers wearing masks and gloves dealing with them.

Dr. Blairmore was listening to the heartbeat of an old man who looked like he hadn't eaten in a month. Len was standing close by also wearing a mask and gloves. He tapped the doctor on the shoulder after he was finished with the old man and pointed at Connor.

The doctor came over. "How can I help you?"

"Dr. Perry would like to take three new blood samples, from a child under twelve, a healthy adult and an older person."

"Yes, of course, I'm hoping she can identify our pathogen quickly. It might be faster if I take the samples and bring them over right away. Would that work?"

"Yes, thank you."

"Wonderful." The doctor seemed unusually happy. "Would it be possible to look at her equipment?"

Not fucking likely. "I'll see what she says, but she's determined to identify the pathogen as quickly as possible and might not welcome other inquires until after that's done."

Blairmore nodded. "Yes, I caught that about her. Very focused. Okay, let me take those samples. I'll bring them as soon as I have them."

Con returned to the lab tent to find all her benches organized with analyzers, a centrifuge, a microscope, slides and other lab tools. "Ready to work?"

"Yes. The blood samples?"

"Dr. Blairmore said he'd have them here as soon as he can."

"Excellent. If this first round of samples doesn't reveal the pathogen, there are other samples I'm going to need."

"Oh?"

"Cerebral spinal fluid, a lung biopsy, and I'd like tissue samples from some of the dead to rule out or definitively identify certain diseases."

"Which diseases?"

"The list is long." She raised a brow. "You were there when Max and I discussed it and came up with eighteen possibilities."

"Yeah, but now you've seen the sick. Can't you narrow it down a little?"

She shook her head. "I make no assumptions, I deal only in facts." She looked at the hospital tent. "Whatever this is, it's deadly. The records Dr. Blairmore showed me are frightening. There aren't any survivors."

"What?"

"Every patient who has gotten sick has died within twenty-four to thirty-six hours."

Holy fuck. "That's not good."

What was worse was the determination on Sophia's face. She was going to figure this shit out or die trying. He'd never backed away from a battle before, but he wanted to abandon this one. Pack Sophia up and get her the fuck out of here.

NINETEEN

"WHY DID YOU think we were sent here?" Sophia asked. "To deal with some run-of-the-mill cholera outbreak?"

"I didn't realize how dangerous your work was outside of your fancy lab at the base."

She studied him and noted wide eyes and white lips. What had terrified her unflappable bodyguard? Was it the thought of losing another teammate?

"This is all part of my job," she said softly. "It's no different than when you deal with explosives. There's always the possibility of them blowing up in your face, but if you handle them right, no one gets hurt."

"Yeah, I get it," he said slowly, his gaze the unfocused one of a person deep in thought. "I've been assuming this would be like anthrax."

"If it were Akbar's anthrax everyone here would already be dead. No, this is something else. Something deadly, yes, but the symptoms are different. The timing of the disease, too."

"What does your gut tell you?"

"I don't know enough to guess."

When he didn't answer, she glanced at him and found him staring at her microscope.

"This isn't a puzzle or mental exercise. This could be something relatively benign, once we know what it is and if we have a treatment, or it could be something entirely new. The problem with viruses, in particular, is their ability to evolve rapidly. Sometimes that evolution is to our advantage, sometimes it isn't."

"H1N1," he said with a nod.

"Yes. It was so close, so very close, to a virus that could have become the next great pandemic. A couple of differences in its genetic sequence and it could have killed hundreds of millions of people. There are literally hundreds of viruses out there like it. And those are the just the ones we know of."

"You live in a scary, scary world," Con told her in a tone that sounded incredulous.

"Why do you find that so strange?"

He looked away. "You look so damn innocent. You talk like you've never seen a single ugly thing in your life and yet you can imagine the deaths of millions of people."

Oh, if only he knew. "Death and I are old companions." She gave him a weak smile. "There was a time, when I was a child, when death looked likely. I suppose I learned how to think around it then." She watched him, noted his stiff posture and rigid neck muscles. "You're a soldier, death can't be a stranger to you."

"No, but I understood the risks and chose to face it. You…you never got that choice."

"No, but I'm okay with that. Lots of people get no warning at all. No chance to decide how they want to die, or have the opportunity to choose to do something with the life they have before cancer takes it away. I was lucky."

"Yeah. I was lucky, too."

He didn't sound like he thought he was lucky. The way he said the word, all growly and low, made it sound like he wished he hadn't been lucky at all.

"You sound like you wished you'd died with your buddies."

"I can't discuss previous missions in an uncleared area like this one."

She was going to challenge him on that, but someone was walking toward them. It looked like Dr. Blairmore. A few seconds later he entered their tent and handed over three vials of blood. "Is this enough?"

"Perfect, thank you." She took the blood from him and asked, "Can I get some cerebral spinal fluid or a brain biopsy from any of your patients? I'd also like a sputum sample and some tissue samples from other internal organs."

"Sputum won't be too difficult. Tissue samples and CSF, I don't know." He frowned. "I'll have to make some gentle inquiries about that."

"Please do. Tissue samples will help with the identification if these blood samples don't pan out."

"I'll do what I can." Dr. Blairmore pulled at his fingers like an addict coming off a high.

"Thank you." Though Sophia's words were clearly a dismissal, she didn't take her gaze off him.

His gaze jerked from one spot to another, her face, her hands and her equipment as he nodded a couple of times, then rushed back to the hospital tent.

"There's something hinky about that guy," Connor muttered.

"If by *hinky* you mean odd, I agree." She took the vials of blood and began making notations in a notebook and on a small electronic tablet. Normally she could sink into her work with utter focus, but the sounds of moaning and the calls for help in a language she didn't understand only a little ways away broke through her mental bubble over and over. Because the sounds changed, grew weaker, until one voice after another was replaced by other, newer voices.

She mourned the loss of a high, childlike voice. Its replacement was the deep bass of a man, yet he spoke the same words in the same panicked tone. A voice that knew it was going out, its flame extinguished by an illness that didn't yet have a name.

She found she had to take a few deep breaths to maintain her composure. She was dying too, just a little slower.

Despite the distractions, or perhaps because of them, Sophia didn't stop working until darkness had fallen and Connor put his hand on her arm.

"Sophia, time to eat."

"I will," she said, trying to slide out from underneath his grasp. "I just have to finish this…"

Connor put his hand under her chin and tilted her face up so she had to make eye contact with him. "It's been hours since you last ate or drank anything." His tone was reasonable, gentle. "Whatever you're doing can wait while you feed your brain."

She was looking at stained slides of the three blood samples she'd been given. They could wait a few minutes.

She sighed, nodded, stripped off her gloves. She threw them away and washed her hands with a waterless antiseptic she'd brought with her. Con handed her an MRE meal and a bottle of water.

Smoke and River joined them, their faces silent and serious. Things in the camp couldn't be going well.

"Are you seeing any sickness in the camp population?" she asked them.

River shook his head. "A lot of fear, though."

She didn't blame them. She turned her attention to eating and shoveled the food into her mouth without really tasting it. It went down better that way. "Thank you."

"You're welcome." Connor steadily ate his own meal, his gaze on their surroundings, roving, evaluating. "Any revelations?"

"I've eliminated most of the bacteria and some of the more common viruses."

"That's something."

"There's still a long list to go."

He gave her a sour look. "That sucks."

"Nothing I can do to change that." She shrugged. "I'm going to need those tissue samples."

"Maybe I'll steal you a body."

He said it so *grab some milk while you're at the store* normal she couldn't help a snort.

They all finished their food at about the same time. Smoke and River went to relieve the marines and let them eat while she went back to work.

She'd be finished with the blood soon, but she wasn't tired and really wanted to keep going until she had an answer. "Can you check with Dr. Blairmore about the tissue samples? I need them as soon as possible."

When Connor didn't answer right away, she glanced at him. He was staring into the darkness like he could see for miles and miles, his body still as a hunter that's sighted prey.

She lowered her voice. "What's wrong?"

"We're being watched."

She looked out into the night, but saw nothing other than what she would have expected, the hospital tent lit by overhead lights powered by the aid group's generator. No one appeared to be overtly watching Connor or herself. "Is that a surprise? I mean, I assumed people would be watching us. We're doing important work."

"Body language betrays what people are really thinking and feeling. You can see hope, anger, fear, joy and malice in the way they move, their gestures, facial expressions and posture." He paused. "Most of the people I observed as you worked looked afraid and tired. A few of them, hopeful. A few..." This time when he stopped talking the expression on his face turned dark and dangerous. "When evil is staring at you, you can feel it. Don't go anywhere alone."

"I get that, I do, but I can't be three places at once."

Con pulled out his radio, but before he spoke into it he turned to her and asked, "What three places?"

"Here, the hospital tent and the bathroom."

"That was a dumb question," he muttered to himself. "Where else would she go?"

"No, it wasn't," she corrected. "I would have asked the same question if I'd been you. Assumptions are never a good thing."

"Sometimes you're exactly like my sisters and sometimes it's like you're from another planet." He gave her a crooked smile

"I didn't exactly have a normal childhood, so I suppose you could say I *am* from another planet. I spent a lot of time in hospitals, going through chemotherapy that was often painful and always uncomfortable. When most young pre-teens and teens were worried about boys, their friends and school, I was worried about whether I was going to go into remission or not."

"Yeah, you're right. You don't look at the world like most people, do you?"

"No. Most people see the world through one pair or another of rose-colored glasses. I threw mine away when I was eleven years old."

He stared at her, his mouth a white line. What was his face saying? Not anger or sadness, more like he was dissatisfied with something. He turned away and spoke into his radio, his words indistinct.

She went back to her microscope to look at the blood smears. Cell morphology she understood. Men, not so much.

She glanced out into the dark, the voices of the dying an unneeded reminder of what she was here for.

"I hate war," she said.

Connor sighed. "It doesn't make much sense."

"It doesn't make *any* sense," she countered. "Can you imagine the things we could accomplish if we took our aggression toward each other and redirected it toward the exploration of space or medicine or renewable energy?" She huffed. "Human beings are really, *really* stupid sometimes."

That made him chuckle, but it didn't last long. "I'll go talk to Blairmore." He glanced at her sidearm. "Keep watch."

She resisted the urge to roll her eyes. "Yes, sir."

Con came back at a jog only a couple of minutes later. "We've got a problem. Blairmore says no more samples."

Well, how the hell was she going to figure this out without samples? "All of them?"

"The local elders are kicking up a stink, especially about samples from the dead."

"Why?"

Con shrugged. "Blairmore didn't give any details." He tilted his head to one side. "Maybe we should ask the locals ourselves."

TWENTY

THE RISING SOUND of voices in the hospital tent caught Connor's attention. Motion followed the noise, indistinct and generalized before breaking apart into individuals, all headed toward Sophia's small lab tent.

The group numbered about eight to ten men, all of whom spoke at once, their hands gesturing in large, abrupt movements that had Con moving to step in front of Sophia and the tent without conscious thought. Smoke, River, Henry and Stalls joined him.

The group paused about fifteen feet away. Their shouting however, didn't stop, and Con did his best to sort out the various complaints and demands they had.

The sickness is your fault.

You're not here to help, you're here to desecrate the dead.

This woman-child should go home to her husband. Her presence here is an insult.

Go home, Americans. Take the sickness with you.

The men kept yelling, but the messages were the same. They didn't want American military help and they thought Sophia was too young and female to be of any use.

Connor replied in Arabic, though one or two of the men were using a dialect he hadn't heard before.

"We're here to diagnose the sickness and treat the sick," Connor told them. "That is all. This woman is a doctor and she won't desecrate the dead. She needs samples from the sick, the living."

A couple of the men stopped shouting, but the others didn't.

This is your fault.

What did you Westerners do to us?

Take your diseased woman away.

Well, shit. He was going to have to shake a stick at them. He lifted his weapon and said, again in Arabic, in a dark, loud voice, "Go back to your families. *Now.*"

Three or four of the men began backing away, disappearing into the dark. The remaining men held their ground and continued to shout.

How hard was he going to have to shake the stick? He flicked the safety off on his weapon, but before he could do anything else, Sophia stepped forward holding up a vial of blood. She didn't say anything, didn't do anything but hold the tube high and in front of her.

The men facing them slowly fell silent, then in the face of Sophia with her blood and the four soldiers with their guns, they slowly faded into the night.

Wow, that was one threat he'd never tried before, and damn if it didn't do the job.

In the hospital tent, a woman began wailing, her grief a knife in the night, reminding Con that the real enemy was one none of them could see.

Except for the woman standing next to him.

Con glanced at her thigh where her Beretta rested in its holster. "Stay here with the team."

She raised one brow. "Going somewhere?"

"Yep. Going to see if I can find a volunteer to give you the samples you need."

"Shouldn't Dr. Blairmore do that?"

"If he was going to do it, he'd have done it. Someone may have made threats." Con shrugged. "Whatever the reason, you don't have what you need to identify the bug that's killing these people." He angled his head at the big tent. "I'm going to see if one of them wants to be a hero."

Despite the four soldiers standing with them, she tucked the tube of blood into a pocket, pulled her gun out, checked to see if her magazine was loaded and slid one bullet into the slide. "Okay."

Holy fuck. Did she have any idea how *amazing* she was? Standing there like a young Valkyrie before her first battle, ready to lay down the law as she knew it.

It was all he could do to keep his hands to himself and walk away from her, walk through the canyon of darkness between them and into the house of dying in front of him.

He pulled a mask out of a pocket, put it on and moved to the center of the large tent, surrounded by hundreds of beds, almost all of them occupied. A few of them with corpses. When he spoke, it was in Arabic.

"There is a doctor over there—" he pointed at Sophia and his men, silhouetted by the light coming from her lab tent "—who is trying to discover what is causing the illness and death here. So far, she's failed. She needs samples of the stuff you cough up from deep in your lungs. She also needs a tiny bit of the fluid that will need to be taken from your spine. The spinal sample will hurt. I can't guarantee you will get better, or you will live." He stopped talking and surveyed the many, many eyes watching him. "But these fluids might be able to tell her what's killing you. Is anyone willing to give me the things the doctor needs?"

For a moment, the stillness in the tent was absolute.

A hand rose from a row of cots at the outer rim of the tent. "I," said a man, sounding weak. "I will give."

Another hand rose and the words were repeated.

Another, and another, until nearly a quarter of the people in the makeshift hospital had their hands in the air.

For the first time since they arrived earlier that morning, Con saw hope on the faces of the dying.

He strode over to Dr. Blairmore, who looked fit to be tied. "Doctor, I'll send Dr. Perry over to collect the samples she needs from the volunteers."

"The local headmen were very specific, no more samples..."

"You told us no samples from the dead. These people aren't dead. At least, that's what I think it means when someone raises their hand and says in a recognizable language, "*I will give.*" What do you think?"

The doctor swallowed hard. "Yes, I suppose...but what if—"

"Doctor, we've got enough difficult realities. We don't need to start worrying about the *what ifs.*"

Dr. Blairmore leaned close and whispered, "Some of these men are very dangerous."

"So am I," Con whispered back.

He walked past the doctor and returned to the lab tent. "I got you about fifty different volunteers."

"I only needed two or three."

"Merry Christmas," he said. "What do you need to get your samples?"

"I've got everything here." She patted what looked like a first aid kit.

"I told that idiot Blairmore you'd be collecting the samples yourself."

"Idiot?"

"He's scared to death some warlord is going to shoot him."

"Is it justified?"

"Only in the sense that if he doesn't start cooperating, *really* cooperating, I might shoot him myself."

Sophia didn't bat an eyelash. "I'd offer to loan him my body armor, but I don't think it would fit."

"Yeah, his hat size is a lot smaller than yours."

She laughed, a throaty, happy purr that speared him in place and held him immobile. It set fire to his muscles in a way he thought he'd lost a year ago, a fire that carried no grief or worry, a fire that gave him joy and... one hell of an erection.

Fuck.

"So," she said, her eyes smiling at him. "How are we going to do this?"

"The team can mind the store. You and I are going to get the samples."

Len met them just outside the hospital tent with a crooked smile. "What did you say to Blairmore? He's *pissed* at you."

"He's a pansy ass who's trying to make way too many people happy."

"Truth." Len waved them in. "Don't drink and drive."

"Yes, Dad."

Ten feet away, they stopped to put on masks and gloves. Sophia whispered, "I don't like him."

"Oh?"

"He's a cynic."

Connor had to forcibly keep himself from laughing out loud. "And I'm not?"

"You're different. You give a shit. He doesn't."

That made Con pause. "How do you know that?"

"He makes no effort beyond the minimum. He's got a sarcastic streak that's the other side of cruel."

"Whoa, cruel?"

"And he..."

"What?"

"Whenever he looks at me, he looks at my boobs. He doesn't meet my eyes, like I'm an object to him." She leaned even closer. "He gives me the creeps."

"He's on the job. Sometimes he has to be an asshole. Cut him a little slack."

She huffed and said, "Fine."

Con cleared his throat. "I have older sisters, and that's the second time you've said *fine*. I know what fine really means."

"Oh, and what does it mean?" she asked, her tone frankly disbelieving.

"Fucked up, insecure, neurotic and emotional."

She stopped walking to stare at him. "Really?"

He shrugged. "Sisters."

She gave him a lopsided smile. "I kind of like it." Then she frowned. "But I'm still reserving judgment on your friend."

"Fair enough."

Several people held up their hands as the two of them walked through the tent. Sophia didn't hesitate, choosing someone who was coughing and even had spittle on his face. Connor spoke to him in Arabic and translated his responses for Sophia. He said yes to the collection of the mucus on his face, but when her hand closed in on his face he yelled and tried to grab Sophia's hands. Connor restrained him by taking his wrists and holding the sick man's arms away from Sophia.

After she was finished, she retreated quickly and changed gloves, a move Connor copied, then went on to another volunteer. Only she didn't choose as quickly this time. Many of the sick put their hands up again, saying *I will give* in Arabic, but Sophia seemed to be looking for something specific.

She wasn't finding it.

"What's wrong?" he asked.

"That man, he seemed coherent enough to give consent, but then he tried to grab me."

"Yeah, it was a little weird, but he's sick, so…"

"The CSF sample I need to take is very painful. If the patient moves, I could damage their spinal cord. They can't move once I've started."

"Come on, let's talk to Blairmore."

The doctor was on the other side of the tent and scowled at both of them as they approached.

Sophia explained what happened with the first patient and asked if confusion of this degree was a common symptom of the disease.

Blairmore frowned, but said, "Not all patients show that much confusion, but some do. We're seeing a lot of seizures."

"I *really* need a CSF sample."

"A meningococcal infection?"

"I should have seen something come up in the blood samples, but I haven't. It could be viral. Will you help me get a sample?"

"You don't understand how dangerous it is to do something the leaders of this camp have refused to allow." Blairmore glanced at Connor, who flashed his teeth. "Plus, you're a woman. One bodyguard isn't enough. Ten aren't enough."

"They'd kill me for trying to fight this, whatever it is?"

"Yes," Connor said. "They will. You're a challenge to their authority, no matter how well meaning."

"Every moment that passes means more people will die."

An old man approached slowly, stopping a few feet away, but making eye contact with Connor.

When Connor met his gaze, the man spoke in Aramaic, a language as different from Arabic as Latin was from French. He had to mime not understanding, but the old man wasn't giving up.

"Doctor?" the man asked, glancing at Sophia.

Connor nodded.

The old man gestured for them to follow him.

"Should we go?" Sophia asked.

"He's speaking a different language than most of the people here. He might have something different to show us, too."

Connor and Sophia followed.

The man led them to another part of the tent, the section where the dead were being wrapped in cloth before burial. The old man stopped and put his hand on the head of a body, that of a young woman. He pointed at Sophia then at the body and pantomimed taking something from the body. The motions were made without hesitation.

"Is he giving me permission to take a sample from her?" Sophia asked Connor.

"No, I think he's *telling* you to do it."

She glanced around. "Do you think if I did it quickly, would anyone notice?"

"Let's find out." Connor moved to stand next to the old man and angled himself so he was blocking Sophia from view from the majority of the tent's occupants.

Connor tried asking a few questions, looking to see what words in the languages he knew corresponded to words in Aramaic. From the blank look on the old man's face, not too many.

Sophia knelt next to the woman, putting her pouch of collection equipment on the floor between her knees. "Can you turn the body?" she asked Con softly.

He complied, using a flashlight as if they were just examining the body for outward signs of disease. Then he tried talking to the old man some more, using a tone that was loud enough and frustrated enough that anyone listening in would think he was trying to ask questions about the woman's health before she died.

With the woman on her side, Sophia was only visible from the eyes up and she kept those down as if she were praying.

After a couple of minutes of charades, she whispered, "I'm done."

"Don't get up yet," he cautioned her. "Put everything away now, so it doesn't look like you just took samples from a dead person. Have a look at a couple other bodies, too."

She stayed where she was for several more seconds, then got to her feet and bowed a little to the old man.

She turned and walked a little ways to look down at the body of a boy. She didn't touch him at all, just examined what she could see with a sharp gaze. "Do you see the sweat?" she asked Con, gesturing at the stained blanket on the cot.

"Yeah." He glanced around. "They all look like that. Is it from the fever or something else?"

"I don't know. It just seems excessive, and yet they look dehydrated. See how the eyes are sunken and the lips shriveled."

"What does it mean?"

She tilted her head to one side and looked at body after body. "I don't know." Her voice had a hard edge to it.

Dr. Sophia Perry didn't like it when she couldn't understand a disease.

TWENTY-ONE

"Dr. Perry?"

Sophia looked up to find Dr. Blairmore coming toward her. "Yes?"

"What are you doing?" he asked in a tone so accusatory she wanted to smack him. Idiot. She was doing her job whether he liked it or not.

"I'm doing the only kind of examination you'll allow," she said, not caring that she sounded snotty. She hoped she sounded snotty and completely out of patience. "A visual one. I've noted a few other symptoms that you failed to mention."

He reared back at that. "You have?"

"Look at these people," she ordered, pointing at the bodies. "Excessive sweating, yet there also signs of severe dehydration. Add those to the confusion and seizures and I'm comfortable narrowing down the pathogen to one that attacks the brain or CSF."

He shrugged. "I would tend to agree with you. What does that get us?"

"Closer to the answer." She forced herself to look at him the same way she looked at Max while trying to solve a problem, like he was part of the solution. "Please, talk to whoever is in charge of the camp. Explain that without a sample of brain tissue from one of the dead, I may not be able to identify the pathogen. Without that answer, no one else is going to come to help, and hundreds more *will* die. I don't have to have anything to do with the collection. Obviously, you're the best person for that. You have a relationship with the people here." Some of them, anyway. "I don't."

He squared his shoulders. "I'm glad you understand that, Dr. Perry. I've invested a lot of time and effort in the care of these people." He glanced over at Len, who watched them all from a distance. Len, who was paid to protect him.

So, that's what his problem was. He didn't want to take second seat to a military doctor who looked young enough to be in med school. Maybe he was writing an article for a medical journal or was hoping to sell his story of sacrifice in the desert sands to one of the big US media outlets.

"I'm going to go back to my tent to eat and rest," she said. "And wait for you to come to me with any news. I do have a sputum sample to test, but I doubt now that anything will come of it."

Surrounded by dozens of dead bodies, Dr. Blairmore's smile was out of place. "Thank you."

She nodded at him, glanced at Connor and walked out. The farther she got from the moron the madder she got.

Connor caught up to her as they left the hospital tent and said in her ear, "Unclench your fists."

She did it, but it was harder than it should have been. "I want to strangle that guy. Just a little." She snorted. "No one would notice, right?"

Connor choked. "You look so innocent when you're planning to murder someone. How do you do it?"

"Which part?"

He opened his mouth, then shut it again. "If you have to ask, there's no point in discussing it further."

"Discussing what?" asked a voice behind them.

They both turned, Connor thrusting Sophia behind him as he brought up his weapon.

Len held up his hands. "Sorry, didn't mean to startle anyone."

"You shouldn't sneak up on people with semi-automatic weapons in their hands," she said.

Len put his hands down and Connor relaxed his stance, but he didn't lower his weapon all the way to the ground.

"What do you want?" she asked the mercenary.

"To, ah, apologize for Blairmore's shitty attitude. The guy is a little paranoid."

"He's a pompous ass," Sophia told Len, then pasted on the fakest smile she could manage. "But then, what do I know, I'm a glorified cheerleader." She turned on her heel and entered the lab tent.

She unpacked the two samples and wasted no time in noting them in her journal and preparing them for testing. She put both samples through the Sandwich, a portable analyzer that could determine most of the common pathogens, bacteria and viruses responsible for the majority of lethal diseases, and waited impatiently for the results.

Negative for pathogens.

How could both samples be negative? Something had caused the dead woman's symptoms and killed her.

As she set up more tests, Sophia considered the puzzle of the disease. If it wasn't bacteria or viruses detectable in blood, sputum and CSF, what was it?

The symptoms were fever, hallucinations, dehydration, confusion, seizures and death within twenty-four hours or so. A short time span for any micro-organism. None of it fit any disease she could think of.

Sophia went in search of Connor and found him still talking with Len. Both men turned to look at her.

She was struck by the differences in their expressions. At first glance, they looked the same, blank and businesslike, but while the corners of Connor's eyes were crinkled with concern, Len's were puffed up with a contempt he couldn't hide.

Her body jerked with the need to back away.

"Sophia?" Connor asked. His voice saying her name gave her a little boost.

She didn't want to discuss the results with Len standing right there, so she asked, "When is the first supply drop scheduled?"

"Dawn," Connor answered. "Do you need something?"

"Yeah, I've started a list."

"Did the spit you collected give you any answers?" Len asked.

"No. It tested negative for everything, but I'm not giving up. I'm going to collect more blood samples from people near death. It may be that the pathogen isn't present in the blood until then." She rounded her shoulders, slouching as if tired. "Would you mind telling Dr. Blairmore that I'd like more blood samples, approximately fifteen to twenty, taken from a cross-section of the population here, the closer to death the better? He can collect them if he prefers or I can do it. Just ask him to let me know how he wants to do this."

"Can do." Len punched Connor on the shoulder. "Later."

As Len walked away, Sophia said to Connor, "Can you give me a hand with the Sandwich?"

"Sure." They went into the tent.

Sophia stopped in front of the analyzer and crossed her arms over her chest. "How much do you trust Len?"

"Not as much as I used to. He's pretty casual about a whole lot of people dying."

She nodded, thinking hard. She couldn't see a way around making a lot of people angry. "I need something."

"Right, the list of supplies."

"That's the easy stuff. What I really need is not so easy."

"Sophia," he said in an aggrieved tone. "Just tell me."

She sighed. "I need you steal me a dead body."

CON STRUGGLED NOT to laugh at the *I'm sure you're going to say no* expression on her face. "Most girls ask for flowers or chocolate."

She rolled her eyes. "Well, I'm not most girls, am I?"

"At least you know what you want." She wanted him, she'd been very clear about that. "Speaking of which, could you be more specific about the condition and type of body?"

"An adult whose time of death is within six hours." She frowned. "Is that too specific?"

"No, that's good. Do you need an entire body?"

"Well, no. I need brain tissue specifically."

"What if we went to where they're piling the dead so you can grab a sample?"

"That would work. I thought around the same time as the supply drop in the morning. People will be distracted."

"Good idea." He smiled at her. "Did you really want to ask for more supplies?"

"I suppose I should. Things the aid group could use. I'll make the call and check in with Max at the same time."

Con went out to check on Henry and Stalls. "Anyone paying too much attention to us?"

"No, sir," Henry said. "That kid you hired has been back and forth a couple of times. We gave him some rice and water purification tablets for his family."

"That's no problem. Things might get a bit dicey, so when he comes back, give him some more food and tell him we're not going to need him for a while. Anything else?"

"A couple of men from that mob that tried to get close earlier have been hanging around the perimeter, but they haven't done anything threatening."

"Make sure you change up the schedule of your perimeter patrols randomly, so they don't decide to ambush us. If they start to make noise, don't let them distract you too much from the rest of the perimeter."

"Sir, Sergeant Smoke and Sergeant River are out on a reconnaissance of the camp. They said you'd know."

"Very good."

"They weren't sure how long they would be."

"Don't worry about it. They're keeping an eye on the refugees in the camp. We won't see much of them unless things are about to blow up in our faces."

"Yes, sir."

"Sir, are gloves and masks enough to protect us from the disease?" Stalls asked.

"None of the health care workers have gotten sick, so

yeah. Dr. Perry is ordering more safety gear, but that's just a precaution."

He saluted them and they saluted back.

Con went back inside the lab tent and found Sophia cleaning up and shutting things down. "Done?" he asked.

"For now. It'll be a few hours until the morning supply drop. A good time to get some sleep."

"Excellent." He took up a position where he could see her and the entrance while she finished.

After a few seconds she looked up from what she was doing. "Are you waiting for me?"

"Where you go, I go."

She glanced out at the silhouettes of the two marines guarding their small encampment. "Why do I feel like we're outmanned and outgunned?"

"More men isn't always the answer. If we come storming in with a couple of platoons, these people would have felt like they were in a police state. Since that's what most of them are running from, we would've had a lot more trouble from the refugees."

She scowled at him. "People are still dying. We may still have trouble."

"It is what it is." He crossed his arms over his chest. "All we can do is our jobs." He dropped his arms and took a couple of steps closer to her. "Stay focused. I won't leave you vulnerable for any length of time."

"It's not me I'm worried about," she said, her voice vibrating with tension. "Every time you step in front of me to protect me, I want to scream. You're the one in danger, not me."

"It's my job to stay close to you, to protect you." He tried to catch her gaze, smile and ratchet her apprehension down. "Four sisters, remember? They'd kick my ass if I let you get hurt in any way."

"Ha," she said lifting her chin. "I bet you've been standing in front of them, taking the punch or the hard words, since you could walk."

This woman's intelligence stunned him and turned him on. "Who me? Never."

"Oh yeah?" She narrowed her eyes and poked him in the chest. "Give me their phone numbers."

Her request caught him off guard and he laughed with real humor for the first time in…months.

Since the explosion.

He'd come out of that injured in a way no one could see, no one could heal. He'd been filled with so much anger and self-destructive guilt he had actively looked for ways to get revenge or get killed, preferably both.

Sometime since he met Sophia, he'd changed. The reckless rage had been transformed into purpose. She had given him a new reason to be human again. Given him something to fight for, instead of against.

For the first time since the explosion, he felt a sliver of fear for himself. What if he died? Who would protect her then?

He gave her all four phone numbers, and made a mental note to talk to his sisters about Sophia. Tell them how special she was, how fragile she was.

As she added the numbers to her contact list, her shoulders came down a fraction.

She'd been stressed.

He should have noticed sooner, but with all the crap going on and all the dying happening a stone's throw away, he'd misinterpreted her body language.

"I have one other question," she said as she put her phone away.

"Shoot."

"Where can I use the bathroom?"

"We've got a primitive camp toilet. You might have to squat."

"Oh no, I have a thing that allows me to pee standing up. I just want a little privacy."

"You…have a *thing*?" She had his brain going places he never wanted to visit.

She looked at his face and laughed. "Yeah, it's a female urination device made out of medical-grade silicone."

"Oh." Thank God she'd explained that.

"Here," she said, one hand reaching into a pocket. "I'll show you."

"No." He flashed the palms of both hands at her. "Not necessary. I believe you." He led her to their primitive toilet, then turned his back while she did her business.

Her grin was almost smug as she entered the low-slung sleeping tent in front of him.

Henry and Stalls were already asleep, their gear, packs and weapons taking in most of the available space.

Sophia gave them a long look, shook her head and turned around to crab-crawl out.

"Hey," Con said in a whisper, following her. "Where are you going?"

"To sleep in the lab tent."

"Is that safe?"

"I'm a little nervous about leaving all the equipment

and samples unattended. Not that any of the samples have tested positive or anything."

"That's not an answer, and that's not like you at all."

She sighed and stopped walking.

He stopped a couple of feet away, expecting her to talk to him, but she moved in closer. Close enough that he could catch a hint of something coconut-scented. Her shampoo?

"Okay, I'm just going to say this and hope you don't fall over laughing." Her voice was low, tight and it quivered on the last word. She swallowed hard and said, "I can't sleep in a space that small with a bunch of guys I don't know. I looked at them in there and it seemed deliberate, you know? Them taking up so much space. There wasn't room for me in there the way it is now, let alone you, too."

She was right. Those two assholes could have organized themselves better. "It's my fault," he told her. "I should have made sure, when they sacked out, that they'd done so like professional soldiers rather than a couple of weekend warriors who don't know any better." He smiled at her surprised face. "So, let me ask again. Is sleeping in the other tent safe?"

"Yes."

"Then let's go."

The interior of the lab tent had a blind turn before it branched out in its starlike shape. It meant no one could just look in from the outside and see equipment, you had to go in and around before anything became visible.

Con and Sophia lay down on the floor in the center of the tent. It was warm enough out that a bedroll wasn't strictly necessary. While sleeping in full gear was uncomfortable, it shouldn't have stopped him from falling asleep. Hell, he'd slept through gunfire and wicked turbulence.

Nope, what kept him awake was the soft snore of the woman who slept two feet away in front of him.

And the smell of coconut.

STEPPING IN SAND is not soundless.

Con came awake all at once at hearing more than one person moving around within a few feet of the tent. Their movements and whispered words were hardly stealthy. He counted at least three, maybe four or five different people. People who were inside the perimeter Macler and Norton were supposed to maintain.

Con rolled to his feet, carefully and quietly, then he put a hand on Sophia's shoulder. She didn't immediately wake, so he gave her a little shake.

She came awake with a soundless start and stared at him for a moment before she took a breath.

He put a finger over his lips, then gave her hand signals to tell her to stay where she was, but arm herself with the Beretta. When she nodded, he backed away, readying his weapon.

He eased around the blind corner, presenting as small a target as possible to anyone outside.

Several shapes and shadows were in motion, moving past the tent he and Sophia were in. Now they were all concentrated around to the sleeping tent.

Not three or four or five, but eight distinct people were moving in, all carrying some sort of weapon or implement that could be used as a weapon.

In his experience, the only people who snuck up on other people in the middle of the night were people up to no good.

Con took three steps forward, then set off a flare and tossed it in between the men and the tent Henry and Stalls were sleeping in.

Smoke emerged out of the dark from the direction of the desert. He moved in to cover the left side of the lab tent on fast, silent feet, his weapon up and ready to fire.

River ran in from the hospital tent, his compact body in a tight crouch that distorted his shape into something scary in the night.

The movement and light sent men yelling, shouting and running in about six different directions. Henry and Stalls stumbled out of the tent without gear. Just a weapon in their hands.

One man ran past Con, and he tripped the guy so he could find out just what the hell was going on.

The man shouted in Arabic that he hadn't done anything wrong.

Con pointed his weapon and the guy and replied in the same language. "Only a guilty man runs away." He flashed a hand signal at Smoke and River and they dissolved into the darkness again. If there were a half-dozen men where he could see them, how many were there where he couldn't?

"Holy shit," Henry said, running up to Con and pointing his weapon at the local on the ground. "What the fuck is going on? Did this guy do something?"

"I don't know. Get geared up and find Macler and Norton." The fact that both men still hadn't appeared, and there was no way they would have missed all this commotion, was not a good sign.

Henry glanced around. "*Fuck.*" He took off for the tent to get his gear. "Come on, Stalls, the sergeant says gear up."

"Smoke, River," Con said to the two men who looked more like shadows than real people. "Keep an eye on the camp. See if you can figure out who's stirring up trouble."

Both men nodded and faded out of sight.

"Con?" Sophia's voice was low and tight behind him. "What can I do?"

"Stay where you are for now. I may have to move. If I do, it'll be your job to defend yourself and the lab. Don't let anyone in. If it isn't one of us, shoot them. Got it?" He wasn't going to lose her, not to anyone or anything.

"Len, too?"

"Yeah, Len, too. If it comes to that, tell him I ordered you to shoot him."

TWENTY-TWO

SOPHIA TRIED TO regulate her breathing, but she had too much adrenaline in her system. Having someone wake you in the darkest part of the night, then tell you to be quiet and get your gun out, had that effect on a person.

It was the first time it had happened to her.

It sucked.

It seemed like there were a hundred people running around the tent site, some yelling in a foreign language, others carrying what looked like pieces of pipe or tools. Her hands shook with the need to do something, *anything*, but right now the best thing for her to do was stay still and quiet and let her brain process what was going on.

Con had a man on the ground, his fancy rifle, or whatever they called it, aimed at his chest. Henry and Stalls exited the other tent, now wearing their body armor and carrying their rifles properly.

Their delay in responding to what could've been a dangerous attack wasn't going to look good on any report.

Seconds ticked past and the noise and movement of people slowly calmed down, until she had no problem hearing every word Con said to his captive, despite the fact that she didn't understand any of it.

Henry and Stalls came back around the tent.

"Sergeant, we found Macler and Norton. They're unconscious about thirty feet away. Looks like someone bashed them on the head with something."

"Probably a pipe or whatever the men who hit them could get their hands on," she said.

Con said something to the man he'd been questioning. The man got to his feet, and backed away, keeping all of them in his sights until the darkness swallowed him whole.

"Sophia," Con said, his gaze telling her to take care, or else. "We'll be right back."

She nodded, her throat too constricted to allow her to swallow.

The three soldiers vanished and she focused on the surrounding darkness. Shouts were still echoing through the cool, still air, but they were much farther away now.

If I were a bad guy I'd pick now to do something awful. Sophia backed into the tent until the shadows in the blind corner of the entrance hid her completely. She tilted her head and listened hard, not just in front of her but all around the structure. If someone wanted to stop what she was doing, damaging her diagnostic equipment would accomplish that.

There was movement in the darkness between the lab and the hospital. Two people emerged, walking toward her.

She took a step forward, intending to order them to stop, just as someone shoved a knife through the tent wall behind her.

Unknown parties coming at her from two directions. Wonderful.

She grabbed her open bottle of water and as soon as

the head of the person who cut the hole in the tent came through, she tossed the contents in his face.

She pointed the Beretta at the two coming toward her from the other direction. "Stop."

They didn't stop.

She fired a warning shot in the air.

They stopped and put their hands up.

Behind her, the man who'd cut the hole in her tent had stumbled back and fallen, yelling in a language she didn't know.

A large body whipped around the wall of the tent.

In the darkness, she couldn't see who it was and shifted to point her gun at him, but he hurtled past her, launching himself through the slit in the tent.

Connor.

A brief intense wrestle on the ground knocked Connor and the man she'd doused against the tent. A couple of seconds later, Connor dragged the man by his neck around to the front where she could see him, then dropped the man on the sand and put the muzzle of his rifle under his chin.

He crouched there, his hands steady on the weapon, his gaze seeming to take in everything at once. The calm competence he exuded was palpable, and it bolstered her own confidence.

Henry and Stalls arrived a moment later, fireman-carrying Macler and Norton. Both men were still unconscious.

She took a step toward them, but Connor's voice stopped her. "Wait."

Smoke appeared on the other side of the sleeping tent. He flashed a couple of hand signals at Connor, who replied in their secret sign language. Smoke disappeared again.

"There's trouble brewing in the camp," Connor said in a whisper that didn't carry. "River and Smoke are keeping an eye on it, but it could blow up on us."

"We have to help them," she said between clenched teeth, looking at the two unconscious men dangling from the shoulders of Henry and Stalls.

"We will, but we're going to do it when we're sure the threat is over."

"Put them inside the sleeping tent," Sophia called out.

Henry and Stalls followed her orders without hesitation.

One of the two men who had stopped with their hands in the air yelled out, "It's Len and Dr. Blairmore. Can we help?"

Sophia looked at Con, who gave her a short, single nod.

She lowered her weapon, but kept both hands around the butt. Just in case.

The man who'd cut the hole in her tent yelled something.

Connor and Len didn't react, but Dr. Blairmore jerked liked he'd been shocked.

Dr. Blairmore rushed to the man she'd thrown the water at. "What did you throw on him?"

"Excuse me?" Sophia couldn't quite believe the accusation in his voice. "That man came through the tent with a knife in his hand. Would you have preferred I shot him?"

"What did you throw on this man?" Blairmore asked again, anger giving his voice an edge.

Connor's body had gone still. "How do you know she threw anything on him?"

"Well, he's covered in something wet, so she must have thrown something at him."

"There's no cause and effect to connect me to someone with a wet face," Sophia told Blairmore coldly.

"You speak Dari," Connor said to Blairmore. It was an accusation.

"What's wrong with that?"

"Nothing." Connor's teeth gleamed white in the darkness. "Except you inferred that Len was both a bodyguard and a translator."

"I speak enough Dari to get by," Blairmore retorted. He glared at Sophia. "What did you throw on this man?"

"I'll answer your question if he explains why he used a knife to cut himself a new entry into my tent," Sophia answered with a thin-lipped smile.

No one said anything.

"Aren't you going to ask him?" Sophia asked him, rapidly running out of patience.

"Well, I thought one of you would ask," Blairmore said, looking at Connor and Len.

"Doctor," Connor drawled. "If you want to know what Dr. Perry may or may not have thrown on this idiot's face, an idiot who cut up an American Army tent with a knife long enough to fillet a camel, *you're* going to have to ask him his motives."

"I'll ask," Len said with a laugh as plastic as his personality. "Just to cut through all this bullshit."

"No," Sophia told him. "Dr. Blairmore is a big boy. If he's fluent enough to understand what this man was yelling, he's fluent enough to ask a simple question."

Blairmore glared at her, then haltingly asked the intruder a question.

The man spit on the sand.

Blairmore opened his mouth, to say what, Sophia wasn't sure, but she didn't care either. "I got it. A spit is a spit in any language."

Blairmore opened his mouth again and again she spoke first. "Water. I threw water in his face. Clean bottled water."

Blairmore said something in Dari to the man, who relaxed a fraction.

Blairmore looked at her and sneered. "Stupid woman. We need these people's cooperation, if not respect, in order to continue our work here."

"I need for someone to not stab or shoot me," Sophia replied. "So I can do my work and leave. Now," she said, taking a step toward him, "tell me what awful thing you, and this man, thought I'd thrown on his face."

Blairmore's jaw sagged for a moment, before he drew himself up and retorted, "I don't understand the question."

"Both of you were quite worried I'd thrown something dangerous on him. Something that could pass as water, or be transported in water. What is it?"

"I don't know what you're talking about."

"Sergeant Button." She turned to Connor. "Please tell us what the penalties are for impeding this investigation?"

"Penalties?" Blairmore sputtered. "What are you talking about? You're here to help *me*."

"The United States Army Biological Response Team," Connor said in a clear, loud voice, "has been tasked with, and granted investigative jurisdiction over, this outbreak by the World Health Organization and the government of Lebanon."

Blairmore's jaw dropped again. This time, it stayed down.

"If you are deemed a danger to, or an impediment of, said investigation, the penalty is ten years' incarceration in the country the offense occurred."

"You're here to help us," Blairmore said in a small voice.

"No," Sophia told him. She had no time or sympathy for idiots. "I'm here to determine the pathogen causing this outbreak. My only goal is to save lives. If you can't or won't assist that goal, get the fuck out of my way. If you choose to ignore this last warning, I will make sure you get thrown into the deepest, darkest hole available for every second of those ten years."

He stared at her, so silent and still he had to have stopped breathing.

"I'm waiting for you to respond with your agreement to comply or your departure plan," she said. "Which is it?"

Blairmore swallowed so hard she could see it from where she stood. "I... I understand."

"Good. What did you think I threw on him?"

Blairmore took a long time to respond. When he finally did, he stuttered through the whole sentence. "I was told that...that you might try to steal the credit for all the work I—We've done here."

She waited.

"One of the local leaders told me you might try to test a new vaccine for Ebola here." He shrugged with one shoulder. "He'd heard a rumor that the American military wanted to test a vaccine made from the live virus. That you needed an isolated population and that this vaccine could be delivered by mixing it with water, and consumed or even absorbed through the mucus membranes in the mouth, nose and eyes."

"And you believed this shit?" she demanded. "No reputable doctor would condone such an action."

Blairmore sneered at her. "*You* aren't a *people* doctor."

She examined his face and saw nothing but disdain colored by fear.

She would get no help from him, nor could she trust him. She took another step forward. "You are a fool. Stay out of my way, stay away from this area and if you do or say anything to jeopardize this investigation, you will find yourself in that hole."

Dr. Blairmore lost the sneer, but not the disgust as he turned and hurried back to the hospital tent.

"What about him?" Len asked, pointing at the guy who'd knifed his way through her tent.

"Check with me later," Con told him. "After I've questioned him."

"I've seen him around," Len said. "He's well known in camp. If he stays missing for long you're going to have an even bigger problem on your hands."

Con flashed his teeth. "Won't be a problem if he's found on the other side of camp, dead of a couple of knife wounds, will it?"

Len shrugged. "Probably not." He looked at her and nodded. "Let me know if you need any help." With that, he headed back to the hospital.

Sophia watched him walk away. It was almost a swagger. "Still taking your water plain?"

"I think so."

"Wonderful."

"Con? Doc?" River's voice floated out of the dark.

"Here," Connor answered. "We're okay, but we're down two marines."

River came around the lab tent and crouched next to the man Connor had taken captive. "He's been missed. You've got maybe ten minutes before a very large angry crowd comes looking for him."

Sophia stepped closer to look down at the man on the ground, his damp face reflecting the low light from the flare. "Do you understand me?"

He didn't respond.

Connor translated.

She saw a tightening of his lips. Good enough for her.

"I am a woman," she began slowly so Connor could translate as she spoke. "I didn't come here to kill or hurt or experiment. I came to help the women and children of this camp. I came to help the fathers and brothers and leaders of this camp. Men make war. I am not a man."

The man spoke rapidly for several seconds. Connor translated.

"One of our brothers swore on his life that you came to kill our women and children with your poisons."

"I don't know your brother. I have never met him, but I can show you why I would never do that to anyone else." She began to unbutton the sleeve of her left arm.

"What are you doing?" Connor hissed.

"I need to show him my pain."

"You don't need to show him anything." Connor shook his head, saying, "This is totally fucked."

She started rolling up her sleeve and though the man on the ground tried to shy away when she bent to give him a good look, he did look.

She turned her arm to show him every scar, every bruise. "I had a cancer when I was a child. The doctors did many things to me to save my life. Many painful things." She turned her arm again and the man stared at her arm with eyes gone wide. "None of it worked. I grew weak and everyone thought I would die. But I didn't. I began to get better. Not because of the things doctors did. My body simply...got better."

"Allah," the man whispered.

She nodded. "I made a promise to try to help everyone. Until my dying breath, I would do nothing to harm, only heal." She rolled down her sleeve and buttoned the cuff.

The man pointed at different places on her arm, and said something.

Connor translated. "You are sick now. How can we trust you, when sickness is still inside your body?"

TWENTY-THREE

SOPHIA REGARDED THE man with sober eyes and said, "Can you show me a person who is without blemish, without sadness or fear? We all have flaws. Some people have visible flaws, while others hide theirs. I choose not to hide mine."

The man stared at her, but for the first time since Connor got a hold of him, his face wasn't twisted with hate and fear. He looked...thoughtful.

"Were you trying to kill the doctor?" Connor asked him.

The man reared his head back a little. "No, killing a woman is cowardly. I only wanted to destroy whatever is in that tent."

Con relayed that information to Sophia.

She sighed. "I admit, I'm not sure what to do next. If people in the camp are upset that he's disappeared, should we let him go?"

He'd prefer to make the bastard disappear. Permanently. It was guys like this who killed his friends, his teammates. It was guys like this who thought they were on some holy crusade, that their deaths meant something, when all they really were was cannon fodder.

"Do you have a wife and children?" Con asked him.

"Yes," the man answered.

"Are they sick?"

"No."

Well, fuck. It would be so much easier if he could just kill the guy and leave him to be found in the desert.

"Go," Con told him in a clear, cold voice. "If you come back and try to attack us again, I will kill you."

The man lay still and silent for a moment, then scrambled to his feet and backed away, never taking his eyes off of Con. A little ways away, darkness consumed him.

"I can't decide if that was a good idea or not," Sophia said, staring after him.

"Neither can I," Con told her.

"Is it true about the ten years in jail?" she asked. "I thought he would just get deported."

"I have no idea," Connor said with a shrug. "Jail time made for a better threat."

"I better check on our marines." She glanced at him, sighed, then went to the sleeping tent.

Con didn't follow, there was too much shit going down and too many people willing to blame their hard times on the easiest scapegoat—the United States Army.

An odd bird sound flitted past Con's ear. One of Smoke's early warning signals. The man himself followed after a couple of seconds, barely distinguishable from the darkness.

"How much trouble are we in?" Con asked the other man.

"About half an hour ago, it looked like a mob was forming, but several people collapsed, some with seizures. It broke things up when family members came to take the sick away and bring them to the one place where they'd just been talking about erasing from the face of the earth." Smoke snorted. "That's a direct quote."

"So, it's a good news, bad news situation."

Smoke shrugged.

"I caught a guy who tried to slice up the lab tent. It turns out someone in camp has been telling everyone that all this is our fault. Sold them some bullshit that we've been experimenting on them, creating some kind of vaccine for Ebola using a live virus."

"Akbar?"

"A possibility. Keep an eye on Dr. Blairmore. Turns out, he's a pompous ass who's only looking out for himself. He made threats against Sophia."

Smoke nodded.

"Can you and River keep the rest of the camp under surveillance? Let me know if things are about to blow up again?"

Smoke nodded again and left.

Sophia came out of the sleeping tent, frowning.

"How bad is it?"

"They both have concussions. They've regained consciousness and I don't think they have any fractures, but I'd like to X-ray them to be sure, but that's one piece of equipment we don't have."

"Yeah. Until you figure out what's going on, no one is going in or out of here."

She deflated a little. "They're on bed rest until I say different. It's all I can do for now."

"You're the boss."

"How soon until dawn?" she asked, staring out into the desert. Her hair had come loose from its tidy bun and she looked no more than sixteen, until you looked into her eyes. There was knowledge in her gaze that told you she'd seen and lived through horrible things. Things that would have broken a weaker person.

She might look fragile and bruise easily, but there was a toughness inside her he recognized on a visceral level. She was a survivor. When she set her mind to solve a puzzle, she didn't give up.

"Probably less than an hour." Less than an hour to prepare for a new day and all the deaths it would bring.

She looked at him, unblinking for a moment. "I still need samples from a dead body."

"Get ready. We'll go when the air-drop is made."

She gave him a grim smile and walked around him and into her lab. A light came on inside and he could hear her moving around.

Henry came out of the other tent. "I'll stand watch, sir."

Con nodded. "Very good. We're going to get a supply drop at dawn, but it's supplies for the camp, not us, so maintain your station."

"Yes, sir."

Connor did a sweep of the area, looking for people or things that shouldn't be around. He took a couple of photos of the slice in the tent, then pulled out a roll of duct tape and sealed it up on the outside. The edges were already tacky due to the sticky, weblike stuff the material of the tent was coated with, so sealing it was relatively easy.

The deep purple of dawn turned the unending darkness of night into a shadow realm.

Time to set the stage for a little body snatching.

Con headed for the hospital tent and nodded at Len who was standing just inside. "That supply drop is going to happen soon. We've got nothing coming for us this time. Everything they're dropping is for the hospital or the camp in general."

Len's face perked up. "Where are they dropping it?"

"North of here, maybe a quarter mile. Two of our guys are down. Concussions, so we're not going to be much help to you. Have you got enough people to get what you need?"

Before Len could answer Blairmore charged over to them. "What now?" he demanded.

Con smiled at him. "Just reminding you that there's going to be an air-drop of supplies this morning for the hospital and camp. You're going to need to get some people to the drop site or the refugees might take it all."

"We've got it covered, right, Doctor?" Len asked Blairmore.

"Absolutely." Blairmore's face twitched like he didn't know if he should be angry or appreciative.

"Awesome." Con nodded at Len and headed back to his own territory. About ten feet away, he turned back. "I wonder, two of our guys were hit over the head during the scuffle. Dr. Perry thinks they both have concussions, and we're under a quarantine order, so if we need help, can we come to you?"

"Of course," Blairmore said, as if he'd been grievously insulted. "I'm well aware that Dr. Perry might have other things on her mind."

Yeah, he was a prick.

Con made himself smile and wave. "Thanks."

He walked back to the lab tent and went in. Sophia was finishing up the work she'd started last night.

"How long will it take to get your samples?" he asked her, watching her look at a slide under the microscope.

"Not long."

"What are you going to do, drill a hole in someone's head?"

She glanced at the big knife strapped to his left leg. "Ever open a coconut?"

She'd surprised him again. "Okay, that's quick. I can work with it."

"Excellent. When are we going?"

"As soon as we hear the plane's engines. Anytime."

She stepped away from her microscope, changed her gloves, then donned a mask and grabbed two sample containers big enough for about one cup of something. She shoved those in her pants pockets, then picked up two scalpels, holding one while the other got stowed in another pocket.

"You're taking two samples?"

"Well, I figure, since we're there..." She shrugged, but looked more energetic than she had since they arrived.

He grunted. "I'm going to ignore how creepy it is that you sound excited about this."

"What I'm excited about is figuring this shit out, helping these people, then getting out of here."

"Amen." Con put a mask and gloves on, too.

Airplane engines, big ones, droned in the distance. Connor angled his head toward the hospital and the pile of dead bodies on the other side of it. "That's our cue."

She followed him, watching a number of people from the hospital, and the camp beyond it, run past them toward the sound of the airplanes.

They skirted the path most of the people seemed to be taking, headed toward the hospital at an oblique angle then kept going until they were fifty yards away.

The smell hit first, like a punch to the gut, rotting meat and far, far too much old blood.

Con gagged and thought about taking his mask off so he could puke.

"Breathe through your mouth, not your nose," Sophia said to him. "It'll take a few minutes, but the smell will get easier to tolerate."

"I forgot, you doctors have to work with a lot of corpses."

"Yes. In medical school it's common to name your cadaver. I called my first one Reginald, because he looked so uptight and British."

"You give them names?" That was a disturbing thought. "It's not like they're pets."

"You'd be surprised what some medical students do with their cadavers. One guy took his to a frat party dressed as a clown. The stiff made a hundred bucks in tips."

"That is a very weird kind of awesome. I'm oddly impressed. Did you do anything like that with yours?"

"No, not really."

"Not…really?"

"There was one guy who used to torment me because I was only sixteen. I removed the testicles of his cadaver and put them in his shoes."

"You *what*?"

"He kept calling me a ball-buster, and I didn't want to be the only one doing it."

"Holy shit." He shouldn't find that funny, not with so many dead bodies lying in front of them, but it hurt not to laugh.

The dead had been stacked like logs in a pile reaching about three feet high and stretched for about twenty feet. Most of the bodies were wrapped in cloth, but not all of them.

Sophia looked at the bodies, walked around the pile, then pointed at a wrapped one, whose head was easy to access.

Connor cut the cloth away, then sheared off the back of the skull with the big knife he had strapped to his left thigh. Sophia took a sample of brain matter, screwed the cap on the sample container, then quickly pointed out a second body.

Con repeated the process and she had her second sample in about the space of a minute. He cleaned his knife and slid it into its sheath. The two of them walked calmly past a corner of the hospital, glancing at the people inside. Most of the healthy staff and helpers were missing—gone to the air-drop—leaving only the sick and dying.

Every cot was taken. A few people lay on crude pallets on the sand around the edges of the hospital. Not a problem now, but when the sun was higher in the sky, it would be. Anyone not in the shade would probably die of dehydration and sun exposure very quickly.

When they got back to their tiny territory, Smoke and River had returned and were playing guard by standing in plain view with their rifles in their hands. Henry was with them and the three had set up a reasonable perimeter around their two tents.

Smart. Let all the people coming and going from the air-drop see sufficient guards to keep them wary of trying anything stupid.

Sophia walked straight to her lab tent and disappeared into it.

"Any problems?" Con asked River.

"Not so far. We're not as interesting as we were a

few hours ago. That air-drop might do more to keep the refugees from mobbing us than anything else."

"Satisfy a few basic needs and people are always happier and less willing to take risks."

"Did you get what you need?" River asked, glancing at the lab as he spoke.

"I think so. There's a lot more people in the hospital than there were last night."

"How many is a lot?"

"They're bursting at the seams."

River's mouth tightened. "We could be looking at another mob situation tonight."

"If the rate of sickness keeps going up, that's a definite possibility."

Excited yells caught their attention and a few older kids ran past carrying smallish sacks of rice and boxes of MREs. Con kept watch with Smoke, River and Henry while people moved around, either going or coming from the area of the air-drop. Things didn't calm down for at least an hour.

River and Smoke headed out to snoop in the camp while Con went into the lab to check on Sophia. "How's it going?"

"Not good. I ran both samples through the Sandwich, but the results are negative." She clenched her fists and stared at the piece of equipment like she could change the answer with her mind alone. "I don't know what this is, and it's driving me crazy."

"So, you've tested for everything this machine can test for, right?"

"Yes."

"So, what's left?"

"A surprisingly large number of viruses."

"What about those brain-eating amoebas I heard about on one of those medical mystery shows?"

"Not likely. You need to dunk your head in warm standing water and get it up your nose. These people don't have enough water to do that, and it still takes two to three weeks before symptoms appear."

"Can you test for it?"

"No, we're in the middle of a desert, I didn't bring anything to test for that."

"So, what could you do a rapid test for that the Sandwich doesn't?"

She turned to look at him, but she wasn't really seeing him, her brain was moving at Mach 10 and he just happened to be in the way.

"I could check the morphology of the tissue with some different stains," she muttered, "and rule out several possibilities…"

"Like what?"

"Oh, mad cow disease, West Nile, even malaria…" Her voice trailed off again.

"So, I should let you work?"

She didn't answer. She was already grabbing her samples and moving to another of the tent's arms to do something else.

"Okay then." At least she was working and doing something productive. He still had to get his hands on Akbar.

TWENTY-FOUR

SOPHIA WANTED TO throw her microscope across the room. Negative, negative, negative. Every stain she'd tried for every virus, fungus and parasite she knew of that fit the symptoms turned up exactly nothing.

She growled at the offending piece of equipment and clenched her fists to keep from doing something very stupid.

"What's wrong?"

Connor stood behind her, looking much too awake and alert than should be allowed. Neither of them had had more than two or three hours of sleep and it was now noon. The heat of the day made her want to curl up on the sand and snore.

"All the tests I've conducted are negative." She gripped the narrow counter her microscope sat on until her knuckles were white. "I've tested for every disease that could match the symptoms, but there's nothing."

Connor nodded slowly. "Okay, here's what you're going to do. First, you're going to eat something and take a nap. Then, when you've gotten some rest, you can come back at this problem with fresh eyes."

She snorted. "I'm not sure I can sleep. I'm too wired up. Too fucking angry at everything."

"Did I ever tell you how I survived the monthly week from hell when I was growing up?"

"Week from hell...oh, your sisters."

"Yeah. My sisters. The only thing that kept me alive was my ability to judge when a woman needed to eat, and you, Doctor, are overdue for some food."

"You're not going to go away until I agree, are you?"

"Nope. Max gave me strict instructions to make sure you ate. He seems to think that you forget to do that when you're working."

"Tattletale." Max was a great boss, but his tendency to over-protect her was infuriating.

Might as well get the eating over with, then maybe she could get some work done. She walked out of the tent to find that the team had erected a sun shelter just outside. Smoke and River were both asleep, the remains of consumed MREs beside them. Stalls was awake and standing under the tarp that composed the shelter, his rifle in his hands.

"Where's Norton, Henry and Macler?"

"In the sleeping tent," Con replied. "Henry is grabbing some sleep."

"How are Norton and Macler?"

"They're doing okay. We're waking them every couple of hours, but there's been no change."

"Good." She took a seat and Con handed her an MRE.

Chicken Dinner. All MREs tended to taste the same, but this one wasn't too bad. By the time she was done, she was half-asleep.

Con smiled at her.

She rolled her eyes. "Yes, I'm tired. Happy?"

"Only if you actually sleep."

"I'm going to. It would be stupid not to." She gestured at the lab tent behind her. "In there."

He nodded and continued eating his own meal.

Sophia got up, dusted herself off and went into the tent. She lay down in the same place as she'd slept last night.

Had it only been last night? It felt like it had been a week already since they'd arrived, not less than twenty-four hours.

Con slipped into the tent and lay down behind her.

He wasn't touching her.

Unacceptable.

She rolled over and came face to face with him. "I need you to agree to something."

He blinked and took in a breath, but she spoke again before he could.

"When we find Akbar, before you do anything, I want to punch him in the face."

He waited, then said, "Every time you open your mouth you surprise the shit out of me."

She stared at him for a moment. "Is that a no?"

"You're that frustrated?"

"I've never failed to figure out a problem like this before. I'm so angry I want to scream and pound the sand." She had a clenched fist in the air before she realized what she was doing. Sophia forced herself to relax her hand and lower it. "But I'll settle for hitting him."

Connor examined her face for another moment. "Thomas Edison was once asked how it felt to fail after ten thousand failed attempts to create a commercially viable light bulb. His response was, '*I haven't failed. I've just found ten thousand ways that don't work.*'" He cupped her face and rubbed a sandy thumb over her cheek. "You only fail if you give up." He raised one eyebrow. "Are you giving up?"

She scowled. "No."

"Then shut it with the failure talk." He drew her closer and kissed her, long and slow. "Now roll over and go to sleep."

She did as he ordered and was rewarded with him spooning her from behind, his arm coming over her waist. It felt safe and sexy at the same time.

She laced her fingers through his and finally let herself drift off.

SOPHIA WOKE FROM a dreamless sleep. Con was gone, the impression on the tarp floor behind her unoccupied.

She checked her watch and discovered she'd slept for a couple of hours. Not enough, but it would have to do. She stood and went to stare at her microscope and decided that since all her testing had turned up no useful results, it was time to change tactics and start testing for pathogens that didn't necessarily fit the symptoms.

Something nagged at the back of her mind.

The mid-afternoon sun beat hot wings over her face and neck as she walked the short distance to the sleeping tent. Stalls stood guard between the lab and the sleeping tent. Inside Henry and Macler were talking softly. Norton appeared to be sleeping.

She crawled over to the two men with concussions, pulled out her pen light and checked their pupils. Then she went out the same way she came in.

"Hey," Henry whispered, having followed her out. "Um, are they okay or are they dying?"

"They're fine. I would have said something if they weren't."

"So, you're a no news is good news person?"

"Yeah." Wasn't everyone?

"Okay." He went back into the tent.

Sophia entered the lab and considered all the work she'd done. She'd tested for everything that matched the symptoms. Time to try testing for things that didn't match exactly, but were sort of close. Viruses that affected the brain were a good place to start.

She prepared new slides of the samples and performed a test that had been used in the field in Tanzania and showed excellent accuracy.

She looked at each slide with the microscope.

Then she did it again.

Both samples were positive.

Positive.

For rabies.

The symptoms didn't match, but maybe someone, Akbar, had tinkered with the virus like he had with his anthrax strain. The problem was, viruses were harder to work with, control and produce in any amount. This particular virus had been plaguing humans for thousands of years, but had never caused widespread disease for a reason.

Rabies could only be transmitted under specific circumstances, and could hibernate inside its host for anywhere from weeks to months. Once symptoms manifested though, it was universally fatal.

This variant of rabies killed in a day, not weeks or months.

One day.

If it was Akbar, he seemed to want to speed the disease process up. Not a good prospect for the people he was making sick.

Something dropped onto her hand.

She glanced down. A blood drop. As she was studying it, another hit her glove. Crap, she was having a nosebleed.

Sophia stripped off her gloves and grabbed a couple of squares of gauze to wipe her nose, but it kept bleeding.

She sat down, pinched the bridge of her nose and let her mind consider the puzzle she'd discovered. What variant of rabies presented like this?

None.

No one had so much as hinted at any animal bites. So, where did it come from and how was it infecting so many people?

She didn't have an answer for those questions either.

Her nosebleed seemed to stop, so she left the lab, but Con wasn't in sight. Neither was Smoke or River. Stalls still stood guard.

"Where is Sergeant Button?" she asked Stalls.

"He went to talk to that Len guy. He said he'd be back."

Sophia returned to the lab tent and called Max. At least she tried to call Max. She couldn't get a signal. That was strange. Her satellite phone was working a couple of hours ago.

She strode out again and headed straight for the hospital tent. Before she got there she could see Dr. Blairmore listening to a patient's chest. She walked straight toward him.

As soon as he saw her he snapped, "What do you want?"

"I've determined the pathogen."

He seemed to come to a complete stop. Not even breathing. "What?"

"I've determined the pathogen."

His tone changed entirely, became hopeful. "What is it?"

There was nothing hopeful about a rabies virus that killed in approximately twenty-four hours. "Can we speak privately?"

He hesitated, she could see him arguing with himself about it, but good sense won over pride. He led her to a sheeted-off area where he and his team must rest, wash and eat. It was empty.

"It's rabies," she said to him, her voice just louder than a whisper.

He frowned. "It can't be. The clinical picture doesn't match and no one's been bitten. Death occurs too rapidly to be rabies."

"I know that. I tested for everything I could think of that could match what you're seeing, but everything came up negative."

Dr. Blairmore's frown deepened. "You can only diagnose rabies from infected brain tissue."

"I snuck over to your pile of dead and took two samples while everyone was busy with the air-drop."

He shook his head and threw up his hands. "Do you have any idea how large a mistake that was? If the local leaders find out—"

"Do you have any idea how many people this virus can kill?" she interrupted. "Because it's killing in a day, Doctor." She pointed at the sick and dying people on the other side of the tarp. "I know it's rabies, but I don't know how people are being infected. Especially, in the large numbers we're seeing here. I studied rabies in university. There are no known variants that do this."

He stared at her blankly.

"Have you noticed any bite marks on any of the sick?"

"No."

"Are the aid workers getting sick?"

"Only a few."

"So, it's either airborne, ingested or perhaps contact with contaminated body fluids."

For the first time since their first encounter, he looked thoughtful rather than hostile. "I think if it were airborne, we'd be seeing even more sick."

"Do you have any rabies immunoglobulin?" she asked.

"We always bring a little in case someone on the team is bitten by an animal, but only enough for a couple of people."

"I tried to call out a few minutes ago, but I couldn't get a signal. Could you try?"

He nodded and walked stiffly over to a locked box. He pulled out a cell phone, turned it on and dialed a number. His face froze after a few seconds and he slowly lowered the phone. "I don't have a signal either."

She glanced around. "Where's Len?"

"Oh, he said he was going to sleep…" Dr. Blairmore glanced around. "But he doesn't seem to be here."

"Well, that's not good." Getting help was her next priority. "Can you keep this quiet until I can consult with my CO? We don't need to have the population here panicking."

"Yes, of course. Panic would be…bad."

Very bad.

She left the area and headed out of the hospital, but stopped walking halfway to the lab tent.

Stalls wasn't visible, when he should be standing guard.

She walked a little closer and saw something dark and shiny on the sand between the lab and sleeping tents. A little closer and she could tell what it was.

Blood. A lot of it.

Her breathing seemed to echo in her ears as she looked in the sleeping tent first. Henry, Macler and Norton were all there, but the knife wounds on their necks and blood all over the tent told her they were dead.

She slithered out, her mind intent on getting herself out of the area as quickly as possible and finding Connor.

Len was standing between her and the lab tent, the rifle in his arms aimed at her, an entirely unsavory smile on his face.

Len, who she hadn't liked from the first. Len, who was supposed to be Connor's friend. "You killed them." It was a statement, not a question.

He shrugged and said like he had all the time in the world, "Collateral damage."

His confidence made her stomach hurt. She looked around, but there was no one to help her. "Where are Connor and the others?"

Len's expression was coldly calculating. "Somewhere nice and safe and out of sight, just in case I need them."

"For what?"

He walked toward her slowly. "To make sure you do what you're ordered to do."

"By you?"

"No, sweetheart." He reached out to grab a lock of her hair that had come loose.

She shied away, but that only seemed to make him happier. "I'm the muscle, my business partner is the one who needs you for your brain."

Idiot.

"I knew you were stupid the moment I met you," she said to him, letting disgust bleed into her words. "Stupid and, very soon, dead."

"Who's going to kill me, *sweetheart*?" Len asked stressing the name. "You?"

She grunted. "The person behind all this death. You're only useful to a point, and when your usefulness ends, you'll just be another one of those poor bastards over there." She pointed in the direction of the mass grave. "Dumped in a hole."

"That would be bad for business," said a voice she'd never heard before.

A man emerged from her lab tent and walked toward her. He looked to be in his late forties, balding and bearded. He stood about five foot ten at the most, and looked incredibly average.

"Mr. Akbar?" she asked.

The smile he showed her did nothing to warm his eyes. "Dr. Perry. I'm very happy to meet you at last."

"Why would you want to meet me at all? I'm young, female and in poor health. Hardly a threat."

"Of all the people I consider a threat, you're in the top three."

Now she knew for certain he was nuts. "Why?"

"Your knowledge of the rabies virus, of course. I knew it wouldn't stump you for long, and I see I am right."

She deliberately slouched and rolled her shoulders

forward. "You didn't destroy anything in there, did you? That's my favorite lab."

"Certainly not. I need it and you."

That didn't sound good.

She glanced at the sleeping tent. "Or what, you'll kill me like you killed them?"

"Wouldn't you like to know why I wanted you?"

"Whatever it is, it can't be worth setting fire to a hotel and killing those men in that tent. They were good men."

Akbar's insincere politeness disappeared like it had never been. In its wake was a very, *very* angry man. "Yes, yes, good men who take orders and do what they're told."

He came closer and she had to force herself not to back away.

"It was good men like them who killed my family. My wife, children and parents." He came a little closer to her. "They were good people too, but there was no mercy for them. I have none for you or any other American soldier."

"Dude," she said, her lips twisted with irritation, "I think the butter has slipped off your noodles."

He frowned. "I don't understand."

Len laughed. "She means you're crazy."

Rage transformed Akbar's ordinary face into that of a monster as he yelled at Len in Dari.

Len looked utterly surprised for a moment before he managed to control his reaction.

"Now do you see what I see, Len?" Sophia asked. "Do you see death on his face?" She moved her gaze from Len's face to Akbar's. "He'd kill the whole world if he could."

Akbar controlled himself enough to let his facial

muscles relax and settle into a cold expression devoid of emotion.

His eyes couldn't hide it though, his hatred for everything and everyone. When his family died, any conscience this man had died, too.

He walked toward her, stopped a couple of feet away, then hit her hard enough to knock her off her feet.

Stunned, she lay on the sand, one hand landing in part of the blood pool that had belonged to Stalls, the other braced to defend herself from another strike.

"Now you will listen to me, you stupid woman." He said the last word like it was something dirty. "You will do as you're told or I will kill you and the remaining men who came here with you."

She stared up at him and tried not to give away how ridiculous she thought he was. She was *already* dying.

But Connor, Smoke and River might still be alive. She would have to play his game until she knew for certain what their conditions were.

"I'm guessing you want me to manipulate your rabies virus in some way?"

He nodded.

"That is not a fast process, nor is it an easy one to control." Disgust and contempt stretched the muscles of her face. "Besides, it looks to me like you have a perfectly good killer virus as it is."

"No, it's missing something."

"Like what?"

"Easy transmission from person to person."

Good God, combined with its rapid onset and death, that would give it the potential to wipe humanity off the face of the Earth. "You don't need me for that. You did a good job of speeding the lifespan of the infection up."

"Methods of transmission was one of the key things

you studied in your dissertation," Akbar said. "Some of your conclusions would have required a deep understanding of how the rabies and related viruses are transmitted. Some are transmitted more easily than others."

He'd read her dissertation. That was unfortunate. She couldn't hide what she knew and didn't know. What she didn't know was how to change a rabies virus's mode of transmission. It wasn't something she'd even thought of at the time.

"That's true, but I don't know how to change the ease of transmission for rabies. It doesn't survive well outside the body." She glanced at the hospital. "Humans die from it, they can't carry it like some bats or foxes can. It's just not a good candidate for causing a pandemic." What she couldn't understand was why he'd chosen it in the first place. There was a legion of more easily transmitted deadly diseases. "Why rabies?"

"Death is painful, for both infected and non-infected," he said like he was some kind of emotional vampire, excited at the prospect of feeding off other people's pain. Then he looked at her again and said, "You will work on the problem or you will die."

"How am I supposed to do that? My little lab is great for diagnostic work, but not research. Not for what you want me to do." It would also take time. Time this nut bar didn't have. If she and Connor didn't report in, Max would know there was something wrong and investigate.

"Don't worry, Dr. Perry, I have additional equipment waiting for you at another location. As soon as my transportation gets here, we'll be leaving, but you can start now." He strode closer and she shrank away. "You're smart for a woman. Figure it out, make progress, or I will kill one of them right now."

TWENTY-FIVE

"How DO I know you haven't killed them already?" Sophia asked. There was no trusting a man whose only goal was death on a mass scale.

Akbar glanced at Len. "Show her."

The mercenary grabbed her by the arm and hauled her into the refugee camp.

At this rate, she was going to have bruises on her arm for the rest of her life. That struck her as so ironic, she laughed.

"What's so fucking funny, sweetheart?"

"You're gonna die, asshole, and I think that's hilarious."

"You should be a little nicer to me," he said in her ear. "I'm the only thing standing between you and all these sick, hungry, desperate people."

"Well, aren't you Mr. Good News today."

The idiot thought that was funny.

They passed down a narrow walkway between makeshift tents and shanty-type dwellings until they arrived at a ruined collection of buildings made of rock and clay.

People drew back from Len like he was the carrier of a deadly disease.

So, he was known to the populace. That meant he'd been working for Akbar for a while, maybe even the entire length of time he'd been here. Perhaps he'd used Dr. Blairmore and his aid group as a cover.

"You do know that as soon as your usefulness ends," she said to Len, "he's going to kill you."

"Only if I don't kill him first."

Wonderful, she was dealing with two sociopaths instead of one.

He dragged her past two men holding Russian-made rifles into a stone-walled room with a roof made of rotting wood. Four vaguely human shapes huddled against the far wall, either lying on the sand or sitting up at awkward angles.

She recognized two of them immediately. Connor and Smoke.

She surged forward, but Len yanked her back.

"Connor? Smoke? Are you all right?"

"You touch her, you motherfucker, and I'll make you hurt for a very long time," Connor said in a voice so broken and ragged it was barely discernible as his.

Len leaned close to Sophia's ear and said, "He's got a thing for you."

She ignored him, her focus on Connor. The shadows created by the uneven roof made it hard to see. "Are you injured?"

"We all are," he said.

Only Smoke moved. Were the other two so badly injured that they were unconscious or unable to move? Panic welled up, unfamiliar and uncomfortable. She shoved it down with cold logic. She couldn't help them if she had a meltdown.

"Details," she ordered.

"Does she give the orders in bed too, Button?"

"I wouldn't know, asshole." Connor's laugh was full of pain. "Stab wound to my left thigh and possibly a couple of cracked ribs. Smoke took a John Wayne shot to the shoulder. River caught a bullet with his arm and kept fighting. Len kicked him in the head and he's been down ever since. Stalls got stabbed too, but he lost consciousness a little while ago."

She finally looked at Len. "I need to check them."

"No problem," he said, an evil smile spreading across his face. "Just as soon as you give me a blow job."

"You motherfucking son of a bitch," Connor yelled as he tried to get up. "Don't you touch her."

Len pointed his weapon at him and grinned.

Connor froze with his teeth bared.

She put her face close to Len's and said, "You put anything that close to my face, I'm going to bite it off." She snapped her teeth a couple of times.

Len backhanded her, knocking her to the sand. Again. He came at her, violent intent turning his face into a hideous mask, and she laughed.

"How are you going to explain damaging Akbar's prize?" she asked.

He stopped, then snarled, "I'll tell him you tried to escape."

"To where? We're in the middle of a desert. If you claim I tried to overpower you, he's not going to believe that either. I'm too small and weak for that to be a possibility." She sat up and when that didn't seem too difficult, she got to her feet.

"You know what your problem is?" she asked the mercenary. "You think you're in control. You have the combat and weapons skills, so you pretend to bow down to Akbar. Until your final paycheck is in the bank, and then you think it'll be easy to kill him and disappear."

When he didn't respond right away, she knew she was right. "The reality is, he's crazy and no one's life means anything to him. Certainly not yours, not even his own. He has no plans to let you live one second longer than necessary."

"Shut up, you stupid bitch."

"I'm going to examine them now," she said. "I advise you to think about it while I'm doing that. Right now, Akbar needs me a whole lot more than he needs you."

She checked on the unconscious men first. Stalls was dead, and from the amount of blood soaked into the sand underneath him, he'd bled out. She glanced at Connor and shook her head. River was alive, but when she checked his pupils, only one reacted to light. "Concussion," she reported softly. "A bad one."

Smoke didn't say anything when she looked at his shoulder. "Any trouble breathing?"

"No."

"Good. It looks like your collarbone is broken. Try not to move around or it could pierce your lung." She wished she could do more for him, but advice was all she could give.

He gave a short nod but never took his eerily light blue eyes off Len.

Connor had his hands wrapped around his thigh, but his pants were so blood soaked she couldn't tell where the wound was. "Is the wound on the outside or inside the thigh?"

"Outside, but it's still bleeding like a bitch."

He wasn't going to be able to hold it forever.

She pulled off her shirt, leaving her in just a tank top, and tied it around Connor's leg, wadding up what she could to press against the wound he revealed when he removed his hands.

"What does Akbar want from you?" Connor asked very softly.

"To make his virus easier to transmit."

"*Fuck.*" He hissed as she tightened the fabric hard around his leg. "You know which one it is?"

"Rabies."

"Is that even possible?"

"He's read my dissertation and has made certain assumptions. I mapped the virus's code, so I know which changes would need to be made…" She tried to pin a confident expression on her face, but seeing him so bloody was doing something to her insides. Something painful and cold. "He says if I don't do what he wants, you're all dead."

Connor glanced Stalls's body, then at his own leg. "We're all dead anyway."

"Yeah," she whispered. "That's what I think, too." She was going to die, in a matter of weeks most likely. She wanted her life to count for something. Maybe this was it. Maybe she could save Connor, Smoke and River. Maybe she could take out Akbar with his own weapon.

She leaned forward and whispered in his ear, "Don't blame yourself. I kinda knew I'd die first."

"What the fuck are you whispering?" Len asked, his gun pointed at Connor's head.

Sophia rolled her eyes and said to Con at a normal volume, "I really, really wanted to have sex with you." Then she was on her feet and walking away.

"Not going to happen," Len said with a disgusting sneer on his face. He put a hand on the back of her neck and pushed her faster.

She glanced over her shoulder to see Connor staring after her, the confused, irritated expression on his face reassuringly familiar.

RAGE AND PAIN combined and roiled inside Connor until he felt like he was going to explode.

"Sex?" Smoke asked.

"Don't fucking go there, man," Connor said with a glare at his friend. "Don't."

Con glanced at their jailors. Two guys who held their weapons like they'd had some training.

Probably not enough though.

Stalls was dead and River was halfway there. Their jailors likely thought this was easy duty, standing guard over a bunch of bloodied and dead guys.

Connor groaned and grabbed his leg like it really hurt, then whispered to Smoke. "Collarbone?"

"Not broken," he whispered back.

She'd lied out loud to give them an advantage. *Fucking A.*

Connor switched to Dari and said to their guards, "I have information about an American military attack."

They looked at him, but didn't move.

"I want to trade this information for my life."

One of the two men came toward him. "What attack? This is a refugee camp."

"The United States knows there's a terrorist group with people here. They're going to destroy the entire camp, then apologize later and say it was a mistake."

The man came closer, his rifle pointed at a spot halfway between Smoke and Connor.

Connor lunged upward, putting his weight on his good leg, to grab the rifle and push it so it was pointed up and away from anyone.

At the same time, Smoke rolled and reached for the knife strapped to the terrorist's leg, pulled it out, then threw it at the other guard.

He fell to the ground, the knife embedded in his eye.

Connor wrestled the rifle away from the other one, then bashed him on the side of the head with the butt.

He handed the rifle to Smoke. "I'll carry River."

"Hospital?" Smoke asked.

"Yeah, best place to hide him."

"Wait here." Smoke slipped out of the room, and came back with three traditional Middle Eastern robes long enough to cover up their uniforms.

"Where'd you steal these from?"

"Not far. Laundry."

It took both of them to get River into a robe, but they managed it and Connor hoisted him over his shoulder. Good thing the guy wasn't Smoke's size.

They walked relatively slowly to the hospital. No one paid them much attention, mostly because they weren't the only ones. By the time they got there, they were part of a procession of about four groups taking someone to the hospital.

Connor got River into a cot. "Stay with him. I'm going to look for the doctor," he said in Dari. There were a lot of people in the hospital tent, most of them were on cots, sick or already dead, but there were still a lot of aid workers amongst the ambulatory family members taking care of the sick.

But no Dr. Blairmore. Where could he have gotten away to?

He found the good doctor behind the tarp of the staff-only area. He was sitting on a cot staring at his feet like they were fascinating.

Connor limped over and crouched next to him. "Hey, Doc. I need you to check out my friend." He spoke in

English, but Blairmore didn't seem to notice what language he was using.

"I'm sorry, your friend will have to wait his turn." He glanced up and understanding flooded his face. "Sergeant Button? I thought you were dead. I heard gunshots and saw bodies at your camp."

"Not quite there yet."

Blairmore glanced around uneasily. "So you know Len is a...a murdering monster?"

"Yeah, my cracked ribs let me in on that little secret. Has he hurt you or the other aid workers?"

"No, not yet, but he says he will if we interfere with whatever he and that madman are doing."

"That madman the same guy who told you Dr. Perry was a problem?"

"Yes." Blairmore shook his head and his bottom lip quivered like he was going to cry. "I was a fool."

"There's a lot of that going around." Con patted his shoulder. "Listen, there are only three of us left and my buddy Len kicked River pretty hard in the head. Can you take a look at him?"

"Of course, but be careful. Len comes through the hospital every so often. He might notice your man."

"As soon as he realizes we've escaped, he'll probably be too busy searching for us to bother with your patients or you." Con smiled at him and winked. "You're no threat to him, right?"

Blairmore stared at him, blinked, then nodded and said slowly, "Yes, of course, I'm no threat and far too busy with people who really need my help to watch for some stupid soldiers. Besides you guys are a bunch of arrogant assholes and that woman with you needs to be taken down a notch or two."

"That sounds good. He'll buy it sight unseen."

Con led Blairmore to River's cot, and the doctor did a quick exam.

"He's got a nasty concussion, and I don't have the equipment here to do anything about it. I can give him some medication that might help reduce the brain swelling, but that might not be enough."

"Any help is better than none," Connor said, working hard to sound like Dari was his first language and English was an afterthought. "Do you have a way to call for more help? More medicine or machines?"

"No, I can't seem to get a signal."

Shit, Len must be blocking it.

"Battery dead, maybe," Con said, then gave him a little bow and limped away with Smoke beside him.

"Now what?" Smoke asked, sticking to Dari.

"Now we figure out how to get Sophia away from Akbar before he makes her design the next great plague."

TWENTY-SIX

IF ONLY CONNOR had had time to teach her more of the martial arts stuff he promised, Sophia could have done something about the asshole twisting her arm damned near in half.

"I realize I don't matter much, but if you keep hurting my arm like you are, I won't be able to use it at all."

He didn't answer or change the way he held her.

"Don't take my word for it," she said. "Have a look at it." Her uniform shirt was around Connor's thigh, leaving her arms free of fabric.

He glanced down, then did a double take. "It looks like it's broken."

"No, I have a clotting problem, though."

"Why the fuck did Button bring you out here if you're sick?" Len asked, disgust twisting his features.

"I'm a specialist. Did you think people who could diagnose weird viral or bacterial diseases grew on trees? Your boss is a dangerous man whose only goal is to kill Americans." She gasped, pretending shock, "Oh my, that means you, too."

"Shut the fuck up."

"Or what? You'll hurt me some more, or kill my team? Those threats have already been used."

He pointed his weapon at her face. "Shut. Up."

She shut up.

Shaking his head, Len shoved her in front of him the rest of the way back to the lab tent.

Akbar was pacing outside it. He took one look at her, stared at her arm, then started yelling in Dari.

Len yelled back.

After a minute of this back and forth, Akbar turned to her and asked with some concern, "You're sick?"

Was he serious? He was going to kill her anyway.

Still, she wasn't quite ready to die.

"I have idiopathic thrombocytopenic purpura, ITP."

Akbar stared at her for a long moment. "What does this mean?"

That's right, he wasn't a doctor, he was a chemist.

"It means that if you're stupid—" she glanced at Len "—and you twist my arm, I'm going to look like I was in a car accident. If you shoot me, you'd better mean to kill me, because I'll probably bleed to death no matter how severe the wound." She was laying it on a little thick, but she wasn't telling Akbar anything he couldn't find out on the internet.

He and Len exchanged a few more words, then Len headed off, leaving her with Akbar and at least a dozen of his well-armed friends.

Akbar stared at her like he was trying to take her apart. "Death does not scare you." It was a statement.

One she disagreed with. "I've seen a lot of death, some of it violent, some of it…peaceful. However it happens, the result is the same. The loss of a person. All their knowledge, memories, culture, everything that makes them unique, is gone. From one second to the next, wiped out as if it had never been." She narrowed her eyes. "Facing death has made me stubborn. I'll fight death with everything I have, but I'm still afraid."

"You think like a woman," he said with a sneer.

"This is a surprise?"

He continued to stare at her like she was dirty underwear. "You saw your men. Will you comply with my order?"

"If I do as you ask, will you allow my men to have medical treatment?"

He nodded.

Hmmm, say no and get them killed or say yes and give them time to escape or get rescued? Yes, it is.

She swallowed hard, hunched her shoulders a little and nodded. "You want me to make your virus easier to transmit, right?"

"Yes."

"That's not the only consideration when evaluating the virulence of a virus," she offered tentatively. No use in angering the nutcase. "There are others, like the immune status of the host, how quickly the host can adapt to the virus and mount a defense. How hardy the virus is or if it can survive outside the body for any length of time. What kinds of cells the virus can invade and multiply in or not, and how efficient the virus is at replication."

"Replication has already been altered. As you can see—" he pointed at the hospital tent "—it runs its course in hours instead of weeks."

"But there's been no person to person transmission, has there? You're infecting people one at a time."

"Correct, but rapid person to person transmission is my goal. I want a rabies variant that can spread quickly through the population."

"Airborne?"

"Yes."

She shook her head. "The rabies virus isn't the measles. It's extremely difficult to become infected without a bite. Rabies has been around for thousands of years, it's relatively stable for a virus."

His expression was cold. "I changed it. I accelerated the progression of the disease."

"Okay, so one change worked. Doesn't mean another one will."

His mouth tightened brutally.

Her hindbrain read the danger and kept her tongue talking. "How *did* you infect all these people?" She glanced behind her at the hospital with its hundreds of occupied cots.

For a moment she wasn't sure he was going to answer or if he was going to have her killed on the spot. Finally, he said, "The water supply. I've used up almost all of the virus I have. Creating large quantities will take time, even for me."

"You thought you had already solved the problem of person to person transfer without a bite?"

"Yes, but it appears that the virus isn't viable in water for longer than an hour, and infection takes a fairly large quantity of virus."

He was treating this camp full of people like his personal lab rats. There was no way she could do what he wanted, but she needed to give time to Connor to find a way out of his predicament, and for Max to investigate why she hadn't contacted him at their regularly scheduled check-in time.

She sighed, hoping she wasn't making it too theatrical. "I suppose I'd better take a closer look at it. I only did a Direct Rapid Immunohistochemical Test on a small sample of brain tissue." She gave him a frustrated look. "Most of the equipment I have with me is diagnostic."

He didn't say anything, just gave her a brief nod.

She went into her tent and took another look at the test samples she had on slides. The samples looked typical, but it wasn't designed to reveal anything probative about the virus itself.

She went back to her initial brain tissue samples and began to prepare them for several new tests. All the tests she could think of. Anything to take up time.

Come on, Max. We've missed a check-in. Where are you?

CONNOR AND RIVER took up seated positions at the outskirts of the hospital tent, as if they were waiting on one of the patients near them to die.

Con was not happy with what he was seeing at the lab tent.

Sophia had been talking to Akbar, though not loud enough for them to hear what was said, then she went into the lab with Akbar's permission.

Surrounding the tent were a dozen or more armed militants. Akbar himself didn't appear armed. Though for all Con knew, he carried around containers of anthrax just for the sole purpose of tossing it at people, then running the other way.

Sophia seemed uninjured, except for her arm, which looked badly bruised even from this far away. He was going to have a short but painful conversation with Len very soon. The bastard had killed Stalls and had a hand in the deaths of the other marines. Sophia was safe, sort of, for now, but the lust on Len's face meant she wouldn't stay safe.

"Would she?" Smoke asked.

Con frowned. "Would she, what?"

"Design a plague?"

The contents of Con's stomach turned to ice. "Fuck, no she wouldn't. A guy like him, fucking around with shit and killing people…she'd find a way to fuck him up six ways to Sunday."

Smoke's face looked even colder than Con felt. "Do we stop her or help her?"

"Yes."

Smoke's only response was a grunt.

"We need to get some of those guards away from here."

"Missed a check-in."

"Yeah, so Max will send a fly-by to see if there's a problem or if it's a technical glitch. He won't wait long. He's kind of paranoid."

"The guards will disappear at the first sign of an aircraft," Smoke said.

"Got a laser pointer in one of your pockets or did Len take it?"

Smoke smiled. "I've got it."

"Find a position where you can signal any aircraft that flies over and be ready to send an SOS."

Smoke nodded, got up slowly and disappeared into the hospital and into the camp.

Con considered moving to a closer location, but before he could decide where, Len arrived at the lab. He went inside, then came out with Akbar.

The two men talked quietly for a few minutes. There was head nodding and finger pointing. Akbar called a couple of his goons over and there was some more discussion, then he went back into the tent.

Len sat down on an overturned bucket under the tarp at the entrance to the lab and seemed to be content with whatever was going on.

Akbar came out of the lab, spoke to Len again, then took four of the armed goons and headed into the camp.

Looking for supplies, water or fresh victims?

The rumble of a couple of fighter jets became audible and got louder fast.

Len shouted in Dari, "Everyone smile and wave."

All the goons smiled and waved on cue. Too bad Smoke was signaling for help at the same time.

Fucking crazy son of a bitch, you just got made.

The fighters didn't circle back and everyone relaxed. Len went around to give orders to a couple of the goons, then went into the lab tent.

Alone.

The fucking asshole. He was going to put his hands on Sophia.

He needed a reason to go there, to approach the lab. Looking around, he found a tray with a row of hypodermic syringes on it. He picked it up and began walking toward the lab with a businesslike air.

At the first challenge, he said in Dari, "I was told to give these samples to the American woman." He held out the tray.

The guard glanced at the tray and nodded.

Con went into the tent.

"Take your hands off me." Sophia sounded mad. "I'm up to my elbows in rabies virus and you want to play snatch and grab? Are you stupid? I've got enough of the virus here to kill ten of you."

"I'm on your side, sweetheart." Len's back was to Con and he backed up a step as he lowered his voice.

"I'm double-crossing Akbar. Put down the container of brains and come with me. I'm going to get you out of here."

"What about Connor?" she asked in a tone that told him she hadn't seen him standing behind Len.

"I'm sorry, Akbar had him and his buddies killed." He held out a hand to her. "Come on, let's go."

The son of a bitch.

Connor shifted his weight to take a step closer, to take Len down, but Sophia spoke before he could move.

"There is nothing that would make me go with you willingly," she told him in her *I think you're stupid and therefore uninteresting* voice. "You're a terrible liar."

Len's posture changed. He shifted toward her, crowding her against the bench behind her. "Akbar has already promised to let me have you when he's got what he wants," Len told her in a disgusting purr.

That's it, you're done. Con rammed the tray, rim first, into the base of Len's skull.

He dropped like a stone.

Sophia stared at Con with wide eyes for a second then set what she was holding on the bench with a shaking hand, stripped off her gloves and threw herself at him.

He staggered for a moment, his injured leg a little wobbly. "Are you okay?" he whispered, running his hands over her. She was badly bruised everywhere he looked.

"Yes. No." She shook her head and wiped tears away. "I was so scared they were going to kill you."

"Hey, it's been tried, but I keep bouncing back." He rubbed her back, kissed her temple then coaxed her chin up so he could make eye contact. "We've got to get out of here."

"How are we going to do that?" Her voice quivered with enough stress to make him look around for another asshole to beat up.

But they were alone. "Good question."

She pulled back to stare at him incredulously. "You came in here with no plan to get out?"

"I saw Len go in and knew he was going to…" Con glanced down at the SOB and had to fight the anger that made his hands tighten with the need to bloody his fists on the other man.

"You…you…" she sputtered, smacking his chest with the flats of her hands. "You can just go out the way you came in." She pointed at the exit. "Shoo."

"I won't leave you here with nut bar."

"Juvenile," she muttered, then stretched up and kissed him so quick he didn't have time to respond. "Someone has to tell Max what's happening," she whispered. "Akbar is trying to weaponize rabies. It's not going to work, I'll make sure of that, but he introduced large amounts of the virus to the water supply here. He just couldn't get it easily transmissible from human to human. That's why he wanted me."

"Rabies is fucking deadly."

"Yes, and it's a terrible, painful way to die, which is his secondary goal." She poked him with her index finger. "You've got to tell Max to get rabies immunoglobulin, passive antibodies and the vaccine to the camp as soon as possible. We might be able to save some of these people, but only if it happens quickly."

She was a saint, an angel, and insane if she thought he'd leave her here. "You're coming with me."

She shook her head. "I'm the only one who can stall Akbar long enough for help to arrive."

"*No.*"

"Yes." She gave him a watery smile. "Please. I'm a lousy shot, I don't know the first thing about hand-to-hand combat and I'm too breakable to really learn, but I can do *this*."

He got right into her face and bared his teeth. "Can you stay alive?"

"Can you?" she asked just as fiercely, grabbing the fabric of the robe he wore so she could give him a shake. "Will you?"

She knew. Goddamn it, *she knew* he'd planned to never get out of this alive.

He couldn't leave her and he couldn't let her leave him. The grip the ghosts of his battle brothers had on his heart burned away, leaving only Sophia in possession of it.

"I will if you will," he snarled at her. "You might have terrible depth perception, spatial orientation and aim, but you're smarter than Einstein and when things get tough, you get mean. I need you to look after yourself and knock this guy on his ass."

"I have the perfect motivator," she whispered, smiling and wiping some dirt off his cheek. "I'm going to have sex with you, remember? You promised."

Well, if she had to have a goal, he'd be happy to sacrifice himself. "Is sex all you think about?"

"No, sometimes I think about the very small things I can see with my very nice microscope."

He hcsitated. He hated this. It fucking *sucked*, but she was right. Someone had to get help, someone had to delay Akbar, and he couldn't do both. He had to trust her not to do anything self-destructive.

He kissed her, hard and quick. "Don't disappoint me. We're going to have lots and lots of sex."

TWENTY-SEVEN

As soon as Con left, Sophia bent down to check Len's carotid pulse. The mercenary was still alive, but she suspected the blow Con had landed may have done more damage than just knock him unconscious.

She picked up the scattered syringes, disposed of them, then grabbed the metal tray and was trying to decide what to do with it when Akbar came in.

He took in the situation in one glance and one corner of his mouth rose in a snarl.

"He attacked me," she said, glancing down at Len's unconscious body. "I didn't mean to do this, though."

Akbar swore in a language other than English, then went back out and yelled something.

Two of his men came inside and carried Len away.

"Pack all this up," Akbar said. "We're leaving."

Leaving? Had he decided to abandon the refugee camp? Whatever the reason, it wasn't good. They had him here and they needed him to stay so Max and the Army could catch him. "But I'll have to start testing all over again."

Akbar's jaw clenched. "You will do as you're told or your men will be shot." He took a gliding step toward her that was all the more threatening in its silence. "I won't ask again."

You don't have my men. She examined his face and saw an explosive anger there that hadn't been there before. *He knows they've escaped. Is he running?* "You're bringing them with us?"

His nostrils flared. Had she pushed him too far? "They will follow." He glanced around. "Pack the equipment you want or it gets left behind. We leave in ten minutes." He strode out to call to his men.

She could hear him issue orders and really wished she could speak Dari.

There was no way she could go with him. If she did, she was as good as dead with nothing accomplished.

So, how to make him leave her behind?

Outside, the sound of engines approaching had her poking her head out of the tent to see what was going on.

Trucks, three of them, were pulling up to the area around her lab. Fuck. She had less time than she thought.

She went back inside, calmly unplugged her favorite microscope and put it into its hard-shell carrying case. It had a nice sturdy handle on it. The microscope was, like everything else in her portable lab, compact, but it was still heavy. The case with the scope in it weighed in at about eight pounds. She put that to one side then pulled out a couple of bottles, one of formalin, the other methanol.

She used both for fixing tissue samples, preventing decomposition and allowing her to create single-cell-thick cross sections of a tissue sample. These she mounted on slides so she could evaluate their morphology. Both chemicals required caution to use. Formalin was toxic and a known carcinogenic, and both were highly flammable.

Sophia opened the bottles and began sprinkling the tent with their contents. She dropped the bottles on the

sand just inside the tent and walked out with her microscope in her left hand. She stopped about ten feet away.

Akbar saw her, frowned and walked toward her.
"That is all you want to bring with you?" He continued past her toward the tent.

Sure, go right on in.

She put her microscope down and slid her right hand
into her thigh pocket and pulled out a flare.

Akbar stopped a couple of feet away from the entrance. Maybe he saw the empty bottles. Maybe he
smelled the chemicals, since she'd so liberally doused
everything in them. Whatever the reason, he turned,
violence riding him like one of the four horsemen of
the apocalypse.

She lit the flare and threw it into the tent, then threw
herself to the sand and covered her head.

The next few seconds passed in slow motion, as if
she was watching a movie rather than real life.

The armed men around her moved, or started to,
some to raise their weapons at her, others at threats
that weren't there.

The explosion that resulted after the flare ignited the
formalin and methanol tossed all of them on their backs.

Akbar was thrown only a few feet away from her,
facedown in the sand.

She sat up, glanced at him. He seemed down for the
moment, so she grabbed her microscope and walked
away toward the hospital and refugee camp.

People stared at the fire burning behind her with
their mouths open. Well, most of them did. One man,
dressed in a traditional robe, came straight toward her.

She'd know that face anywhere. Connor.

He met her halfway between where her lab had been

and the hospital. He had no rifle or weapon that she could see, just a grim set to his mouth.

Now what had she done wrong?

He took her by the arm.

"Ouch."

He adjusted his grip instantly and asked through clenched teeth, "Are you injured?"

She shook her head. "Just a lot of people grabbing me there today."

Behind them someone yelled in Dari.

"Fuck," Connor breathed, looking past her shoulder at something.

"Is there more than one?"

"Not yet."

"How close is he?"

"Ten feet."

"Wait here." She turned, then nodded at the man with the rifle and walked toward him.

Behind her, Connor sucked in a breath.

Four feet away from the gunman, she stumbled, then spun and bashed him in the shoulder with the microscope.

He went down with at yell, and Connor was on him within a second or two, punching the man a few times, then taking his rifle.

"Come on," Connor said, looking angrier than she'd ever seen him.

They made it into the hospital tent, where everyone ambulatory was rushing to see what was going on and watch the fire.

Connor pulled her into a cluttered corner of hospital supplies and made her sit down in the middle of them. "Was Akbar with you?"

"Yes. He brought in trucks. He was trying to get me to pack up my lab so he could move it."

The rage on Connor's face hadn't lessened a bit. "And you, too."

"I suppose. I doubt that's going to happen now. I sort of blew him up with the rest of the lab."

"How do you sort of blow someone up?" Connor asked, his voice rising. "Is it the same as getting sort of pregnant or sort of dead?"

"Why are you so mad? Would you rather I let him kidnap me and my stuff?"

"No, but I do mind you trying to kill yourself." He leaned down to say, in a dangerous tone, "And you promised you wouldn't."

She smacked him on the chest. "I wasn't. I was doing my best to prevent a problem from getting any bigger."

"Which problem? We have several to choose from."

"The Akbar problem. He needed to be stopped and I had no time to consult with you. He only gave me a few minutes to pack up."

"So that's when you thought…*hey, what the hell, I'm going to blow myself up*?"

She smacked him again. "No. I thought what a great opportunity to take away the lab equipment he had a hard-on for, and maybe kill him at the same time."

"What kind of explosive did you use?"

"I opened a couple of bottles of flammable liquids, tossed the stuff around, then threw a lit flare in."

"Fuck, you're lucky you didn't create a crater the size of a house with that shit."

Yelling and movement of people had Connor pushing her to the sand behind the boxes and crates of supplies.

"Don't go anywhere. It doesn't sound like Akbar

stayed blown up." He gave her a glare. "I'm going to see if I can do some permanent damage to the bastard."

"Max might want to question him."

"That's why I only said damage, not kill." Connor stood and was gone the next moment.

Sophia took a look at herself. She was dirty, bruised and her hands were shaking like crazy. At this rate, the aid workers were going to think she was sick.

What she was, was thirsty, but drinking the regular water supply was out. Even knowing whatever rabies virus was in there was most likely non-viable didn't make it safe. Didn't Blairmore have any bottled water? That must be why he wasn't sick.

She opened a cardboard box and found bottled water. Score. She grabbed one, broke the seal and drank it all down. She grabbed another, but caught sight of something behind the box, stashed where no one would see it unless they were raiding supplies like she was doing.

It was a backpack, a lot like the ones Connor and the other Green Berets wore, filled with gear. Interesting. She opened it and found it full of all kinds of stuff she normally wouldn't touch with a ten-foot pole. Explosives, Primacord, a couple of nasty-looking knives, a Russian Tokarev pistol with ammunition. She was used to a Beretta, but a gun was a gun.

Beneath that was a small device that looked a little a remote control with a short antenna poking out the top.

It hit her. This was Len's pack and this device must be a signal jammer to prevent anyone from calling for help.

The off button wasn't immediately obvious, so she fiddled with it until she got the battery compartment open, pulled the battery out and threw it away.

She still had her cell phone in one of her pants pockets. She pulled it out. It was almost dead, but there might be enough battery power to let her make a quick call. She punched in Max's cell number and prayed for him to answer as it started to ring.

"Sophia!" he yelled after the second ring.

"Max," she said as loud as she dared. "We need help. Lots of help from soldiers with guns." Idiot, she sounded hysterical.

"Help is on the way. Someone signaled the jets I sent on a fly-over.

"It's rabies, but Max—"

"Rabies? Slow down. What happened? Was Akbar involved?"

Pain exploded in the side of her head as someone knocked her down and ripped away the phone. Disoriented, she tried to grab the phone, but it was kicked away.

Akbar stood over her, bleeding from multiple cuts on his head and neck. His lips peeled back to expose his teeth at her and he grabbed her by the neck with one hand. Then he dragged her through the boxes and crates she was hiding behind and past the hospital's cots, occupied and not.

He didn't seem to care if she avoided any obstacles or hit them with her body.

Once they reached open sand, he ruthlessly forced her to the ground on her back, his hand tightening on her throat.

"You have cost me far more men, money and time than I can afford."

She tried to talk, but his hold on her throat was too tight. She tried again anyway. His curiosity must have got the best of him, because after the third try to talk, he let off on the pressure so she could speak.

It was probably a fool's errand, but she was going to try talking to the human being who used to inhabit this monster's body.

"Why?" she asked in a tone made harsh by the pressure he'd already put on her neck. "These people didn't hurt you. Why kill them in such a horrible way? Why kill them at all?"

For a moment she thought her question might have reached him. Might have given him pause, perhaps a moment to realize just how terrible the things he'd done were. He looked at the hospital, at all the people, some of them dying only a few feet away of a virus he'd given to them. His face relaxed a little, his jaw sagged and he sucked in a breath.

A moment later, yelling and gunfire turned his face to stone.

She sucked in a breath while she still could.

His hand tightened on her neck again and this time she knew there would be no reprieve. He was going to kill her. An insane smile spread over his face as he pressed harder. "Every one of the people I love has been murdered. Why should anyone else be free of the pain and suffering I live with every day? Until I know peace, no one else will know it either."

Goddamn it, she hadn't beaten cancer as a kid, then become the youngest medical doctor in the USA with a double speciality, just to cave in to the whim of a madman.

She closed her eyes, fisted some sand and threw it in Akbar's face. He reared back, so she lunged up and managed to punch him on the side of the head, hoping his current injuries made him more susceptible to a strike there.

It loosened his grip on her neck and she slid away, but he followed, backhanded her and grabbed her again. This time he had both hands around her neck.

She wasn't going to get away. Death was looking at her and he seemed much too happy to see her.

She'd accomplished one of the two things she wanted to do before she died. She'd done something worthwhile. Something worth dying for.

Please, let Connor be safe.

Spots crowded her vision and she struggled to take in a breath, began to panic, claw at his hands until blood coated her fingers, but the world was going dark and...

The vise around her throat suddenly disappeared.

She coughed and sputtered, her battered throat still tight as she sucked in air. Wonderful air.

Nearby, a sharp cry of pain caught her attention. Two men were struggling together, fighting, one with a knife. Connor and Akbar.

Connor should have been able to subdue Akbar, but he'd been stabbed in the thigh and lost a lot of blood. And Akbar had noticed. He kept punching Connor's leg.

She forced herself to her feet and moved to interfere in their death match, but three of Akbar's armed guards were running toward them. Akbar's back was to them or they likely would have shot Connor. As it was, their shouts distracted Connor enough for Akbar to break away.

He yelled at his men and pointed at Connor and Sophia.

Their weapons came up.

Sophia dove behind a crate, her attention split between Connor and Akbar's goons.

Connor hesitated.

"Con!" she shouted. He'd promised, promised her he would stay alive.

At her shout he threw something at one of the gunmen. His knife struck the chest of one of the men so hard, he fell backward.

The others scattered, their shots going wide.

A distant gunshot rang out and one of the men dropped to the sand. The other two ducked and backed away just as another shot hit one of them in the neck.

Akbar grabbed the injured man's rifle and he tried to wrestle it away, but the next shot hit Akbar in the arm.

The uninjured man grabbed him and ran, putting the hospital between them and whoever was shooting at him.

Sophia crawled over to Connor and began to check him for new injuries. Her shirt bandage on his thigh had come loose and he was bleeding again. She clambered to her feet and moved to look for a proper bandage, but he grabbed her hand and pulled her back down.

"Stay down," he growled at her. "Can't you see someone is shooting at us?"

"Whoever it is," she said, jerking her hand out of his grip, "isn't shooting at us." She got away from him this time and went to the supply area Akbar had used her as a battering ram to destroy.

Aha, she had upended a box of bandages. She grabbed a couple, then went back to Connor, who was now sitting up and looking grumpy.

"You didn't know the shooter wasn't shooting at us."

"I did the moment he didn't shoot us."

"What the hell does that mean?" he demanded.

She took a long look at his leg, then inserted her fingers through the tear in his pants and ripped it open.

"Ow!"

"Oh, shut up, you big baby." She gave him a glare as she bandaged his leg. "Or would you rather bleed to death?"

People were running around, but between the explosion, fire and gunshots, most of them were giving Sophia and Connor a wide berth.

A tall man wearing a robe about six inches too short for him walked toward them like a panther approaches prey.

"Hello, Smoke," Sophia said. "Please tell Connor you were the one who shot those guys over there and made Akbar stop trying to kill us."

Smoke shrugged. "Okay."

"Oh for fuck's sake," Connor said. "Did you actually do all that?"

"Yeah."

Connor shook his head, frustration and irritation making him look dangerous, wild and out of control.

"Max called," Smoke said. "He's on his way. We should see some support in an hour or so."

"Wow, I almost don't know what to do with that good news," Connor said with more sarcasm than Sophia felt was required.

TWENTY-EIGHT

"Bad news, Akbar left in a truck," Smoke said.

"Feel better now?" Sophia asked Con, rolling her eyes as she wrapped a second bandage around Con's thigh.

He wanted to shake and yell at her for taking the insane risks she constantly took. "No. You could have killed yourself lighting the lab up like that."

"I wasn't going to let Akbar take my equipment or me with him."

Her steady tone had him on the verge of exploding. "So, it would have been okay if you'd died?"

She didn't look up from tying off the bandage. "Yes."

Wrong answer.

He took her by the arms, gently because she already had too many bruises, and brought her nose to nose with him. "Who the fuck brainwashed you into valuing yourself so little?" Whoever it was, he was going to hurt them.

"Who brainwashed you?"

"What?"

"You wanted to die, don't try to tell me you didn't. I'm a cancer survivor, remember? I've seen lots of people make the decision that death would be better than living. Sometimes, when you thought no one was looking, you'd look like that. Like you were telling your battle buddies you just had one more mission to do before you joined them."

His mouth tightened. He should have known she'd figure it out. For someone so young, she saw with old, wise eyes.

"I don't feel like that now."

"Good." She sighed and all the starch seemed to go out of her. "We're all going to die someday."

"Flippant comments like that are going to get you handcuffed to a bed so you can't get into any more trouble." He wasn't kidding.

She reached out and stroked one hand down his face with a sad little smile on her face. "Sounds like fun to me."

She was all misty eyed, like his sisters got when they were really emotional. It was so unlike her, a tsunami of cold concern washed away his anger in one sweep. "What the fuck is wrong with you?"

She laughed, but it was bitterly sad. "Would you like the entire list or just the highlights?" A tear tracked its way down her face.

"Sophia?"

She blinked at him, a little frown creasing her brow. "I don't feel very good." A trickle of blood came out of her nose, her eyes fluttered shut and she sagged in his hold.

Con cradled her against his chest and yelled, "Smoke, I need some help here!"

Smoke swept into Con's field of view. "Find Dr. Blairmore. Sophia just passed out on me."

Smoke took one look at Sophia and disappeared into the hospital.

"Come on, gorgeous, don't do this to me," he whispered. He wiped the blood off her face, but it kept coming in a slow, steady drip that worried him more and more with every passing second.

Dr. Blairmore arrived, took one look at Sophia's bruised arms and bloody nose and sucked in a breath. "Was she tortured?"

"She says she has a clotting problem," Connor said. "But this is the second nosebleed she's had in the last few days. She gave herself a plasma transfusion at the base in Bahrain before we left."

Blairmore shifted on his feet with the anxiety of a man who had really bad news for someone. "Can I do a couple of tests?"

Con glanced at the woman he held. He'd let her have her secrets because he had no intention of living past his chance for revenge. She'd changed him in ways he was still trying to process, but two things were clear. Death no longer appealed to him, no longer offered the solace he longed for. *She* gave him that and he wasn't letting her go. "Absolutely."

Blairmore drew some blood, then disappeared with it. An aid worker found a cot for her and Con moved it so it was next to River's. The staff started an IV with saline for Sophia and after a look at Con's leg, one for him, too.

"Without the supply drop this morning we wouldn't have been able to help," the aid worker said. "We haven't seen a new case of the illness in six hours."

Because Akbar had run out of his poison.

"Do you think the worst is over?" the aid worker asked.

"Probably," Con said wiping the blood off Sophia's

face for the umpteenth time. "Unless someone starts a riot."

"People are much calmer now. Someone would have to work really hard to start a riot today."

Smoke set up a patrol around the hospital, keeping an eye on everyone and everything.

Blairmore came back, and from the lack of color on the man's face, the news was going to be bad. The doctor cleared his throat. "She's very sick. Not with rabies," he said quickly. "But her platelet count is dangerously low, the rest of her cell counts aren't good either."

A numbing cold flowed over him. "She had leukemia as a child," Con told him. "It went into remission."

Blairmore just nodded. "Most childhood leukemias are curable now, but there are always a few that…come back after the patient is an adult." He swallowed, then added, "I'm not certain, you understand. I can only do cell counts here. She'll need further testing at a fully equipped hospital to determine if I'm right."

Con looked at the woman who held his heart, his life in her hands, and vowed to make sure she got the best care there was. "Thanks."

Smoke drifted over after Blairmore left. "Does she know?"

"She had a nosebleed back in Bahrain. She knows." And she didn't tell anyone, not him or Max.

"Huh," grunted Smoke. "I thought you were the suicidal one."

"Not anymore," Con said. Unconscious and without the force of her personality, he noted how pale Sophia was, how black her eyes were. Her bones stood out against her skin and her lips looked bloodless.

She'd come close, perilously close to working herself

to death. If she thought he was going to stand back and let that happen, she was in for a rude surprise.

A unit of Army Rangers arrived first. They secured the entire camp and Smoke finally ceased his unrelenting watch over the hospital and crashed on a cot alongside Sophia's.

They were going to need their own wing at this rate.

Max arrived three hours later, took one look at their beat-up-looking group and ordered them all back to the base in Bahrain. River was going to need surgery, Con a blood transfusion and Smoke was ordered to take forty-eight hours to rest.

When Max found out about Sophia's cell counts he calmed down to an extent Con knew was not good. He stopped talking, standing and looking at her for so long, Con had to say something.

"She lied to us?"

"Yes." Max's gaze met his own and Con could see that her lies had hurt the other man deeply.

"Why would she do that?"

"I don't know."

"You're both stupid," Smoke said.

When they looked at him in confusion, the big man added, "Cancer doesn't just hurt the victim."

"She didn't tell us because she didn't want either of us to worry?" He was going to spank her ass when she was better.

Max nodded. "Yes, that feels right."

"Fuck, Smoke," Con said to his friend. "Ever think of becoming a therapist?"

For a moment Smoke looked completely disgusted. Then he said, "Killing bad guys is my therapy."

"I'd say that's fucked up, but I've been doing the

same thing." Con shook his head. "What about you, Max?"

"Let's just say I'm a workaholic and leave it at that." He gave Sophia another long look, then nodded at Con and Smoke. "Keep an eye on her. Consider it an order."

Max left to take care of a number of details left behind after Akbar's departure, not the least of which was replacing the water tank and making sure the water was clean and safe to drink.

He came back and woke Con from a deep sleep. "A medical helicopter will be here in thirty minutes to transport you all back to the base. Keep me apprised as information comes in." The last sentence delivered with a glance toward Sophia.

"Yes, sir."

She was still asleep. How had she managed to do all the shit she'd done? It spoke of a mental fortitude that was stronger than anyone's he'd ever met.

The chopper arrived and everyone got loaded on. They'd been in the air for twenty minutes when she woke up.

The first thing she did was grab for his hand.

Who needed painkillers when all it took to make him feel like a superhero was her reaching for him without thinking?

He was sitting next to her gurney, strapped into the large helicopter. He leaned close and yelled, "You've been asleep for a few hours. I think all the crap we've been through caught up with you. We're heading toward Bahrain and Max wanted to keep us together. River is going into surgery as soon as we land."

She relaxed more and more as he talked. When he finished, she closed her eyes briefly, then smiled at him.

"Max gave strict orders," Connor added. "You're not allowed to do anything until he comes back."

That made her frown.

"I did, however, talk him into letting me continue to give you Tai Chi lessons."

She grinned and nodded.

The big sneak. He knew she'd never be satisfied with that. She dozed for the rest of the trip, but he could see her reliving things in her mind. Her fists would clench and a couple of times, she screamed as a rough bump woke her.

He'd hold her hand until she got herself out of the nightmare or memory, then settle in to covertly watch her.

Back at the base, all of them were taken to the medical clinic for a thorough check.

Connor had lost more blood than he thought and got a couple units.

River made it through the surgery. A small hole was drilled into his skull to relieve the pressure from his concussion. He woke up wondering what the hell happened.

Smoke ended up getting a unit of blood, too, then slept for almost twenty-four hours straight.

Sophia tried to tell the staff that blood tests weren't necessary. Even argued with them, until Con asked for a minute alone with her, then told her quietly, "Blairmore did some cell counts while you were out. He told us they were really low."

"Big mouth," she muttered.

"No, he was doing his job." Con thumped her gently on the head. "What were you thinking, going into an outbreak situation with an unknown pathogen, knowing you were sick?"

"I was thinking this was my chance to do something important." She dropped her gaze and picked at the blanket under her fingers.

"You're not going to pull that shit again," he told her in a hard tone. "You're going to take care of yourself and do everything you can to get better." He should take his own damned advice.

"Wow, listen to you, Dr. Button," she shot back, pink warming her cheeks.

"I've been hanging around you long enough for some of it to sink in."

She seemed pleased by that.

"So, why did you do it?" Con asked her.

"Max needed me to do my job. I decided what I could do in the here and now was worth the risk."

"You lied to me," Con said.

She opened her mouth, but he wasn't finished yet.

"You also lied to Max. Me, I'm just a soldier, but Max? He's not happy with you and I think you're going to find out there's a steep price to pay for what you did."

"Just a soldier?" She stared at him, her mouth hanging open. "You're my *partner*." She narrowed her eyes and said, "Let's talk about the price I'm going to pay." Fuck, he was going about this all wrong.

"My lifespan isn't going to be counted in decades, Connor. Where else could I make the most of the time I have than in this team?"

"This isn't some suicide squad," he barked at her. "The Army needs you long-term."

He had never seen a more resolute face than hers. "I don't have a long term to give them."

"Don't say that, Goddamn it, don't even think it." He wanted nothing more than to hunt Akbar down and finish killing him.

"I had to do this," she said after a moment. "I had to keep the truth to myself. If I had told Max, he would have immediately put me on a plane and sent me back to the United States."

"Damn straight."

"Then we wouldn't have found out just how insane Akbar is. We almost did catch him, and now we know his goal isn't just to kill, it's to cause as many people as possible pain while they die."

She wasn't listening. He needed to try a different tactic. "You wanted to do something worthwhile with your life. Something worth dying for. Isn't that what you said to me the day we met?"

"I can't believe you remember that."

"Hell, yes, I remember that. It's almost word for word what I said when I wanted to get back on active duty." He leaned down and said in her ear, "And it was the truth, as far as that goes, because I also wanted, in the worst way, to die in the performance of my duty."

"I figured that out the night those goons tried to kidnap me. You threw yourself into taking those men down with no thought to yourself. None at all." She held her breath for a moment. "There I was, fighting so hard to live just a few weeks longer, and you were trying so hard to die."

"I'm not trying to die anymore. I hung around this crazy, gorgeous doctor for too long. I have something to live for now. I'm hoping she feels the same way."

She stared at him with tears in her eyes and it nearly killed him to act casual and say, "Now stop arguing with the lab tech and let her take some blood so you can figure what's wrong with you and fix it."

"It's never that easy," she whispered.

"You're the smartest and most stubborn person I know." He kissed her on the nose. "I've got some paperwork Max is squawking at me to fill out. I'll see you later."

"You're not just a soldier, by the way," she said before he could go three steps. "You're *my* soldier. Remember that."

For the first time since the explosion, he smiled with no hint of sorrow at all. "Sounds good to me."

An hour later, one of the doctors came around to talk to Sophia. Twenty minutes after that, a nurse set up a unit of blood plasma for transfusion for her. Then a unit of blood.

He asked when he could visit her and was told he couldn't. She'd requested no visitors.

What the fuck?

Smoke distracted the nurse so Con could sneak into her room.

"How did you get in here?" she asked, glaring at him.

Wow, where did Miss Crabby come from? "Smoke is making your nurse's life difficult."

"I don't care." She looked away. "Get out."

Something had happened to cause this about-face. He wasn't leaving until he knew what it was. "No."

She frowned at him, then deliberately turned on her side and stared at the wall.

"What's wrong with you?" he asked her.

"You're what's wrong with me."

"Sophia."

"I told you before, all my cell counts are low."

That didn't sound like cancer.

He had to work to keep excitement out of his tone. "You don't have leukemia?"

"No."

No cancer. "The nosebleeds?"

"Not enough platelets and too much stress from idiots who can't take a hint."

Not cancer.

Thank *God*. "I'd go, but we have some unfinished business."

"Tai Chi lessons?" she asked hesitantly.

She was pushing him away, probably thinking it was for his own good.

Sometimes, it was good to be bad.

If he told her how he really felt, how much she really meant to him, she'd fight him every step of the way. It was time for a little tactic called fishing, and he had the perfect bait. He bent down so he could whisper in her ear, "Sex."

Her breath caught right before she inched away. "I've changed my mind."

"You? Ms. *I'll get it done or die trying*, you've changed your mind?"

She didn't answer for a long time, then she sighed and said, "It was a nice idea, but the reality is, I'm in no shape for it now."

"Nice?"

She rolled over to stare at him.

"Sweetheart, you're covered in bruises and every time you sit up you have a nosebleed. I know I can be an idiot sometimes, but I'm not that stupid."

"Max is going to have me on a plane for the lower forty-eight within the next twenty-four hours. I don't know if I'm ever going to see you again, so there's no point in...discussing it."

He'd deal with the *I don't know if I'm ever going to see you again* statement in a minute. "Why is Max putting you on a plane so fast if you're not dying?"

She sighed. "Because he thinks, and I agree with him, that I have aplastic anemia—my bone marrow has gone on strike—and I'm too sick to remain on active duty. I need to have more testing to determine what my next treatment steps are, but I will likely receive a medical discharge."

"But not dying?" he asked, holding steady to his determination. Hope was too wild an emotion to let loose inside him.

She hesitated for a long couple of seconds. "It's just as deadly as any cancer if my bone marrow doesn't respond to treatment."

"So, that's it?" He couldn't believe it. "You're just giving up?" This woman always had a will of steel. Where had that gone?

She rolled over to look at him, and he saw that her face was wet. "I'm so glad you've decided to live. I was incredibly lucky to have you as a partner and battle buddy. You're big and sexy and you make me laugh. I wish I could have had more time with you, but it's not going to work out that way." She smiled. "I hope you continue to kick terrorist ass, and you find happiness, because you deserve it."

Her words gutted him. She was leaving him so she could die where he couldn't be with her, comfort her, love her.

This wasn't a casual brush-off.

She was saying goodbye forever.

No fucking way.

He'd fought for her, lived for her and he wasn't about to let her give up on herself.

TWENTY-NINE

SOPHIA HURT SO MUCH, like someone had taken her right arm and ripped it off. The last thing she wanted was to be away from Connor, but her cell counts weren't going up on their own. It was looking like her bone marrow had given up the ghost and wasn't producing much of anything.

Losing Connor, never seeing him again, not being able to touch him, was a sort of emotional torture, but he had a life to live and now he might actually want to live it.

She hated the confused hurt she saw on his face. She'd done that, wounded him, but she couldn't take it back. It was better than letting him watch her die.

He froze, absolutely motionless for a second, then his expression morphed into confusion and uncertainty.

So much pain on his face, and she'd put it there.

She wanted to take it all back, apologize for hurting him and promise whatever he needed to give her back her confident soldier again, but her death would hurt him so much more.

This was the lesser of the two evils.

The pain receded from his face, replaced by anger, irritation and resolve.

Uh oh. The soldier was back.

"You shut that shit up."

Great, he was going to get stubborn. "Connor, this

isn't something you can bulldoze your way through. You can't stare it into submission, or order it to stop. I'm deathly ill."

"Exactly," he said, bending down.

What was he doing? Unlacing his boots?

"You think I'm going to leave you to deal with this alone?" He toed his boots off, then began unbuttoning his uniform shirt. "I'm not going anywhere you aren't."

"But—"

"No buts. You can order other people around. Not me." He threw his shirt on the floor and crawled onto the bed.

"What are you doing, you stupid man?" she hissed. He was supposed to leave. Hurt, yes, but better than the prolonged agony of watching her die a slow death. "The nurse could come in at any moment."

He gathered her up, sliding one arm under her while the other coaxed her into rolling up against him. It didn't take much coaxing. He gave heat off like a furnace and she was so cold. Despite her brain telling her body to push him away, she snuggled into him and returned the full-body hug. "You are the biggest stubborn idiot I know."

He rubbed her back and nuzzled her hair, temple and the back of her neck. "But I'm your stubborn idiot."

She was glad, so *glad* he was, but oh how she was going to hurt him.

She started to cry.

He held her, his hands cradling her close as he murmured gentle words in her ear.

Someone opened the door to her room, paused, then closed it again.

At some point, she fell asleep.

She wasn't sure where she was at first when she woke, but it came back to her in a flash. The rustle of paper pulled her attention to the chair next to her bed. Max was sitting in it, reading out of a file folder.

Connor was gone.

"Max?" She tried to sit up, but he raised his hand and gestured for her to lie back down.

"Relax, Doctor. Everything is okay."

She doubted that very much. "Did you find Akbar?"

Max's face grew cold. "No, the bastard got away."

"Oh no."

Max nodded. "He's leading us on a merry chase. He's even started a correspondence with me."

"How is he doing that?"

"He's writing messages on corpses and leaving them where they'll be found."

He was devolving? "He's turned into some kind of mass serial killer."

"Yes, and unfortunately, he's not done killing."

Her throat was so tight, she could hardly swallow. "How many people died in the refugee camp?"

"One thousand six hundred and four. We've done anti-mortem testing on several of the dead. All of them had rabies." Max gave her a questioning look. "What's your feeling on Akbar? Will he continue to use rabies?"

She sighed. "He'd gone as far as he could go with the virus and he wasn't satisfied with it. That's why he wanted me. He thought, with my knowledge of the virus, that I could manipulate it in ways he couldn't."

"Is that why you destroyed your lab?"

"One of the reasons." She thought about Akbar, how he talked, and what he said and didn't say. "I think he'll move on to a different pathogen. He doesn't want us ready to combat anything he releases."

"That's not good news."

"I did make an observation about him. He's a chemist, not a doctor, so he approaches disease from a different perspective than we do. He looks at what he's doing like a mathematician looks at a math problem—A plus B equals C. But diseases aren't rational or linear. A plus B could also equal F or Y depending on any number of other factors that he's not aware of."

"Perhaps he doesn't care about the other factors, or he's willing to take risks to see if it makes things even worse than he intended?"

"That, too, could be true." She looked at Max. "He's completely uncaring about the pain and suffering of other people."

"Oh, he cares." Max looked particularly grim. "He wants them to feel as much pain as possible." He put down the papers and leaned forward to rest his elbows on his knees. "I'm sending you home. Your cell counts are all down. Without transfusions, you'd be impossible to transport."

"My bone marrow has shut down."

"Likely, but we're not going to do a bone marrow aspiration here to prove it. I want it done in a hospital that can provide the right treatment immediately after a determination is made as to what's going on."

"Are you discharging me?"

Max frowned. "Here's what I would like to do. It's likely that you'll be forced into a medical discharge. I want you to take it. After you've recovered, I can hire you as a contractor, much like Grace's man, Sharp. I want access to your brain even if your bone marrow is misbehaving."

If she survived. "Assuming I *do* recover."

"I have a friend, another hematologist, who's got some outside-the-box ideas," Max said with a hint of challenge in his gaze. "I'd like you to meet him. I think, between the two of you, there's a possibility of a creative solution."

"You're grasping at straws, Max."

His mouth tightened. "I'm trying to save one of the best minds I've ever had the pleasure of working with," Max said with strained patience. "You're a doctor with unique skills. I never brought you in because you're killer soldier material. You're here to save the lives of soldiers and civilians alike from weapons they can't see or combat on their own. Believe me, you are highly respected for what you did at the camp. Even General Stone, though in public he claims not to be happy with some of your more explosive actions. In private, he wishes he could have seen the look on Akbar's face when he realized you were blowing your lab up rather than let him have it."

One corner of her mouth quirked up. "Angry, that's how he looked."

"I refuse to think anything other than positive." Max smiled. It had a sad edge to it, but it was still a smile. "I don't want to lose my friend and colleague, period."

Her throat was so full of unshed tears all she could do was nod.

"River is going Stateside too, and Smoke is going on a six-week leave to rest and build strength after the bullet wound he took in the shoulder. He's been on deployment for almost eighteen months, so he's due for it."

She cleared her throat and managed to ask, "What about Connor?"

"I'm keeping him with me for a little while," Max said. "We're going to work on predicting Akbar's next possible moves and targets."

"That's good," she managed to say, though her throat was so tight she found it difficult to breathe. "He's very intelligent."

"He's still your official partner-slash-bodyguard. If you're a contractor, no one can cry fraternization either."

Heat infused her face. Max had known about their intimate relationship?

He gathered up his papers and stood like he'd just delivered a weather update. "I promise to return him to you undamaged."

"When is that going to be? Six months? A year?" She blinked away tears and couldn't help asking, "What if I don't get better?"

Max shook his head. "Are you with me on the plan or not?"

"Yes, sir."

"Good."

An hour later, Eugene and Jones arrived, but didn't have time to fill her in on their adventure, which started the moment they got on their transport plane. It hadn't gone to their planned destination.

Though they didn't touch each other, Sophia could see they were together in every sense of the word. "You're not going to fool anybody," she told them.

"About what?" Eugene asked.

"You two. No canoodling where anyone can catch you at it."

"Who the fuck says canoodling?" Jones demanded.

"I'm sick, I can say whatever I want."

Eugene was laughing too hard to add much to the conversation after that.

An hour before her plane was to leave, Connor invaded her hospital room. He glanced around at the air-med-evac people and said, "I need a minute with the captain."

Nobody argued, though a couple looked irritated with the interruption.

As soon as they were gone, Connor kneeled on the edge of her bed and leaned across her to brace his hands on the blankets. "You are going to be okay." He paused, his shoulders tense, his knuckles white. "Say it."

She had to fight tears, but managed to croak out, "I'm going to be okay."

He clenched and unclenched his jaw. "Again."

Tears rolled down her face. He looked terrified but tenacious, so she repeated, "I'm going to be okay."

"Again."

She smiled and cupped his cheek. He needed a promise to convince him. "Kidnappers couldn't stop me, a fire couldn't stop me, rabies couldn't stop me and an insane madman couldn't stop me. I'm going to be okay."

He bent his head and let out a huge breath. "Okay." His chin came up and he kissed her. "That's my girl." He kept kissing her until she was dizzy.

Was *he* going to be okay?

She should remind him she needed him, too.

"I'm sad," she whispered to him as he nuzzled and nipped at her neck.

"About what?" He seemed only partially interested. His focus was on her neck, and it felt so good.

She pulled her blankets away, took one of his large hands and curved it around her breast. "I'm still a virgin."

He reared back. "*Fuck.*"

"Yes, please," she said with a small smile.

He stared at her, his eyes hot and his face ruddy. "I made you a promise," he said lowering himself until his lips brushed hers. "I plan on keeping it."

"You're going to have sex with me?"

He shook his head slowly. "I'm going to make love to you."

She sighed, "Okay." And he kissed her again.

SOPHIA STOOD IN front of a group of soldiers who were beginning the process of becoming Green Berets. There were about thirty men present and she was showing them how she collected samples for the Sandwich.

It was slow going because she wasn't officially Army anymore. She was a contractor working for the Biological Response Team, which meant she was considered fair game in the sexual sense. One of the trainees was particularly persistent. Said he had a thing for women with white-blond hair.

She was trying to impress upon the entire group how important it was to work closely with their Biological Response Team teammate. "Communication is key. You don't always know what piece of information might impact the situation."

"Baby," Mr. Persistent said, "you can say anything you want to me, just take off your clothes while you're doing it."

Some of the men laughed, but there were a quite few in the group who looked as irritated as Sophia felt.

She'd given him two warnings already and she was done. She shut up and glared at him until the quiet got uncomfortable.

She kept on staring, until he asked, "Can't take a compliment?"

"Reducing me down to nothing more than a sexual object is not a compliment." She glanced around at the rest. "You're here to learn about biological weapons and how to detect and identify them, correct?"

"Yes, ma'am," the group answered.

"I have two hours to give you information you might need to stay alive." She checked her watch. "Mr. Persistent here has wasted fifteen minutes of that time. How many more minutes are you willing to waste?"

There was a moment of silence, then some general grumbling. Finally someone said, "None."

"Excellent." She carried on with her lecture.

At the end, before she could dismiss them, someone behind her cleared his voice. She turned to find Connor standing near the doorway.

Connor.

Wow, he looked good. Better than good, he looked healthy, in even better shape than the last time she'd seen him…lickable. The closer he got, the better he looked. Big, his muscles defined, his face shaved, his body fit. She could eat him all up.

Connor moved up to stand next to her and she had trouble keeping her hands to herself.

He was *here.*

"My name is Communications Sergeant Connor Button. Dr. Perry is my counterpart on the Biological Response Team. If you're successful in your application to join the Special Forces, my job for the next six weeks will be to take over for Sergeant Stone, who gave you your first taste of our combatives program. In addition to all the other training you'll be doing, I'll be picking out a few of you to work with the Biological Response Team. If you have an interest in working with them, let me know."

He turned to nod at her. "Carry on, Doctor."

"Thank you, Sergeant." She gave him a professional nod and regarded her students. "As you can see, trust will be an integral part of your relationship with your Biological Response teammate. It's important to establish that early, so if things do go wrong, there aren't any hesitations or questions in your mind about what should happen next or who should make which decisions. You both have a role and sometimes you're going to lead, other times you're going to have to let your teammate lead."

As the men filed out at the end of the lecture, Connor turned to give her a thorough visual examination. "How are you, Sophia?" His voice contained no emotion, no intonation from which she could interpret how he was feeling.

"Very well, thank you." She watched him for any sign of happiness at seeing her, but he'd completely closed himself off. Trying to ignore the cold ball of grief at his unconcern, she asked, "And you?"

"Fine."

A burst of hysterical laughter escaped her. "Fine. You mean fucked up, insecure, neurotic and emotional?"

His nostrils flared and he took a menacing step toward her. "Yes, fine, because Max had me on a covert mission that didn't allow me an opportunity to call you for three fucking long months. Fine, because during that entire time all I could think about was you and if you were getting better or if you were going to die on me while I was under."

He took another step toward her, close enough to touch. "Fine, because after three months of being away from you, the only thing I want is to get us both naked and stay that way for as long as you'll allow."

"Oh." When had she started to pant?

"The only reason I haven't started is because I know this building has a security camera pointed right at us, and what I want to do with you isn't meant for anyone else's eyes but yours and mine."

"So," she said, breathless. "That all sounds…really good. What *do* we do?"

"When are you off?"

"In a couple of hours. You?"

"The same. You've got a place?"

"Yes."

"Give me the address."

She did and he put it into his phone.

He speared her in place with a hot look. "If I touch you now, even for a hug, I'll lose it." He lowered his voice until it was only a growl. "God, I've missed you."

She sniffed back the tears and managed to say, "I've missed you, too."

Two hours later, she arrived at her apartment outside the base at Fort Bragg, NC, kicked off her shoes and hoped Connor would arrive before she hyperventilated.

He'd be here soon. Would he be hungry? Thirsty?

Before she could decide what to do her cell phone rang. She answered it, "Yes?"

"It's Connor. Buzz me in." It wasn't a request, and that didn't bother her in the slightest.

She let him in, then paced in front of her apartment door until the heavy knock announced his arrival.

She yanked open the door.

He seemed to fill up the entire space between door-jambs.

He stared at her, and if she thought he looked hot under the collar before, it was nothing compared to how he looked now. There should be steam coming off him.

"Hi," she said, suddenly nervous. "C...come in."

He took two steps inside, dropped his duffel bag on the floor, then closed and locked the door.

She bounced on her feet and smiled, but she was afraid it was as unsteady as the rest of her. "Um." Wow, he looked so good. "Take your boots off."

He shook his head no.

"Why? What's wrong?"

A slow grin lit up his face. "I love how focused you are, sweetheart, but we need to have a conversation before I remove any of my clothing, or we won't get any talking done."

"Even your boots?"

He laughed and the sound brought her to the brink of tears. She'd never heard him laugh like that before. Happy. Completely happy, without a ghost or regret in it. Then he took off his boots.

THIRTY

IT WAS KILLING him to not touch her.

Connor gave her a slow once-over, to be certain what he'd seen earlier in the lecture hall had been accurate. She looked great. Her skin had a healthy glow and he couldn't see evidence of any bruises. It looked like she might have put on a few pounds, but she'd needed them. By the end of their ordeal with Akbar, she'd been underweight.

"Max said the stem cells they used to treat your anemia worked."

She smiled and it damn near made him kneel. "Yes, my bone marrow seems to be functioning very well now. This is a new treatment."

"No more bruises or nosebleeds?" He couldn't see any bruises, but that didn't mean anything.

"Nope."

Her hair was down. He'd never seen it down, clean and brushed out since that very first night he saw her. It had come out of its bun during their skirmish with Akbar, but she'd been covered in sand, sweat, bruises and blood. Now she looked...whole and happy.

Beautiful.

He couldn't stop staring, couldn't believe she was in front of him, healthy and apparently excited to see him after three months apart.

"I'm sorry I couldn't contact you," he said with a

wince. "Max swore he explained it all to you, but that doesn't mean the same thing as hearing you say you were okay with it."

"Ha," she snorted. "I may not have been able to talk to you, but Max kept me up to date on your status during our daily consultations. You really impressed him," she said with a proud tilt of her chin. "You found out more about the biological weapons black market in Syria in three months than we'd managed all the previous year."

"Thanks, but you taught me a lot about what to look for."

"We make an excellent team." She said it like they were about to win a Nobel Prize.

"Yeah." He blew out a breath. He had so much to say, but didn't know how to tell her what had been on his mind, and in his heart, for most of those three months. Where to start.

"Connor?" she asked, looking a little uncertain. "Are you all right?"

"I'm good." What an understatement. "I'm better than good. Just seeing you looking so…" He swallowed hard. "Healthy and…gorgeous."

She smiled at him and it hit him in the chest with the power to stop his breathing altogether. "I missed you, too." She held out her hand.

He took it and her touch calmed something in him that had been wounded by her absence.

"Are you hungry?" she asked. "I could make you something—"

"No," he told her, pulling her slowly closer. "The only thing I'm hungry for is you."

"Oh," she said, a blush coloring her cheeks. "Good."

"We need to talk before anything else happens."

She gave him a frustrated huff. "Why?"

Yep, Sophia hadn't changed a bit. A little too honest, too direct. *Thank God.*

He was going to follow her lead. "This is not a one-night stand."

"You promised to teach me how to have sex," she reminded him. He didn't need the reminder, he'd been dreaming of all the ways he could have her every night since she'd left Bahrain. "To achieve a complete understanding will take some time."

He had to chuckle. "God, I love how your mind works." He cupped her face and brought her even closer. "But let me be clear. It's going to take the rest of our lives."

His statement caught her attention and she blinked at him. "It will?"

"Do you want me to have sex with another woman?"

She frowned. "No."

"Good, because I don't want you to have sex with anyone else either."

"Oh. Good."

"I love you."

She blinked. "You... I..." She took a couple of deep breaths, put her free hand on his shoulder and clutched at him. "I never believed I'd have time to fall in love until I met you. I love you so much it hurts my heart."

"No more pain, for either of us." He gathered her up, enfolded her in his arms and hugged her. She smelled of home. He kissed her neck, tiny kisses on her soft skin.

She made a distressed noise and he pulled back far enough to see her face. "What's wrong?"

"I want to touch you. I want to hold you and sleep with you. I feel like I've been starving my entire life."

"Touch starved," he whispered. "We can fix that."

She nodded and pulled away, taking his hand to lead him down a short hall into a bedroom.

He closed the door behind them then pulled his shirt over his head and dropped it on the floor.

Her wide gaze made him smile. "I intend to love you until you're drunk on your own pleasure. I refuse to rush."

She lifted a hand and reached toward him, but didn't move, so he closed the distance between them until her palm was resting over his heart.

"I missed this," she whispered. "Your heat and strength." She put her other hand on his chest too and stroked him. "I feel like I'm petting a wild animal."

He couldn't stop touching her. His hands swept up her back and pulled her in to his body. He nuzzled her hair. "I missed you."

She kissed his chin, the corner of his mouth, her hands exploring his back and shoulders. "I wake up sometimes, cold and alone. I've taken to sleeping with extra pillows."

"If it's heat you want, sweetheart, you can have all of mine."

She kissed him on the lips and he couldn't hold back his own need any longer. He deepened the kiss, loving her taste, the touch of her tongue, the moans she made as his hands moved, stroked her body, palmed her breasts.

She pulled away to work on her shirt. "I want to feel your hands on me."

"Excellent idea." He removed his pants, but left his boxers on.

She got her shirt off, then unhooked her bra and slid it off as well.

He damn near came in his pants again.

He did let one hand cup a breast, his thumb stroking the nipple. "You're so gorgeous." He walked her backward, both of his hands on her breasts now, until she hit the bed and sat down on it.

He went to his knees and began kissing her again.

She went for his boxers, pushing them down and off. His cock bounced and curved up toward his navel.

"Wow," she said, running one finger up the sensitive skin. "I forgot how big you are."

"We'll go slow," he told her.

"I'm not afraid." She smiled at him, and for that smile, he'd conquer the world. "I'm considering all the pleasure spots you'll hit when you're inside me. Multiple orgasms are definitely possible."

He laughed. "I love that brain of yours. Now turn it off and just feel."

Her jaw dropped open like he'd said something completely alien. "Oh."

He kissed her before she could say anything else. He shifted her until they were both lying on the bed, then he lifted her up so he could suck a nipple into his mouth.

She cried out, her hands grasping at his freshly cut hair.

He laid her down on the bed, stripped her of her pants and panties, a naughty pink thong he was going to have to take a second look at later, and crawled over her until he reached her breasts again.

He went after her other nipple this time, while one

hand plucked at the wet one and his other hand teased her clit.

She bucked and moaned and wrapped one leg around him like she was afraid he was going to run away.

He left her breast to kiss her mouth and took himself in hand to tease her clit and the entrance to her body with the head of his cock. Around and around, a little dip inside and around again. Over and over, until he thrust his middle finger inside her hard and fast.

It pushed her into an orgasm and he kept thrusting until she began to calm a little.

"You're so wet," he whispered. "So tight and silky, I can't wait to feel you all around me."

"Yes, I want to feel you," she moaned. She looked so luscious it was killing him to take things slow.

"I've got to get a condom," he said, pulling away.

"I bought some." She smiled. "I didn't know when I'd see you, so I thought I'd better get some so we wouldn't have to waste time purchasing any." She reached over to the side table, opened a drawer and pulled out an unopened box.

Her hands were shaking, so he took it from her and got a condom out, got the package open and rolled it over his cock.

He kissed her and petted her until she was moaning again, then he teased her until she demanded, "Connor, please, make love to me."

"I don't want to hurt you."

"It hurts now."

They were lying on their sides, so he rolled them until she was on her back and began entering her.

"*Holy fuck*." He shook with the need to bury himself, but he kept it slow and steady until he felt some resistance. Shaking, he rested his forehead on hers. "Love you."

He retreated and thrust again, one smooth unhurried move, until he was buried up to his balls. "God, you're so tight."

She wiggled and panted. "I need you to move."

"You're killing me, gorgeous. Just hold still a minute."

She sucked on his earlobe and said, "Now where would the fun be in that?" She wiggled again, then lifted her hips, changing the angle a little, and he lost it.

He pulled out and pushed back in and it felt so fucking fantastic he did it again and again. "Sophia," he growled. "Are you with me?"

"Ohmygod," she whimpered. "*Ohmygod*. Go faster."

When he didn't immediately follow her order, she smacked his ass. "Faster!"

"Fuck, fuck, *fuck*." He couldn't stop himself, digging in and picking up the pace.

She shattered, screaming, and her internal muscles milking him sent him into outer space.

He came down from the high to discover she was crying.

"Fuck, did I hurt you, darlin'?" He searched her face, then moved to pull out, but she put a hand around his back.

"No," she cried. "Don't leave me yet."

"I hurt you." He was going to beat himself up for doing it.

"Maybe a little, but then it was so beautiful." She sniffed. "I don't know why I'm crying."

Her tears made him feel like beating the crap out of the guy who'd hurt her, but that guy was him. He stroked her face and gathered her close. "You're sure you're okay?"

She nodded and held him tighter.

He hugged her right back.

"Thank you," she said with a lick at his ear. "That was even better than I expected."

The ball of worry in his gut relaxed a little. "I'm glad."

They held each for a few minutes until she cleared her voice and asked, "So...when can we do it again?"

He laughed, happiness a bright light inside him. "Just as soon as you agree to marry me."

She froze. "You want me to marry you?"

"Yup."

She stared at him for a long moment before saying, "I'd have to be an idiot to turn that down." She gave him a brilliant smile. "Yes."

Connor tucked her in safe next to him and kissed her long and slow. "That's my girl."

EPILOGUE

COLONEL MAXIMILLIAN FINISHED reading the final report on the rabies outbreak in the Northern Lebanese refugee camp and signed his name on the last page.

The strain of rabies identified as the pathogen was unique in its speed and virulence. Properties the terrorist Akbar had magnified until the resulting symptoms were barely recognizable as rabies.

A sample had been put in storage, along with Akbar's anthrax strain, but the rest had been disposed of.

Akbar had been wounded, but not badly enough to stop him or even slow him down. Max was sure he was busy planning another biological attack, but there were too many possible targets, and too many places to hide for the Biological Response Team to know where to look next. He was watching a number of companies that produced lab supplies and the chemicals Akbar would need to continue his self-proclaimed jihad.

Then there were the messages left on the corpses.

The last great plague is coming.

No one will be safe.

The whole world will know pain.

All of them addressed to Colonel Maximillian, US Army.

This was a new tactic, but not unexpected. Akbar wanted to keep Max and his people off balance, distracted and afraid. But Max had been terrorized before and not only survived, but thrived.

He wouldn't rest until justice had been done.

Or he was dead.

* * * * *

Keep reading for a sneak peek of VIRAL JUSTICE, the next book in Julie Rowe's BIOLOGICAL RESPONSE TEAM series.

There are very few monsters
who warrant the fear we have of them.

~ Andre Gide

ONE

"THEY'RE NOT GOING to agree with your plan, Colonel," Alicia muttered as she stared at the group of military doctors standing several feet away.

Colonel Robert Maximillian, head of the US Army Biological Response Team, bent closer to the tiny, curvy Sergeant Alicia Stone and had to clear his throat before asking, "What makes you say that?"

"Look at their body language," she continued in that almost subvocal whisper. "They've closed ranks and you're on the outside."

He had to consciously hold himself still as he studied the group of men. Military doctors from five different countries. They were positioned in a tight circle, two with their backs to him, talking quietly. All of them stood at just a hair under attention. The faces he could see were set, eyes serious. Understandable. These were dangerous times, and their mutual enemy could be anyone, even someone in your own army.

Stone shifted and her shoulder brushed his arm.

His attraction to the sergeant was irrational and impossible. He wasn't a fan of either.

"They're having a simple conversation, Sergeant, nothing more."

"I've been on the receiving end of that kind of conversation," Stone said, her voice filled with enough acid to melt steel. "If they wanted to include you, they'd have left a space for you to step into, but they didn't. They've already decided and they know you're not going to like their decision."

"That's ridiculous." He knew every man in the group and had earned their respect. "They're professionals and they know I have new information for them."

"It isn't going to matter. Their minds are made up." Stone's voice was so sharp he stopped to really look at her.

"What happened?" he asked her.

"It's not what happened, but what's *not* going to happen that's the problem, sir."

"No." He waved away the reference to the meeting they were about to attend. "I mean, with you. I don't think I've ever seen you this angry before."

"Me, angry?" she said with wide eyes that did nothing to hide the displeasure on the rest of her face. "I'm *grateful*, sir, to be the only female combat trainer for the Special Forces." Her tone made it clear she was anything but grateful.

"Did you break another officer's arm?" Four months ago, an asshole who'd thought he was some kind of martial arts expert had tried to intimidate Stone during a training session. She'd put him on the mats twice before he got angry and attacked for real, thinking she couldn't handle an actual fight. She'd not only broken his arm, but two fingers of the opposite hand, as well.

The incident hadn't ended there. The officer had accused her of assault, but with so many witnesses the charges against Stone had been thrown out, and *he'd* been charged with assault. Since then, however, at least two other officers had lodged formal complaints against her.

The old boys' club, closing ranks.

"Nothing that would show up on an X-ray." Her voice sounded bland. Something had gone very wrong.

If someone hurt her, he was going to find out and make their life miserable. "Is there anything I can do to help?"

She jerked, as if the question startled her. "Don't argue with me if I tell you to do something."

"Arguing with one's bodyguard would be stupid. I try not to be an idiot more than twice a day. I reached my quota an hour ago." Yet, he always seemed to butt heads with her whenever they were involved in the same operation, even if it was just a meeting. Having her as a bodyguard for any great length of time would be uncomfortable at best.

She blinked.

He consulted his watch as several light armored vehicles pulled up nearby. "Gentlemen, I appreciate your early arrival," he called out to the five men. "The summit is scheduled to begin in an hour. Several more countries than expected have sent representatives. As a result the meeting has been moved to a larger venue." He gestured at the waiting vehicles. "If you would? We'll travel together."

Their cluster broke apart and they got into vehicles.

When he glanced back, Stone was staring after him with a profoundly confused expression on her face.

Max rode with Franz Meyer, chief medical officer for the German Army, while Stone got into the vehicle behind his with his British counterpart.

"Militants invaded another Kurdish village in Northern Iraq today." Franz sounded tired. "At least seventy-five dead and an unknown number of women and girls taken." He shook his head. "Last night a group of refugees attempted to cross the border between Bulgaria and Hungary. At least thirty died in a series of fires started by Molotov cocktails they threw themselves."

Stupid. Human beings had a great capacity for stupidity. "The unrest isn't making any of our jobs easier. Which is why we need countries around the world, not just in Europe or the Middle East, to agree to implement a global vaccination plan."

"But, do you understand the pressure we're all under?" Franz turned to him, suddenly intent. "We can't fight a war against an enemy we can't see. Your proposal is simply too expensive."

"We're facing a new era of biological weapons." Max made direct eye contact with him. "Weapons that are in the hands of people who can and will use them against any target they choose."

"We can't arbitrarily begin a counteroffensive against an enemy we aren't aware of yet," Franz replied. "We have to have more information, more proof than two isolated incidents."

Had he *read* the reports? "Akbar isn't an incident. He's a mass murderer who's just getting started. Treating the sick after the fact is what'll be expensive. You can't just ignore the problem because no one is sure how to pay for it."

"What I'm saying is, where do we start?" Franz spread his hands in a conciliatory gesture that didn't fool Max for a second. "Which do you feel is more important, training existing medical staff, or increasing staff numbers in both military and civilian medical aid groups in Africa and the Middle East? We can't afford to do both."

He held on to his temper with both hands. Stone was right. Franz had already made up his mind.

He had maybe ten minutes more minutes to make his case before they arrived at their destination. Once there, he'd have to repeat his arguments to healthcare leaders from all over Europe, Africa, the Middle East and Asia. Franz had probably thought he was going to catch Max by surprise by asking the question now, but Max had been considering solutions to the problem of worldwide infectious disease control for a long time. Ten minutes might just be enough time to change the German's thinking.

There were other delegates in the vehicles in front and behind them, along with a military escort to keep trouble at bay. The decisions about to be made at this meeting would have a long reach, and there were many groups, extremists of one sort or another, who would do their best to disrupt and destroy any agreements or resolutions.

Max answered without hesitation. "Both." He met his German counterpart's gaze squarely. "If Akbar and Ebola have taught us anything, it's that no one country, or even a few countries, can handle a large outbreak alone. There will be a domino effect and the resulting chaos will take even more lives. When the Spanish flu circulated the world one hundred years ago, it took a year and a half to make the trip. Now, it might take a week." Max shook his head. "We can't afford to do the minimum, Franz. There's no time to build the support system *after* the next deadly outbreak occurs."

"But the cost…"

"The current cost of Ebola is estimated to be two point two billion dollars. That's just monetary. We lost a lot of doctors, nurses and other healthcare workers too. It's going to take years for Guinea, Liberia and Sierra Leone to replace those people. If they get hit by a second wave, or a new infection, they've got no more than a skeleton crew to handle it. Which means it won't be handled. It'll be chaos." Max shook his head. "With the Middle East hemorrhaging refugees into Europe, no one is in a position to help without a lot of prep time."

"We can't afford the plan you propose—" Franz began.

Max cut him off with a diagonal slash of his hand. "Then help me find another way."

The German sighed. "I agree with you on principle, but without an imminent threat, my government won't agree to spend that much time and money on an event that might never happen."

Their vehicle slowed and the soldier driving it yelled back to them, "We've got an accident in front of us, sirs. I'll have to take another route."

"That's fine, Corporal." Max turned to Franz, determined to see the German's not-quite-no as an almost-yes. "We start with a framework, an infrastructure—"

Shots and yelling from outside the vehicle cut him off. Their driver stomped on the brakes.

"What's going on?" Max demanded.

The young soldier never had the chance to answer.

The vehicle in front of them exploded.

For a long moment, the world disintegrated into white noise.

Slowly, his vision and hearing returned. But nothing made sense. Smoke obscured everything, and there was such an uproar of shouting and sirens, he wasn't even sure where he was.

Another, much smaller explosion farther away pulled him back into focus. Their vehicle was damaged—how badly wasn't clear—and the way ahead was impassable.

He turned to ask Franz if he was all right and found the German slumped against the seat, blood dripping from his head.

Blood doesn't flow when you're dead.

He put his fingers on Franz's carotid pulse and found it strong and steady.

Thank God.

Flames from the front of their vehicle caught his attention. They weren't safe yet.

He kicked his door open, then dragged Franz out and back down the street several feet. He went back for the driver, but the young man's head was all but disarticulated from his body by a piece of twisted metal.

Son of a bitch.

Max looked at the remains of the lead vehicle, but what was left was little more than a chassis covered in bent metal and melted plastic. No one could have survived that.

Stone.

Fear sank an ice pick into his gut. He whipped around to look at the vehicle behind his and saw her running with the men from her vehicle, returning to the base.

Relief burned away the cold, allowing him to breathe again.

Good, the survivors needed to evacuate in case of a follow-up attack.

Shouts from the other side of the flames grabbed his attention, but no one appeared. He turned to check Franz and discovered Ali running toward him, her rifle in her hands. "Max?" she yelled.

"What are you doing here?" he demanded. "I thought you were escorting the others to safety."

"They're in good hands." She glanced at Franz and the blood on Max's uniform. "You're the one who needs backup."

He couldn't argue the point. That didn't mean he liked it.

"Are you okay?" He put his hands on her shoulders, sliding them down and over her body to check for injuries.

"I'm good," she said, wiggling away from him to inspect him instead. "Are you? Is this your blood?"

"No, it's Franz's blood. Head wounds often bleed profusely."

"Help is on its way. Did you see what happened?"

"No."

She stared at the remains of the lead vehicle with narrowed eyes. "If we were anywhere else, I'd say that was the result of an IED."

"It could have been," Max said. "The Boston bombing was a homemade device." He looked around. "Any injuries in your vehicle?"

"Nothing besides a few bumps and bruises."

Another explosion had both of them ducking and stepping back from the flames and smoke.

A bullet struck the mess of debris where he'd been standing a moment ago. A second later, Stone took him by the arm and yanked him behind the wreck of his vehicle.

Stone snapped her rifle into position and fired back, but the bullets kept coming. "Get to cover," she yelled at him.

Not without her. "You too!"

"Max," she barked. "What did I say about arguing? Get the *fuck* out of here, before *I* kick your ass."

She was right. He could be an idiot later.

Max ducked and found himself using the smoking wreckage to hide from more bullets coming in short bursts all around him. He managed to get back to Franz and move the unconscious man into a sheltered doorway, but he still couldn't determine where the shooter was. There was probably more than one.

Goddamn it, he didn't have time to be assassinated. He had too much to do.

Movement from beyond the remains of the lead vehicle caught his attention, and a man—no, a boy, barely a teenager—walked slowly and calmly through the rubble and ruined vehicles. A bulky package was strapped to his chest and his gaze searched for someone or something.

The boy saw Alicia, but he didn't do anything threatening. In fact, he backed away from her, hugged the wall of the building behind him and kept moving.

That retreat from her, from blowing himself up, was probably the only thing that stopped Alicia from shooting him.

Who the hell would use a child as a suicide bomber?

Extremists, fanatics, madmen. It didn't matter what anyone called them, they were dead men if Max got his hands on them.

He'd taken a vow to preserve life, but the kind of animals who could plan and execute this terrible act of horror, with a *child* as a weapon, could not be allowed to continue breathing.

That wasn't going to improve his immediate situation. The boy was still walking forward and appeared to be looking for something. A target? In a moment, Max and Franz were going to be visible.

He sucked in a deep breath and prepared to leave the relative safety of the doorway. Perhaps he could talk the boy into surrendering. Franz and Alicia would have no doubt argued with him about that plan, but the German was still out cold and Alicia too far away.

He stood and walked toward the teen.

The young man saw him and took a second to stare at Max. An expression of recognition and fear flashed across the boy's face, and Max knew he was in trouble.

Someone had sent a child to kill him.

If he walked away, would the kid follow? How close did the bomber want to get before detonating the explosives? If there were no eyes on the boy, could he be convinced to abandon his mission?

Max sidestepped away from the doorway, then walked backward. "You don't have to do this," he called to the boy. "We can help you, keep you safe."

The boy followed, picking up his pace to close the distance between them. "They said they will kill my sister and brother if I don't," the boy said, his voice bleak and hopeless.

Max was about to turn and run when the young man jerked once, and pitched forward to land on his hands.

Someone had shot the would-be bomber, wounded him.

Shots pinged off the stone wall of the building behind Max and peppered the area around the child bomber. At least one of them hit the boy and he crumpled. Max ducked and ran back to the relative safety of the doorway where he'd left Franz.

Return fire halted the rain of bullets. Max waited for more, but none materialized.

Had Stone taken out the shooter? Or was he being lured out into the open?

He glanced back at Franz. A sizable blood pool had formed around the man's head. His head wound might be worse than Max had first thought.

Since no one had fired any shots at him for nearly half a minute, he took a chance and rushed back to their vehicle and pulled a first aid kit from the rear seat. It looked completely intact. He ran back to Franz, put on a pair of gloves and began searching for the source of the bleeding. It didn't take long to find a deep five-or six-inch long cut along the back of the German's head.

He pulled out a roll of gauze and a large non-stick pad, and proceeded to carefully stanch the bleeding.

The sound of several pairs of booted feet running toward his hiding place had him glancing up.

A contingent of soldiers in US Army uniforms surfaced out of the smoke.

"I need a medical team here now." Max didn't wait for a reply, but concentrated on getting the bleeding under control.

American soldiers filtered through the area, some to look for more bodies, others to investigate, while some stood watch. He ignored them until he had Franz ready to transport. By that time a group of combat medics had arrived and they were able to take the German soldier away to a nearby hospital.

Max searched the wreckage for more injured, but everyone still alive had been identified by the medics, and was in various stages of being removed from the area.

"What the hell are you still doing here?" Stone demanded.

He turned and stared at her and the rifle she carried, a sick feeling churning his gut. "Did you shoot the suicide bomber?"

"I wounded him. The sniper who was trying to nail your ass from the roof over there finished the kid off." She stepped up to him and poked his chest with a finger. "You're lucky I shot that asshole before he shot you. I also saw you step away from cover and allow that bomber to ID you." She paused, then asked with heavily laden sarcasm, "Do you have a death wish, Colonel?"

If he did, he wasn't alone. "You're the one who stayed out in the open to play shooter."

Check out VIRAL JUSTICE, now available in ebook from Julie Rowe and Carina Press. www.CarinaPress.com

ABOUT THE AUTHOR

JULIE ROWE'S FIRST career as a medical lab technologist in Canada took her to the Northwest Territories and northern Alberta, where she still resides. She loves to include medical details in her romance novels but admits she'll never be able to write about all her medical experiences because "Fiction has to be believable." Julie writes contemporary and historical medical romance, fun romantic suspense and military romance. Her most recent titles are *Deadly Strain* and *Lethal Game*, books #1 and #2 of the Biological Response Team series. Book #3, *Viral Justice*, is set to release in February 2016. You can find her at facebook.com/julieroweauthor.

REQUEST YOUR FREE BOOKS!
2 FREE NOVELS PLUS 2 FREE GIFTS!

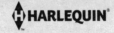

ROMANTIC suspense

Sparked by danger, fueled by passion

YES! Please send me 2 FREE Harlequin® Romantic Suspense novels and my 2 FREE gifts (gifts are worth about $10). After receiving them, if I don't wish to receive any more books, I can return the shipping statement marked "cancel." If I don't cancel, I will receive 4 brand-new novels every month and be billed just $4.74 per book in the U.S. or $5.49 per book in Canada. That's a savings of at least 12% off the cover price! It's quite a bargain! Shipping and handling is just 50¢ per book in the U.S. and 75¢ per book in Canada.* I understand that accepting the 2 free books and gifts places me under no obligation to buy anything. I can always return a shipment and cancel at any time. Even if I never buy another book, the two free books and gifts are mine to keep forever.

240/340 HDN GH3P

Name	(PLEASE PRINT)

Address		Apt. #

City	State/Prov.	Zip/Postal Code

Signature (if under 18, a parent or guardian must sign)

Mail to the **Reader Service:**
IN U.S.A.: P.O. Box 1867, Buffalo, NY 14240-1867
IN CANADA: P.O. Box 609, Fort Erie, Ontario L2A 5X3

Want to try two free books from another line?
Call 1-800-873-8635 or visit www.ReaderService.com.

* Terms and prices subject to change without notice. Prices do not include applicable taxes. Sales tax applicable in N.Y. Canadian residents will be charged applicable taxes. Offer not valid in Quebec. This offer is limited to one order per household. Not valid for current subscribers to Harlequin Romantic Suspense books. All orders subject to credit approval. Credit or debit balances in a customer's account(s) may be offset by any other outstanding balance owed by or to the customer. Please allow 4 to 6 weeks for delivery. Offer available while quantities last.

Your Privacy—The Reader Service is committed to protecting your privacy. Our Privacy Policy is available online at www.ReaderService.com or upon request from the Reader Service.

We make a portion of our mailing list available to reputable third parties that offer products we believe may interest you. If you prefer that we not exchange your name with third parties, or if you wish to clarify or modify your communication preferences, please visit us at www.ReaderService.com/consumerschoice or write to us at Reader Service Preference Service, P.O. Box 9062, Buffalo, NY 14240-9062. Include your complete name and address.

REQUEST YOUR FREE BOOKS!
2 FREE NOVELS PLUS 2 FREE GIFTS!

◆ HARLEQUIN®

INTRIGUE

BREATHTAKING ROMANTIC SUSPENSE

YES! Please send me 2 FREE Harlequin® Intrigue novels and my 2 FREE gifts (gifts are worth about $10). After receiving them, if I don't wish to receive any more books, I can return the shipping statement marked "cancel." If I don't cancel, I will receive 6 brand-new novels every month and be billed just $4.74 per book in the U.S. or $5.49 per book in Canada. That's a savings of at least 12% off the cover price! It's quite a bargain! Shipping and handling is just 50¢ per book in the U.S. and 75¢ per book in Canada.* I understand that accepting the 2 free books and gifts places me under no obligation to buy anything. I can always return a shipment and cancel at any time. Even if I never buy another book, the two free books and gifts are mine to keep forever.

182/382 HDN GH3D

Name _____ (PLEASE PRINT) _____

Address _____ Apt. # _____

City _____ State/Prov. _____ Zip/Postal Code _____

Signature (if under 18, a parent or guardian must sign)

Mail to the Reader Service:
IN U.S.A.: P.O. Box 1867, Buffalo, NY 14240-1867
IN CANADA: P.O. Box 609, Fort Erie, Ontario L2A 5X3

Are you a subscriber to Harlequin® Intrigue books
and want to receive the larger-print edition?
Call 1-800-873-8635 or visit www.ReaderService.com.

* Terms and prices subject to change without notice. Prices do not include applicable taxes. Sales tax applicable in N.Y. Canadian residents will be charged applicable taxes. Offer not valid in Quebec. This offer is limited to one order per household. Not valid for current subscribers to Harlequin Intrigue books. All orders subject to credit approval. Credit or debit balances in a customer's account(s) may be offset by any other outstanding balance owed by or to the customer. Please allow 4 to 6 weeks for delivery. Offer available while quantities last.

Your Privacy—The Reader Service is committed to protecting your privacy. Our Privacy Policy is available online at www.ReaderService.com or upon request from the Reader Service.

We make a portion of our mailing list available to reputable third parties that offer products we believe may interest you. If you prefer that we not exchange your name with third parties, or if you wish to clarify or modify your communication preferences, please visit us at www.ReaderService.com/consumerchoice or write to us at Reader Service Preference Service, P.O. Box 9062, Buffalo, NY 14240-9062. Include your complete name and address.

HI13

REQUEST YOUR FREE BOOKS!

2 FREE NOVELS
FROM THE SUSPENSE COLLECTION
PLUS 2 FREE GIFTS!

YES! Please send me 2 FREE novels from the Suspense Collection and my 2 FREE gifts (gifts are worth about $10). After receiving them, if I don't wish to receive any more books, I can return the shipping statement marked "cancel." If I don't cancel, I will receive 4 brand-new novels every month and be billed just $6.49 per book in the U.S. or $6.99 per book in Canada. That's a savings of at least 19% off the cover price. It's quite a bargain! Shipping and handling is just 50¢ per book in the U.S. and 75¢ per book in Canada.* I understand that accepting the 2 free books and gifts places me under no obligation to buy anything. I can always return a shipment and cancel at any time. Even if I never buy another book, the two free books and gifts are mine to keep forever.

191/391 MDN GH4Z

Name _____ (PLEASE PRINT) _____

Address _____ Apt. # _____

City _____ State/Prov. _____ Zip/Postal Code _____

Signature (if under 18, a parent or guardian must sign)

Mail to the **Reader Service:**
IN U.S.A.: P.O. Box 1867, Buffalo, NY 14240-1867
IN CANADA: P.O. Box 609, Fort Erie, Ontario L2A 5X3

Want to try two free books from another line?
Call 1-800-873-8635 or visit www.ReaderService.com.

* Terms and prices subject to change without notice. Prices do not include applicable taxes. Sales tax applicable in N.Y. Canadian residents will be charged applicable taxes. Offer not valid in Quebec. This offer is limited to one order per household. Not valid for current subscribers to the Suspense Collection or the Romance/Suspense Collection. All orders subject to credit approval. Credit or debit balances in a customer's account(s) may be offset by any other outstanding balance owed by or to the customer. Please allow 4 to 6 weeks for delivery. Offer available while quantities last.

Your Privacy—The Reader Service is committed to protecting your privacy. Our Privacy Policy is available online at www.ReaderService.com or upon request from the Reader Service.

We make a portion of our mailing list available to reputable third parties that offer products we believe may interest you. If you prefer that we not exchange your name with third parties, or if you wish to clarify or modify your communication preferences, please visit us at www.ReaderService.com/consumerschoice or write to us at Reader Service Preference Service, P.O. Box 9062, Buffalo, NY 14240-9062. Include your complete name and address.

SUS13

REQUEST YOUR FREE BOOKS!

2 FREE RIVETING INSPIRATIONAL NOVELS PLUS 2 FREE MYSTERY GIFTS

SUSPENSE
RIVETING INSPIRATIONAL ROMANCE

YES! Please send me 2 FREE Love Inspired® Suspense novels and my 2 FREE mystery gifts (gifts are worth about $10). After receiving them, if I don't wish to receive any more books, I can return the shipping statement marked "cancel." If I don't cancel, I will receive 4 brand-new novels every month and be billed just $4.99 per book in the U.S. or $5.49 per book in Canada. That's a savings of at least 17% off the cover price. It's quite a bargain! Shipping and handling is just 50¢ per book in the U.S. and 75¢ per book in Canada.* I understand that accepting the 2 free books and gifts places me under no obligation to buy anything. I can always return a shipment and cancel at any time. Even if I never buy another book, the two free books and gifts are mine to keep forever.

123/323 IDN GH5Z

Name _____ (PLEASE PRINT) _____

Address _____ Apt. # _____

City _____ State/Prov. _____ Zip/Postal Code _____

Signature (if under 18, a parent or guardian must sign)

Mail to the **Reader Service:**
IN U.S.A.: P.O. Box 1867, Buffalo, NY 14240-1867
IN CANADA: P.O. Box 609, Fort Erie, Ontario L2A 5X3

**Are you a current subscriber to Love Inspired® Suspense books and want to receive the larger-print edition?
Call 1-800-873-8635 or visit www.ReaderService.com.**

* Terms and prices subject to change without notice. Prices do not include applicable taxes. Sales tax applicable in N.Y. Canadian residents will be charged applicable taxes. Offer not valid in Quebec. This offer is limited to one order per household. Not valid for current subscribers to Love Inspired Suspense books. All orders subject to credit approval. Credit or debit balances in a customer's account(s) may be offset by any other outstanding balance owed by or to the customer. Please allow 4 to 6 weeks for delivery. Offer available while quantities last.

Your Privacy—The Reader Service is committed to protecting your privacy. Our Privacy Policy is available online at www.ReaderService.com or upon request from the Reader Service.
We make a portion of our mailing list available to reputable third parties that offer products we believe may interest you. If you prefer that we not exchange your name with third parties, or if you wish to clarify or modify your communication preferences, please visit us at www.ReaderService.com/consumerschoice or write to us at Reader Service Preference Service, P.O. Box 9062, Buffalo, NY 14240-9062. Include your complete name and address.

LIS15

READERSERVICE.COM

Manage your account online!

- Review your order history
- Manage your payments
- Update your address

We've designed the Reader Service website just for you.

Enjoy all the features!

- Discover new series available to you, and read excerpts from any series.
- Respond to mailings and special monthly offers.
- Connect with favorite authors at the blog.
- Browse the Bonus Bucks catalog and online-only exculsives.
- Share your feedback.

Visit us at:

ReaderService.com